Huckleberry Homicide

A FRAN LIGHTFOOT MYSTERY, BOOK ONE

CINDY KEEN REYNDERS

CAVEL
PRESS

KENMORE, WA

CAMEL
PRESS

A Camel Press book published by Epicenter Press

Epicenter Press
6524 NE 181st St.
Suite 2
Kenmore, WA 98028

For more information go to:
www.Camelpress.com
www.Coffeetownpress.com
www.Epicenterpress.com
www.cindykeenreynders.com

Cover design by Scott Book
Design Melissa Vail Coffman

Huckleberry Homicide
Copyright © 2024 by Cindy Keen Reynders

Library of Congress Control Number: 2023951893

ISBN: 978-1-68492-187-4 (Trade Paper)
ISBN: 978-1-68492-188-1 (eBook)

To breast cancer patients and survivors:
facing fear gives us strength, and strength helps us fight.
Despite the struggle, despite the pain, I urge my
pink sisters everywhere to keep the faith.

ACKNOWLEDGMENTS

A S ALWAYS, THANK YOU TO MY HUSBAND and my family for their patience and understanding when I go into my office and disappear for hours. They appreciate my writing addiction and for that I will be eternally grateful.

ONE

Early October

THE YELLOW SPOT ON THE COUNTER in Fran Lightfoot's kitchen wasn't budging, no matter how hard she scrubbed. Determined, she sprinkled cleanser on it, pressed harder with her cleaning rag, and applied more elbow grease.

"Finally!" Fran declared as it disappeared.

"You should put that much effort into getting out and socializing," her sister Lucy said.

"I'm fine," Fran shot back, turning to scowl at Lucy who stood nearby mixing muffin batter.

Two years ago, Fran had divorced her husband, Dan Lightfoot, and returned home to Moose Creek, Wyoming, bringing her teenage daughter, Eva, with her. The marriage, which had started under rocky circumstances, had been troubled. These days, Fran enjoyed her independence and the fact that she answered to no one.

"You need to get out more, Fran. Otherwise, you're going to dry up and turn into a prune with lips." Lucy dropped plump huckleberries into the bowl, and the occasional juicy tidbit into her mouth. She stirred the concoction with a wooden spoon.

"Lucy, I appreciate your concern," Fran returned. "I'm enjoying the peace that comes with being by myself."

"Are you sure you're not lonely?"

"Life is good for me. I have no worries and I'm living near my family again. There's nothing else I could ask for." Fran picked up a muffin pan, doused it with a shot of flour spray, and placed it on the counter.

"I know this guy—"

Fran held up a hand. "Please, Lucy, say no more."

If Lucy wanted her to go on a blind date, she wasn't interested, even if her older sister enjoyed the role of matchmaker.

Lucy studied the purple-speckled batter for a moment, then met Fran's gaze. "You know I only want what's best for you, Sis."

Fran turned on the oven to pre-heat. "It's awesome to know you have my back."

"That's what sisters are for." Lucy began to whistle a tune as she dolloped batter into the muffin tin.

Fran chuckled. As a kid, she'd been jealous of her sister's ability to whistle. Now, she enjoyed the sound. Lucy had always had a positive view of life, and she had a unique way of solving problems. When Fran's world became chaotic, all she could think was to live near her sister again, in the town where she'd grown up.

Simple, every day goings on here had calmed her troubled soul and acted as a balm on her heart. She felt positive about herself again, and loved that her healing process had begun.

"Do you remember playing house when we were kids?" Fran asked as warm memories washed over her.

"Of course." Lucy slid the muffins into the oven and set the timer. "We had good times."

"You'd fix my hair in ribbons and bows and dress me up like a living doll," Fran remembered with fondness.

"You were adorable," Lucy said with a twinkle in her eye. "I couldn't resist the urge to take care of my little sister back then, and I can't resist the urge now."

"Do you have any regrets about leaving teaching to come and run the café with me?" Fran asked.

Lucy smiled. "Not one," she returned. "I do miss the kids, though. However, I like that we get to be our own bosses."

"Yeah, that is nice," Fran agreed.

"What about you?" Lucy asked. "Do you have any regrets about leaving the mortuary business in Tidewater, California?"

"Ah, that would be no," Fran returned. "I appreciated guiding the customers through a difficult time. Also, because I handled the funeral home's bookkeeping, I can handle the café's finances. However, I'd rather cook and bake for a living, thank you very much."

The front door flew open, the bell on it tinkling, as a hungry crowd trekked inside. Fran glanced at the clock, noting the noon hour. She and Lucy could always count on a good-sized lunch crowd.

Lucy, tall and shapely with a mass of golden red hair piled on her head, turned to look at the customers. She wore dark blue slacks, silver hoop earrings, a print top, and a white apron emblazoned with The Saucy Lucy Café's logo.

"Time to get cracking," she told Fran. "Remember, it's your turn to handle the counter today."

"Got it." Fran wiped her hands on a dish cloth and hustled toward the rustic style counter. Lucy's husband Otis, always so handy with woodworking, had built it with reclaimed barnwood. In fact, with his wood working expertise, the sisters had many unique pieces of furniture in here.

Customers gravitated toward different tables, talking and laughing with one another as they looked over their menus. While everyone settled in, Fran's mind wandered. She found it amazing, the unexpected turns her world had taken the last couple of years. All for the good.

Fran found herself moving along with the ebb and flow her life had taken. Swelling with pride, she appreciated her newfound freedom and the future she'd been carving out for herself.

After Fran and Lucy's parents, Reverend James Castleton and his wife, Emma, passed away, the sisters discovered they'd inherited the family home—a beautiful red brick Victorian with white gingerbread trim located in downtown Moose Creek.

Fran suggested that she and Lucy convert the downstairs of the Victorian into a café and the upstairs into comfortable living quarters for herself and Eva. Lucy could work in the café and also share in the profits since she would be co-owner.

Fran suggested they name the café in Lucy's honor, since most of the recipes they planned to use were ones her sister had created. Many had won blue ribbons at the county fair, so the sisters felt certain their customers would love them.

The Saucy Lucy Cafe was born with a simple menu—good old-fashioned soups, jams, jellies, and hearty sandwiches assembled with homemade bread. Or a customer could have a piece of pie and coffee. Whole pies, cakes, doughnuts and other confections were also available for sale. Additionally, Fran and Lucy catered events like weddings, graduations, birthday parties, and similar gatherings.

It wasn't long before The Saucy Lucy Café began turning a profit. Of course, it remained the only sandwich shop in the small mountain community, so that, of course, added to its success.

Lucy eased up next to Fran, placed a hand on her shoulder, and said softly, "Stop by my book club's Fall Feast and Book Exchange tomorrow. It's at Windy Hill Park."

"I don't want to crash your party," Fran said.

"Please come," Lucy insisted. "Henry Whitehead, a fellow member, said he's dying to meet you."

"Are you serious?" Fran asked.

"Serious as a heart attack," Lucy responded. "He's divorced, like you, and has a couple of children a few years younger than Eva. The two of you might enjoy spending time together. You never know."

"I'm not a fan of blind dates," Fran admitted, a sinking feeling in the pit of her stomach. In her mind's eye, she imagined a roller coaster ride on a flaming track. Sure, she wanted to help raise more teenagers. Uh, huh.

Eva had been tough enough at sixteen, especially after ex-husband, Dan Lightfoot, aka, The Undertaker, had left her for Davina Blakely, recent widow and wealthy Silicon Valley business owner.

Fran was left to teach Eva the following lessons for the last twenty-four months—All About Driving, All About Boys, and All About Why Your Father Left Us.

"Henry is a nice guy," Lucy pressed.

"Thanks, but I'm not interested in meeting him," Fran said.

Lucy folded her arms and tapped her toe. "I'm only trying to help."

Fran frowned. Her sister tended to interfere, although she meant well. Lucy had carved out a comfortable life, and Fran sensed she wanted to make sure that her sister had one as well. Since nothing ever stayed the same in Fran's world, she believed her future would continue to hold twists and turns. Nevertheless, she wasn't asleep at the wheel any longer, and she knew she could make the best out of anything that came her way

Thank goodness she'd progressed way beyond what she'd gone through as a young adult. Fran knew her poor choices had caused most of her issues, but she'd been inexperienced and impressionable. Growing up in Moose Creek, the daughter of Reverend James Castleton, preacher at a church where everybody-knows-your-name, had been difficult. She'd felt constricted by her upbringing, and had rebelled by behaving impulsively.

Needless to say, she'd learned her lesson.

Lucy, however, had never challenged authority while living in the Castleton household. Always obedient, she'd done what was expected and stayed out of trouble. She graduated from high school at the top of her class, headed off to college, and earned a bachelor's degree in early education.

Afterward, she'd come home and married a local boy, Otis Parnell, who was now town sheriff. They had one son, Carl, who Lucy believed hung the moon.

Fran's story had more twists in it. She'd disliked school, hated studying, and began dating Dan Lightfoot against her parents' wishes when she was sixteen. She'd gotten pregnant shortly after that, and barely graduated high school.

She and Dan were married, despite both of their parents' protests. In order to flee everyone's disapproval, the couple left for California with baby Eva. There, he'd finished college and entered the funeral home business. Eventually, they'd purchased a place of their own with Dan as the director. Fran ran the office, dealt with the customers, and did the bookkeeping. In the end, Dan began offering too much sympathy to grieving widows.

Before long Fran began to suspect about Dan's affairs, although he denied them. Years passed before she could prove his infidelity. No use crying over spilled milk, her mother used to say, and she took that wisdom to heart. It hadn't been easy to start a new life, but she'd managed it regardless, and now forged along a new path.

"About Henry," Fran said, "is he at least sexy?"

"For Pete's sake, Fran—"

"Well, is he? That would at least be one compensation."

Lucy shook her head. "Honestly, I have no idea if Henry Whitehead is sexy."

"What's the point in me meeting him?"

Lucy tapped her sturdy, solid, gold band. "I thought you might want to settle down again, this time, with someone who is reliable."

"You never give up, do you?" Fran jokingly punched Lucy's shoulder.

"You might be poking fun at the idea of going out with Henry, but I don't think it would be that terrible."

Lucy did have a point.

The kitchen felt like an inferno from the heat of the oven, combined with the heat of the day. Fran pressed her palms against her hot cheeks, as if by holding them taut, she could smooth out any potential wrinkles, and maybe even salvage her complexion from any damage the environment's free radicals might cause.

Lucy had an expectant look on her face, no doubt hoping Fran would agree to meet Henry after all. Fran eyeballed a bag of veggie chips on the counter. She had a crazy urge to bonk Lucy over the head with them.

"Look, Lucy," Fran finally said. "We don't have time for this. Our customers will start ordering soon."

"You're putting me off," Lucy said.

A couple of teenage boys wearing dog collars, scrubby T-shirts, and backward baseball caps atop their purple streaked hair shuffled toward the counter. They stopped to stare at the daily lunch special written on a dry erase board.

"Hi Todd, hi Sam," Lucy called to them, smiling.

"It's nice to see you Miz Parnell," one of them answered, waving at her.

Since Lucy had taught so many of the teenagers in town when they were in her classroom at the local elementary school, she often recognized them.

"Can't we talk about Henry later?" Fran begged.

"I refuse to let you dry up and wither away in this . . ." Lucy waved her hand toward the café on the other side of the order counter. It was filled with plastic molded aqua-colored chairs and bistro tables, tie-die wall hangings, beaded curtains and trailing plants in macramé hangers. "hole-in-the-wall, hippie-retro eatery. You need a life again."

"I like this hole-in-the-wall, hippie-retro eatery. I have a lovely apartment upstairs, I'm putting my daughter through college, and I keep plenty of home-grown bean sprouts on my table, so I'll never go hungry again. What more could a girl ask for?"

"A companion."

"I've got Eva," Fran said.

"She won't always be around," Lucy pointed out. "I realize your opinion of men isn't the best right now, considering the way your marriage ended. Just remember, not all guys are flakes."

"Maybe in your world they aren't."

"Be nice." Lucy wore a cautionary expression, standing there so sure of herself. "And you might try dressing nicer. It's as if you try to hide your attractiveness by wearing unflattering clothing."

Fran glanced down at her faded jeans and old blue T-shirt beneath her café apron. With her pony-tailed, frizzy, ginger-colored hair, she definitely didn't have super model looks. So what?

Two farmers in coveralls, plaid shirts, and green John Deere ball caps walked into the café and stood behind Lucy's former students to read the menu. The boys, obviously having made their choice of sandwich, walked toward the counter.

Showdown time.

As if to indicate Fran needed to make a decision, the oven timer dinged.

"I've got to get the muffins, Fran, so what will it be?" Lucy prodded.

"Okay, I'll go to your book exchange and meet what's-his-name! I'm sure Eva won't mind covering for me here. Now will you please let this go?"

Lucy's brows rose. "Thanks, Fran. I think you'll have fun, even if you are dead set against meeting Henry."

"I realize you're trying to do me a favor," Fran said. "But you don't have to keep worrying about my future."

"We're family," Lucy said. "We're supposed to look out for each other, okay?"

"You're right," Fran said, appreciating the soft kiss Lucy placed on her cheek.

Lucy hustled toward the oven, while Fran picked up a pad and pencil. She met Todd and Sam's gaze as they stood at the counter, ready to eat.

"May I take your order?" she asked in a cheerful tone.

TWO

THE NEXT MORNING, FRAN SHUFFLED DOWNSTAIRS through the empty sandwich shop, and into the kitchen, eyes sticky with sleep. Coffee, coffee, her mind chanted to a primitive rhythm known only to humans, and she vaguely made out the Mr. Coffee machine beckoning to her on the counter. She recoiled as something cold and wet oozed through her toes.

"Holy mother-of-pearl!" An inch of water and soapsuds arched across the yellow and blue linoleum, as if the Great Lakes had taken residence in her kitchen overnight. Fran's gaze traced the pool of water back to its source.

The large, commercial dishwasher.

"Eva!" She shouted over her shoulder, hoping her voice would carry up the stairs.

"What, Mom?" Eva called a few seconds later.

"I need your help. ASAP."

"What's wrong?"

"Just hurry. And bring every bath towel we own."

"Be right there."

While Fran waited for Eva, she dragged out dish towels, tablecloths, and rags, tossing them on Lake Superior. Then she grabbed a mop, sopped up the water, and squeezed it into the sink. Lord, this was going to take all day.

Fran struggled to figure out what in the heck must have gone wrong. It would probably cost an arm and a leg for the repairman to fix it. Just what she needed—another bill.

Eva appeared in the kitchen door, her arms loaded with towels. "Eeeeewwww, what happened?"

Her faded pink flannel bathrobe had obviously been flung on in a hurry, and her long, strawberry blonde hair was knotted in a loose bun atop her head. She sloshed across the floor toward Fran. Having inherited her father's height, she was nearly a head taller than Fran's petite frame.

"I have no idea. But at least the floor will be squeaky clean when we're through," Fran told her. "Throw down the towels, then wring them off the back porch."

An hour later, Fran stood and stretched out the crick in her back. At last, the floor was dry.

Wondering what in the world she could have done to make the dishwasher go on the fritz, Fran glanced over at the guilty beast. Then it all came rushing back. Eva had loaded it. A bottle of dish-washing liquid sat strategically close to the loading zone, with the dishwasher tablets nowhere in sight.

Eva walked in from the back porch, the screen door slamming behind her. "Phewww, what a mess. You're lucky I was here to pitch in. It's going to get hot outside so the towels should dry pretty quick."

Fran nodded. "Hey, tell me something. When you loaded the dishwasher last night, what soap did you use?"

Eva edged over and picked up the dishwashing liquid. "This." Her brows quirked innocently. "Why?"

Despite her annoyance, Fran checked her temper. Eva seemed to live on another planet sometimes, but she'd meant well. "That's used for washing dishes by hand, sweetie." Fran shuffled over, feet and toes withered beyond recognition now, and withdrew the package of dishwasher tablets from under the sink. "This is what we use for the dishwasher. Okay?"

"Oops." Eva winced. "Sorry."

Fran smiled. "I'm glad to know the dishwasher only had a bad case of indigestion."

"Right," Eva said. "I'm gonna go hit the shower. Can I help you do anything else?"

"No," Fran responded too quickly, then decided to change the subject so Eva wouldn't guess her help right now might not be help at all. "Say, how are your college classes coming along?"

"College is cool . . . at least in the three weeks since I started. The cafeteria food sucks, though. Yours is much better. I don't eat there unless I'm starved."

Even though Eva had online classes this fall semester, on occasion she drove over the mountain pass to Westonville University so she could listen to lectures or participate in student activities. Fran had purchased a meal plan for her so when she was on campus, she could eat.

It occurred to Fran that her daughter had offered an unexpected compliment about her cooking ability, and she warmed at the thought.

"I suppose they do their best to feed the students," Fran mused.

"Mom, it'd gag a maggot. And their mystery meat is totally disgusting. Like, it's not fit for human consumption." Eva brushed past Fran and went upstairs.

SINCE FRAN COULD TRUST EVA TO make sandwiches and ladle soup for the lunch crowd, she showered and dressed in a pair of black leather pants, matching gladiator sandals, and a red halter top. Then she hopped in her truck and drove across town toward Windy Hill Park where Lucy's book club picnic was being held.

Under an arching canopy of ancient elms and cottonwoods sporting the golds, oranges, and reds of autumn, she navigated her truck past treacherous potholes on the narrow streets. She wondered briefly when the annual "Potluck and Pothole Day" was going to be held.

As a kid, Fran loved it when community members staged the event. Kids raced around playing while their parents worked with the local asphalt company filling and smoothing out holes in the road. Moose Creek was definitely due for this. She made a mental note to ask Lucy about it.

Tucking strands of hair behind her ears, Fran took note of the parched brown lawns of the neat bungalows lining the sidewalks. It had been a hot, dry fall. Now the small town was under strict water rationing because Mayor Gollyhorn had foreseen a potential emergency situation if the upcoming winter turned out as warm as the last few years.

She recalled Lucy's comment that she might want to remarry. To be honest, Fran did hope that someday, she'd find the right guy to settle down with again. However, Lucy's constant jabs about her being single didn't help. Hopefully her sister would get the hint that marital bliss was a painful topic for her, and she'd stop talking about it.

Ah, good old Moose Creek—it was nice to be back. People had gotten older, old timers had passed away. These days, Fran looked at life through the eyes of a former carpool and cookie mom, instead of a kid with scraped up knees and a runny nose. This place held great memories.

At the park, she pulled into a shade-dappled spot and turned off the truck engine. It shivered, made a popping noise, and went silent. Sliding out, she stuffed the keys in her pocket.

A cluster of people engaged in conversation had gathered near an ancient steam locomotive memorial surrounded by an expansive lawn and tall trees. Piles of potato chip bags were mounded at one end of two picnic tables pushed together. Crusty brown rolls, salads, brownies, and other assorted goodies decorated the red wooden planks. Another table held stacks of books with colorful spines. Paperbacks and hard cover volumes of all sizes stood ready for their new owners to collect.

Pre-school children on playground equipment squealed with

excitement as they streaked down slides, flew through the air on swings, or climbed on jungle gym equipment.

As Fran scuffed through fallen leaves toward a concrete pavilion covered by a metal roof, she scanned the crowd for Lucy. People stood on the dry lawn, tossing horseshoes or flipping burgers on smoking grills. But she didn't see her sister.

When Fran spotted ice chests full of sodas, she made a beeline over to the drinks. Popping the lid of a diet lemon-lime, she took a sip and scanned the crowd again.

"Ah, there she is," Fran murmured, noting that Lucy stood with a group of gabbing women. More like gossiping, Fran figured. Lucy couldn't resist talking about the latest news buzzing around town.

Striding in their direction, Fran called out, "Hey, Luce. What's up?"

"You're late," Lucy said as she turned toward her sister.

Today Lucy wore a floral printed dress, a matching sweater, and fashionable brown leather boots. Her hair had been twisted into a perfect bun.

"Couldn't help it," Fran said. "Our dishwasher went on the fritz and I had to do some extra clean-up," Fran explained.

Gripping Fran's elbow, Lucy steered her away from the group. "Henry is eager to meet you," she said.

"That's nice," Fran said. "But to be honest, I don't think I'll impress him."

"You don't give yourself enough credit," Lucy said.

Fran took another sip of her soda and looked around. "Where is he?"

Lucy shaded her eyes and scanned the crowd. "Ah, there he is over by the horseshoe pit wearing the green shirt. Let's go say hello."

Fran spotted the green shirt. The man she saw was tall and good-looking, and appeared to be near her age. Tall and broad chested, his athletic stature appealed to Fran. She didn't mind so much now that Lucy had insisted that she make an appearance today. And, thank goodness, she'd changed from her jeans and T-shirt into a cute outfit.

She removed the band from her ponytail and shook loose her hair, feeling more attractive with loose, flowing strands. Reaching into her purse, she fished out her lipstick, reapplied it, and smacked her lips. It didn't hurt to primp, considering this guy was way more impressive than she'd imagined.

As they walked toward Adonis, Fran's gaze met his, and he sent her a dimpled smile. Her knees buckled ever so slightly. Maybe Lucy had hit on a good thing.

Fran stopped walking once they reached him, but Lucy tightened her grip on her elbow.

Confused, Fran said, "Wasn't that Henry back there by the horseshoes?"

Lucy looked over her shoulder at him. "Oh, no. That's Kent Braxton. Helen Braxton's husband."

Fran noticed the gold gleaming on his left hand. *Oh, brother!* She should have known better.

With concern, she watched as they approached another man sitting underneath a tree, drinking a beer. He, too, was wearing a green polo shirt, which appeared too large. His jeans bagged and he had dark circles under his eyes. His shaggy dark hair needed a good cut and comb, in her opinion.

However, he offered a pleasant smile and stood when they approached.

"Here goes nothing," Fran muttered to Lucy.

"Don't be so quick to judge, my dear," Lucy said with a chuckle. "Henry took his divorce really hard. He's lost weight and isn't used to living on his own. I'm sure that before long, he'll feel more like himself."

"Divorce can throw you for a loop," Fran said, feeling sympathetic toward him. "I know it did that to me."

"Hello, ladies," Henry said.

Lucy reached inside of her purse and withdrew a jar of the homemade huckleberry jam they sold at the café.

"Henry, I'd like you to meet my sister, Fran Lightfoot," Lucy said as she handed him the treat. "Fran, this is Henry Whitehead."

Fran and Henry shook hands and exchanged pleasantries.

"You two will have to excuse me," Lucy interjected. "I've got to go and make sure we're not running out of soda." With a wink at Fran, she disappeared.

Fran wanted to sprint after her. However, she didn't want to be rude, so she stayed put. After all, Henry understood what it was like to have your world turned upside down. They shared that in common.

"That sister of yours has got a heart of gold," Henry said as he placed the jam on a concrete bench. "Did you know she started the annual Christmas program down at the women and children's shelter?"

Fran nodded, wondering if Lucy considered her a charitable endeavor. "She's mentioned it to me. It's great she did that."

"I know you and your sister own the Saucy Lucy Café," Henry said. "So, I thought you might want to know what I do. I'm a mechanical engineer. I work at Tyler Aviation Plant in Westonville."

"Wow, that's quite a drive to make every day," Fran said, thinking of the long stretch through the mountain pass, which could get treacherous during winter months. Especially with the heavy truck traffic that frequented the highway.

"It's not too bad," Henry said. "I listen to Audible on the way there and back. And since I work 10-hour shifts, I get Fridays off."

Fran noticed a brunette woman in a purple top standing beneath a cottonwood tree. For some reason, she stared daggers at them.

"Do you know that lady?" Fran asked, nodding in the brunette's direction.

"Ah, yeah. That's my ex-wife, Vivian." Henry ran his hand through his mussed hair. "I swear she's stalking me. It's creepy."

Ignoring Henry's ex-wife, Fran fiddled with the bracelet on her right wrist. Beneath the band, her skin tingled with warmth, and she wondered if she was having an allergic reaction.

"That's very pretty," Henry said as he studied the bauble. "Where'd you get it?"

"My mother gave it to me—it belonged to my great grandmother."

"It's unique," Henry remarked.

Fran studied the small turquoise stones set in a pattern of tiny silver roses. "It is, isn't it? My great grandfather, Howard Castleton, gave it to his wife, Etta, on their wedding day in 1920."

"The guy definitely had good taste." Henry chuckled. "I like you. And you're not like I expected you'd be."

"How's that?" Fran asked.

"You know . . ." Henry shrugged. "What's a guy to think? The way your sister talked, it sounded like you didn't date much, and I figured . . . well, you know."

"No, I don't know," Fran responded, wondering what Lucy had told him about her.

"Never mind me," he said. "I have a tendency to put my foot in my mouth, especially around pretty ladies like you."

Fran didn't know whether to be offended or pleased by his comment. For lack of a response, she simply smiled.

"Hey, I'm meeting some buddies and their dates at the fall carnival tonight," he said. "Wanna be my arm candy?"

"I appreciate the offer, but I'm busy," she responded.

"Doing what?"

Think fast, Fran thought. "Uh, I promised my daughter I'd take her out to dinner."

"Can't you take her out another time?"

Fran scrambled for a plausible answer. "Well, tonight's the, uh, anniversary of when Eva lost her first tooth."

"Wow, you still remember that?" His bushy brows shot up.

"Yes. She's an only child, see, and we celebrate small things." Fran's mouth felt dry, as if she was chewing on cotton. She took another sip of soda.

"I'm lucky if I even see my kids these days," Henry said. "They only call when they want money."

Lucy sauntered up, an expectant expression on her face. "So, how are you two getting along?"

"We've been having a nice chat," Fran said. Sensing an ambush, she began to ease toward the parking lot. "I'd better get back to the café, though."

Lucy gripped Fran's arm. "Don't you two have big plans for tonight?"

"Fran says she's busy," Henry said. "It's the anniversary of when her daughter lost her first tooth and they're going out for a celebration dinner."

"Really?" Lucy fixed Fran with her famous, I'm-the-big-sister-and-I-know-you're-up-to-something, look.

"Really," Fran repeated emphatically, praying Lucy wouldn't blow her excuse out of the water.

"It must have slipped your mind, Fran." Lucy grinned. "The anniversary is next Friday. Remember?"

Fran glared at her.

Henry grinned. "That means we're on for tonight."

Busted!

Fran's heart flopped over inside her chest. She withdrew her cell phone from her purse and handed it to Henry. "Put your number and address in my contacts, okay? I'll drive over to your house at seven this evening, if that's a good time."

"That's perfect, now if you'll excuse me ladies, I see someone I need to talk to," Henry said. Winking at Fran, he sauntered toward a group of individuals.

Fran punched Lucy's arm. "Lying is a sin, you know."

"At least I can confess to Reverend Lincolnway," Lucy said with a chuckle, then added in a joking manner, "You, however, must live with your sin."

"You're a pain in my patootie," Fran told her sister. "Do you know that?"

"Come on Fran, Henry's a nice guy. I'm sure you two will have an enjoyable evening."

Fran snorted. "Depends on your interpretation of enjoyable."

"Give him a chance before you draw and quarter him."

"Fine. But after this, I refuse to go out on any more charity-case dates."

You'll feel differently in the morning." Lucy gave a Cheshire cat smile, as though she'd just made the match of the century.

Fran frowned. "Somehow I doubt it."

THREE

FRAN ALMOST FLEW BACK TO THE CAFÉ. Eva had handled the busy lunch hour, and the afternoon consisted of stragglers, so the time dragged. Thinking of the night ahead, her nerves tangled like loose rope in the Wyoming wind.

Why, oh why, had she agreed to that date with Henry?

He seemed like a nice enough guy, but she didn't feel ready to spend time with the opposite sex. She enjoyed spending time alone and didn't believe she would provide very good company. With her current state of mind, she'd probably bore poor Henry to death.

She had half a mind not to even show up, but she knew once Lucy caught wind of her playing hooky, she'd be in big trouble. No, it would be best for her to do her duty and go out with Henry this one time, then go underground. No more blind dates, no charity-case Casanovas.

Nada.

Silence continued to reign at the café, so Fran left Eva in charge once again and headed to her backyard for some garden therapy. She retrieved her gloves and a hoe from the shed and made her way to the dirt plot scattered with withered vines and dried corn stalks.

Pitiful, she thought as she stared at her unproductive attempt to grow anything this past summer. Even the huckleberry bushes lining the back of the yard had stopped producing fruit earlier than normal, which meant she and Lucy hadn't been able to put up as much jam this year.

With the water rationing restrictions, her efforts seemed useless, and her sad harvest didn't seem worth the effort. Only a few wrinkled carrots, crinkled corn cobs, and a tomato or two, pockmarked by hail, remained. She had managed to coddle the pumpkins, giving them extra water, which they craved. They sat on the ground, their long, leafy vines curled like locks of hair.

"Got to have pumpkins for Halloween," Fran commented, feeling a measure of guilt for giving them special treatment.

Time to get down to business, she thought. Chopping thistles and dandelions always calmed the soul. She enjoyed the peace and quiet, along with the beauty of the surrounding mountain peaks covered in blue-green spruce, pine, and yellow-leafed aspen trees. Forty-five minutes later, Fran had half the garden weeded, and she'd cleaned up the dead debris, depositing it in her compost pile.

Fortunately, her mood had improved. After picking several stalks of golden dwarf sunflowers, she slipped back inside, put them in a vase of water, and went up to the apartment to shower.

Energized after the shot of steamy water, she changed into a fresh pair of jeans and a fluffy blue sweater. After applying a spritz of hairspray, her tousled ginger-colored locks looked presentable. A touch of makeup enhanced her facial features and a pair of gold earrings added some bling.

Glancing in the bathroom mirror, she smiled, wondering why she'd been so reluctant to allow herself an evening out. Downstairs she found her daughter seated on a stool at the order counter.

Eva looked up from the language arts textbook she'd been reading, and glanced over Fran's attire with a nod. "Mom. Aren't you going to be late for your date?"

"No, honey, I'm fine." Fran snagged her purse from the closet.

"Is it all right if I use your computer while you're out?" Eva's brows arched questioningly. "I have to write a report about fascism."

Fran winced. She preferred that Eva use the laptop she'd purchased for her college courses.

"I like typing reports on your computer because it has a separate keyboard," Eva added, as if she sensed Fran's reluctance. "It's more comfortable that way."

How could she turn her down her daughter's request?

"Sure, go ahead," Fran told her. "Do me a favor and don't fiddle with any of the settings."

"Sure, Mom. See ya later."

Fran walked out into the backyard where long purple shadows stretched across the ground. Assessing the weeded half of her garden, she decided to finish the other half on Sunday when the café was closed. Making her way down a set of ancient, crumbling concrete steps, which she decided to get fixed soon before someone fell and broke their neck, she entered her old garage.

It had been built long after the Victorian period had ended—probably around the 1940s. Although dark and musty and in ramshackle condition, it did the job of keeping Fran's truck and Eva's little car out of the wind, rain, and snow.

As her truck chugged along the dusty streets, Fran decided that an evening out would help her gain perspective. There are many seasons in life, and she was passing through another one.

It might be relaxing to spend time with Henry's friends and talk about something besides recipes and running a cafe. One caveat, however. It was a good idea that she had told Henry she'd meet him at his place. That way, she would be in control of getting herself home. These days, the idea of remaining independent had become important to her.

The jagged mountains overshadowing the little town rose high into the air, the tips dusted with snow, while the slopes below remained carpeted with green coniferous trees and golden aspen trees. Underbrush added browns, oranges, and buff colors. No wonder painters often depicted lofty heights in their creations—the sight offered inspiration.

Before long, Fran arrived at Henry's man-cave, an old, pumpkin-colored house with scruffy, overgrown bushes. She parked and walked toward it, enjoying the waning warmth of the setting sun. Soon, Daylight Savings Time would kick in and darkness would start cocooning the town much earlier.

Suddenly, a dog leapt from behind a stand of tall, dry weeds, hackles raised, and teeth bared. It was a big mutt with gray shaggy hair and a humped back. He made Cujo look well mannered.

"Nice, doggie," Fran soothed as she backed toward the street. The more she inched back, the more the dog snarled at her.

"Back off, Tiny," a male voice called out.

Fran looked up and saw Henry at the door, a piece of meat in his large hand. Tossing it to the dog, Tiny snagged it between his fangs and scarfed it down with a gulp. Then he stared at Fran again, panting, his tongue lolling from his mouth.

"Tiny?" Fran blinked in surprise.

Henry stepped down the front porch steps. "Yeah, my ex-wife insisted that we adopt him from the shelter, but I had to take him in the divorce. Unfortunately, he keeps getting loose."

Henry grasped Tiny's collar and led him back to the bushes, hooking the canine to a thick chain.

Fran released the breath she didn't realize she'd been holding. Even if the dog had scared the bejabbers out of her, she didn't like seeing it chained. No wonder the pooch was grumpy. She wouldn't like those type of living conditions, either.

Henry smiled and took her arm. "Let's get a move on. Everyone's waiting for us."

"Do you keep Tiny chained up all the time?" she asked.

"Just when I'm going somewhere," Henry said. "I don't want him to chew on anything in this rental. You know what I mean? I put an offer down on my own place, but I'm still waiting to hear from my real estate agent to see if the owners accepted it. Then the dog will have free reign of my backyard."

Fran nodded, glad to hear Tiny's future prospects would improve.

Henry had changed into a nice, button-down jeans shirt, and wore pressed slacks. Looking at him again, Reese didn't feel as critical about his appearance, and she appreciated his attempts to help her mingle.

He smelled of Old Spice cologne. However, in Fran's opinion, or maybe it was her oversensitive sense of smell, she thought he'd applied it too liberally. She sneezed, noting the strong scent was almost enough to peel the socks right off her feet.

In Henry's car, they rode over to the carnival. Fran discovered, to her delight, the fall carnival displayed the same cheesy booths she remembered as a child. Additionally, it offered the familiar glittery, noisy activities. Inhaling the scent of corn dogs, greasy sausage, and powdered sugar dusted funnel cakes, old memories surfaced. Despite the carnival's tacky nature, Fran loved it.

She rode few rides with Henry and his motley crew—two buddies and their girlfriends. The activities thrilled her, and she found herself giggling like a kid. They finally tried the Ferris wheel ride, which gave Fran more cause for amusement after the operator secured her and Henry in the bucket seat.

Henry faked a yawn and performed the ancient slither-the-arm-around-the-shoulders-trick. Fran smiled. This wasn't a date she would soon forget. Despite Lucy's frustrating insistence that she give courting a try, and Fran's stubborn reluctance to do so, she had to admit she was having a good time. How was it that her sister knew she needed an outing like this? Her cares were melting away like ice cubes on a hot sidewalk.

When the ride ended, Fran excused herself in order to use the powder room, explaining she'd catch up with the group. Henry winked at her and sauntered off to join his friends. On the way back to the group, Fran couldn't resist entering the house of fun.

After hooting at her distorted reflection in the mirrors, she hopped on a multi-colored car that took her on a ride through spook alley. It came to a halt near Madame Evangeline's booth, and Fran found herself intrigued by the prospect of being told about her future.

"Hello," Reese said to Madame Evangeline.

"Welcome," The elderly fortune teller said. "Follow me."

Her gauzy scarf, sequined blouse, and dazzling long skirts fascinated Reese. The gold bangles on her arms clinked as she led Fran inside her tent, illuminated by candles and lanterns. She sat on a chair covered with silken, tasseled pillows, and placed her hands palm down on a table covered in a purple cloth. With a wave of her hand, she indicated that Fran should sit in a chair placed nearby.

Madame Evangeline inhaled of the patchouli incense curling around the room in snakes of smoke. She tossed her long black and gray hair over her shoulders, and her crystal chandelier earrings tinkled.

"I have told your fortune before, have I not, my child?" Madame Evangeline asked, her gaze drilling into Fran.

"A long time ago." A shiver crawled up Fran's spine, as if someone had walked across her grave.

"I knew it was so," the fortune teller exclaimed, black eyes flashing. "Back when you were but a child and untainted by the world's cruelties."

"Hmm," Fran said.

Madame Evangeline rested her hands on the crystal ball, long red nails like specks of blood on the glowing surface.

"What do you wish to know about your life?" she asked Fran.

"Whatever you see in the future," Fran answered.

Madame Evangeline nodded and continued staring into the glass ball that had filled with blue fog. "I see danger. Danger that lurks in the darkness. Someone from your past seeks to destroy you. Be mindful of those around you lest you befall their snare. Beware the approaching storms of life."

Fran had to admit she was surprised. She'd figured Madame E. would give her the standard line about marrying someone tall, dark, and handsome, and having six kids. Not that she might be in danger. She didn't want to hear that.

Standing up, Fran removed money from her purse and handed to Madame Evangeline. "Thank you so much."

"Please, I'm not finished."

"I appreciate your concern, but I believe I've heard enough." Fran blew out of the tent like she'd been stung by a bee.

For some reason, the fortune teller's prediction bothered her. She didn't want to believe something dark and mysterious might be headed her way. It unsettled her.

By the time she found Henry, she'd calmed down. He stood at Mort's duck shoot, with its billboard full of yellow feathered critters bearing circular red and white targets. Motorized blue waves curved beneath rows of quackers swimming across a billboard.

Henry lifted his toy gun, took aim, and shot at the ducks, knocking several over.

"Whoo, hoo," he shouted, then smiled with accomplishment.

The carnival worker, a young man sporting a shaggy haircut, announced, "And we have another winner!"

"I'll take the pink teddy bear over there," Henry said, pointing at one on a shelf. After the carnival worker gave it to him, Henry turned to Fran and pressed the fuzzy toy into her hands.

"Here you go," he said. "I thought you might like this."

Fran smiled. "That's sweet, Henry. Thanks."

"You bet," he said. "Want me to try for another?"

"No, and I hope you don't mind if we leave," Fran said. "I'm tired."

"The night is young," he protested.

"I know, and I hate being a party pooper. But I need to get home."

He nodded. "I bet you rise early to start the day, right?"

"Yes," she said. "When you own your own business, it's almost a 24/7 gig."

"We can look forward to next time, then," Henry declared, his gaze expectant. "Would that be okay with you? You know, if we hang out again soon?"

"I'd like that," Fran told him. "I had fun. It was nice to meet your friends, too."

He took her hand as they walked back to the parking lot and got into his car. After a short drive, he pulled up to his house. Then he leaned over and kissed her cheek.

"Come inside for a while," he urged. "Maybe you'd like something to drink like a soda or iced tea."

"No, thanks, but I appreciate the offer."

"Ah, come on. Just for a minute so we can talk."

Fran decided it wouldn't hurt, and got out of his car. She walked with Henry up the sidewalk and they entered his house. Fran dropped her purse next to the coffee table and turned to him.

Without warning, Henry embraced her in a bear hug, then shoved his wet, bumpy tongue in her ear. Fran struggled in his straitjacket embrace.

"Stop it, Henry." Fran continued to squirm. "I do not want to make out with you."

Before she could make her escape, he planted a warm, slobbery kiss on her mouth.

Fran managed to squirm free.

"I'm not ready for this," she said, then hustled outside. As she flew down the porch steps, she wiped her lips on the back of her hand.

"Geez Fran, I'm sorry, I came off too strong," Henry apologized as he followed her, disappointment etched on his face. "Does this mean you won't go out with me again?"

"I don't know—I'll talk to you later," she called over her shoulder." Tiny started to growl from somewhere in the dark bushes.

Digging a ring of keys out of her pocket, Fran rushed to her truck. She peeled out, flinging tiny asphalt rocks in her wake. Rule number one of dating, she decided, was to stay in public places where men had to behave themselves. She fought back tears of frustration. The date had been going fine until that awkward kiss. For some reason, it hadn't felt right.

Darkness draped the neighborhood as she drove home. Anxious to reach her destination, Fran turned down Elm Street and stopped for a red light at the intersection. She reached to turn on the radio, hoping to drown out her thoughts. When she sat back up, she noticed a pair of headlights in her rearview mirror.

To her concern, the vehicle continued to approach. When it smacked her from behind, her head snapped forward, then back. Her brain hammered like it had been bounced across the floor. Outraged, Fran turned around to glare at the dark vehicle.

Amazed and somewhat in shock, she watched as the mystery car pulled out around her truck and shot through the intersection. She attempted to read the license plate or get the make or model. Nice try, no cigar. It was too dark and her head hurt.

The other driver could have at least stopped to make sure she was okay. Then again, why would they do that if they'd planned to hit her truck on purpose?

The light turned green and Fran continued to sit in a daze. At last, she put the truck in gear and drove home. Should she call the cops? No. She really had nothing to report—no license plate, no car description.

She envisioned herself filing a complaint with her brother-in-law, the sheriff. Otis would sit back in his office chair, brows knitted. He would nod occasionally and write in his dog-eared notebook.

Otis would be concerned, of course. They were family and they cared about each other. Otis had been elected to several terms as sheriff, and he did a good job of keeping the peace around here. But with Fran's sketchy details, what action could he take?

Although Fran's hands trembled on the steering wheel, she honestly felt fine. Her old, dinged-up truck would live to fight another battle.

Everything would be all right, she told herself as she parked and went inside her house. The incident had rattled her for sure, but she'd survive.

"Eva, I'm home," she called wearily as she started up the stairs, her feet heavy and her knees watery. In the small living room, she walked past her daughter who plunked away on her computer.

Eva didn't even look up when Fran flung herself onto their old, overstuffed couch. She clutched the pink bear Henry had given her to her chest. Meanwhile, her mind reeled from the night's events.

"Back already?" Eva twirled around in the office chair; one leg crossed over the other. "How'd it go?"

"It was fine," Fran said.

"Come on, I can tell it wasn't," Eva said. "You've got a weird look on your face. What happened?"

"After the carnival, we returned to his house, and, um . . ."

"So, did he kiss you, or what?" Eva popped her gum.

"Slobbered me is more like it," Fran said. "I wasn't expecting that, and I didn't handle myself very well."

Eva made a time out sign with her hands. "TMI, Mom. Too much info."

"You asked."

"Okay, so he doesn't float your boat. But you're obviously a hottie. Consider yourself lucky that at your age you've still got it."

"At my age?" Fran stared at her daughter, wondering how old Eva thought she was.

Eva shrugged. "I just mean that you should be grateful. If you'd been a real hag or something, he wouldn't have asked you out."

"Wow. I'm comforted." Fran stretched her legs out on the wicker coffee table, at last beginning to relax.

"You know," Eva popped her gum again. "I heard you have to date a hundred men before you find the right one."

Fran did not feel well. "A hundred men? I'd rather have a hundred root canals, thank you."

FRAN TOSSED AND TURNED ALL NIGHT. By morning she was tired and stiff. When 5 a.m. rolled around, sleep wasn't an option. That car slamming into her truck last night seemed to have done a number on her, and possibly the jolt caused some muscle damage. A fresh batch of anger washed over her, and she wondered, once again, if the driver had meant to ram into her truck.

"Good morning, sweetie," she said to Eva as she shuffled into the kitchen, surprised to see her daughter seated at the kitchen table hitting the books at this unholy hour of the morning. She headed for the coffee pot that was set on a timer. A rich hazelnut brew called to her, the aroma tickling her nostrils. "You're up way early."

"Morning," Eva mumbled around a mouthful of cereal, then swallowed. "I had to read ten chapters of this history book by Monday or I'm dead."

"We wouldn't have been procrastinating, would we?"

"I got busy." Eva glared at her book.

"Would the busy part have something to do with attending dorm parties when you trek over to the college?"

"No," Eva said sharply, then yawned.

"Come on, sweetie. I always hear when you let yourself in the house late at night."

"Mmm," Eva said.

"I assume you've made friends on campus, friends who invite you to their shindigs."

Eva shrugged; her gaze plastered to the textbook. "All right, yes, I met a girl named Zoe, and I've attended a couple of her dorm parties. Does that make you happy?"

"Honey, you're supposed to enjoy being young and in college," Fran said. "I'm worried, though. You're not drinking and driving, are you?"

"Of course not," Eva said. "I'm not a complete idiot."

"Sorry for prying," Fran said. "But I hate you driving through the mountain pass when it's so dark."

"Zoe offered to let me stay in her dorm room if I ever need to spend the night on campus."

"You should do that next time," Fran poured herself a cup of coffee. "Just call me and let me know."

Eva looked up, her brows raised. "You're not upset about me going to her parties?"

"No, I only want you to be safe. And take it easy, okay?"

"Okay," Eva said.

Leaning back against the counter sipping the hot brew, Fran began to go over her to-do list for the day. Then it hit her.

I left my purse at Henry's house.

Crapola, she'd completely forgotten about it. Growling with frustration, she told Eva, "I left my purse at Henry's house last night. I need to go get it."

"Yeah, I don't blame you for wanting your stuff," Eva said.

"I won't be long," Fran promised. She hurried upstairs and dressed, then drove over to the pumpkin-colored cottage.

As she approached the house, she wondered why Tiny wasn't barking his head off. She checked the bushes and spotted the empty chain on the ground. Had he run away? She knocked on the ripped screen door. No answer. Maybe Henry was probably still in bed. He'd think she was nuts for coming over so early. Oh, well, too bad. She really needed her purse.

To her surprise, the front door stood ajar. Stepping inside, Fran spotted her purse sitting next to the coffee table. All righty then. I'll just slip in real quiet like, get what I need and beeline outta here.

Feeling like a thief and sweating like a pig, Fran tiptoed over and snatched her bag. As she turned to go, her eye caught something in the kitchen that froze her legs in place like pretzels in plaster castings.

In the middle of the floor, Henry Whitehead lay in a pool of blood.

FOUR

FRAN REELED BACKWARD AND PRESSED HER hands against the wall for support. Her mind spun with shock, and a small voice told her to do something, anything.

She needed help.

Fran had no medical training, but from the looks of Henry, he was no doubt beyond any paramedics' ability to resuscitate. His skin had a bluish tinge and his lips were set in a silent scream. The front of his shirt was ripped and covered in blood. Beside him, a broken jar of Saucy Lucy Café huckleberry jelly spread purple goo across the floorboards.

Unable to stomach the sight any longer, she turned away, fumbling for her cell phone in her jeans pocket. She dialed 911 with trembling fingers. Struggling to speak, she told the operator how she had found Henry, and gave her the address.

"I don't . . . I don't think he's alive," she told the operator in a thin, trembling voice.

The operator promised to send help and told Fran to stay on the line and to remain at the scene.

Fran did not want to look at Henry again, so she stumbled into the front room and sat stiffly on his black vinyl couch. She wrapped her arms around herself to try and quell her shaking, then her nose began to twitch. Meanwhile, she answered the operator's questions.

At last, she heard sirens wailing in the distance. She told the operator they were close, and disconnected the call. Next, she dialed Otis and Lucy's number. Since he was the only law around for miles, he needed to be here. She knew his reassuring presence would help to unscramble her brain so she could think sensibly.

"Hello?" Lucy answered.

"Something t-terrible has happened," Fran stammered.

"Fran? What's wrong?"

"Otis needs to come over to Henry Whitehead's place immediately. I think . . . I think somebody murdered him."

Silence thrummed on the cell for a second and Fran heard her sister say something to her Otis, then she heard her brother-in-law answer in a gruff, no-nonsense voice.

"He'll be right over," Lucy told Fran.

Fran disconnected and slipped the cell back into her pocket, coldness seeping into her limbs. Even her toes had gone numb, and her thoughts whirled with disbelief.

Who killed Henry Whitehead? And why?

As Eva would say, this whole thing was so not good. Fran was probably the last person who had seen Henry alive, besides his murderer, and Otis would have serious questions.

A noise on the front porch caused Fran to jump.

"Get your lazy butt up and answer the door, Henry," a female voice called through the open screen. "I thought you was gonna pick up the kids this morning!"

Henry's ex-wife, Vivian, Fran thought. Maybe she'd off'd him last night after Fran left. She seemed resentful enough toward him, so she had the motive. And Henry said it seemed like she'd been stalking him. But why would she show up on his doorstep this morning? Maybe to throw off suspicion? And what would she do if she found Fran here?

Stop being paranoid, Fran told herself. What did she know about solving crimes? She was no Sherlock Holmes.

Fran walked toward the screen door, immediately recognizing

Vivian standing on the porch in a gray running suit and track shoes. The brunette gave her a she-devil look, the same expression she'd worn at the picnic.

"What the heck's goin' on? Where's Henry?" Vivian scowled, her eyes flashing with obvious concern. "Oh, I recognize you. You're one of Henry's new floozies, right?"

Fran's face filled with warmth. "This isn't what it looks like."

"Geez, I knew Henry was a sleaze ball, but couldn't he at least lay off his escapades long enough to pick up his kids like he promised? He was supposed to be over to my place a half hour ago." Vivian heaved herself inside.

"I don't think you should be here," Fran said. "There's been an . . . incident."

"Sure, and I'm the queen of Sheba." Vivian shoved her hands on her hips and hollered, "Hey, Henry Horatio Whitehead, get yourself out here."

As unpleasant as Vivian was, and as much as she seemed to dislike her ex, Fran still figured she would not want to see him laid out on the kitchen floor in a pool of blood. She was the mother of his children, after all.

"He can't," Fran said.

"Can't what?"

"Come out here. Like I said, there's been an incident."

"Oh, I got it." Vivian tossed her dark head. "You two had a hot and heavy night so he's sacked out cold in bed. Far be it from me to disturb his lordship. Do me a favor, toots, and go get the jerk for me."

The wail of a sirens became louder, and Fran decided there was no point in trying to spare Vivian Whitehead any longer. She pointed into the kitchen. "He's in there."

Swearing, Vivian stomped into the other room, complaining about the stack of unwashed dishes and dirty counters. She fell silent, then stumbled back to stand beside Fran, her face pale. "Why'd you go and kill him?"

Fran hugged herself and shivered. "I didn't. I found him like that."

Vivian shook her dark locks of hair. "I always told him he'd better start playing it safe or some pissed-off husband would take him out." She blinked several times, made a gagging sound, and ran outside.

Fran heard her dousing the bushes with what had probably been her breakfast.

Standing outside now, clutching her purse, Fran watched as Otis' brown and white sheriff's car appeared, lights flashing and siren blaring. He parked, then heaved himself from the car and slapped his hat on his head. In a loud voice, he directed his deputy, Cleve Harris, to verify the ETA of the Westonville Police Department.

Westonville was much larger than Moose Creek and had a decent sized police force that was more accustomed to handling murder cases. Which is why Otis had probably called them for assistance.

Otis studied Henry's house, then looked at Fran and said, "Are you all right?"

She nodded, but her hands still trembled.

"You sit tight and I'll handle this," he said. "But I need to talk to you, so don't go anywhere." He disappeared inside the pumpkin-colored cottage with Harris following.

"Rough day, huh?" Cleve said to Fran as he walked past her, scratching his chin.

"You could say that," Fran responded, her voice sounding deadpan.

"This can't be easy. Sorry you wound up in the middle of it."

"Me, too," she answered.

Backup from the Westonville Police Department arrived a short time after that, along with the Westonville Coroner's van. Uniformed officers, along with an elderly man wearing a jacket emblazoned with CORONER, on the back, hustled into Henry's house. Another officer set up a perimeter by looping yellow crime scene tape around the yard.

Fran shook her head, finding it difficult to believe all of this was happening. She could almost believe she'd stepped into a television program or a movie, and that all of the characters involved had been cast to play various parts. The sunlight's warmth offered welcome relief, and she breathed deeply of the fresh morning air.

She sidestepped past Vivian, who was sitting on the edge of a brick planter chewing her nails and crying. An old webbed lawn chair beneath a large cottonwood caught her eye, so she sat down in it. To her frustration, neighbors stared out their windows or stood on their front porches rubbernecking.

Their gazes lingered on her, as if she'd grown two heads, and she wanted to hide somewhere. Being stared at made her skin crawl.

Archie and Janie Spooner, who must have been at least in their eighties, exited the house next door. Fran knew them from church, when she used to attend as a kid. So far, she still hadn't managed to drag herself back inside the place of worship.

Dressed in thick terry bathrobes and slippers, they walked up Henry's driveway and approached Fran with questioning glances.

"What happened?" Archie queried.

"I'm sure you'll read all about it in the newspaper." When they continued to look at her with prying glances, she added, "I'm sorry, I don't know what else to tell you."

"Come on, you can trust us, Fran," Janie urged. "Did someone get hurt?"

Fran nodded. "It's Henry Whitehead. He's been murdered."

"Holy cow," Archie said, and started walking toward the house.

"Don't go in there," Fran said. "It's, it's ugly."

"Yeah, and I know from cop shows that the less people stomping around a crime scene, the better," Janie said.

"I suppose that makes sense," Archie admitted.

Janie patted Fran's shoulder. "You look like you've seen a ghost. Come on over to our house and have some coffee. Maybe it'll make you feel better."

"I need to stay here," Fran told her. "I appreciate the offer, though."

The couple shuffled back into onto their porch, shaking their heads and whispering to themselves.

The community had one small newspaper called the Moose Creek Chronicle. Fran figured it wouldn't be long before one of their reporters caught wind of the trouble and came to investigate. What a story this would be—murder in little old Moose Creek. There probably hadn't been a homicide here in decades.

Lucy pulled up in her blue Ford sedan, parked along the curb, and got out. She hurried toward Fran wearing jeans and a stylish black sweater, and knelt down beside her. "Are you all right?"

"Of course. I find bodies all the time."

"Don't joke. This is not funny," Lucy scolded.

"I know it's not, and I didn't mean to sound so flippant," Fran said. "I'm still in a daze after finding Henry. I can't imagine who would do such a thing to him."

Lucy met Fran's gaze. "What happened? Did you and Henry have a fight?

"That's not at all what happened, Lucy."

"Then tell me, what were you doing here?"

"I left my purse at Henry's house last night," Fran explained. "I didn't remember it until this morning, so I came over here to get it. That's when I found Henry d-dead."

"This such a shame," Lucy said. "Poor Henry."

"He didn't deserve this," Fran said. "And I sure hope the police don't think I had anything to do with his murder."

"I can't believe they would," Lucy said.

"If they do, you might be visiting me at the women's correctional center down in Chamber City," Fran said, then gave an uneasy chuckle. "Do you think you'll be able to fix me up on dates if that happens?"

Clanking noises drew their attention and Fran watched the coroner's technicians rolling what appeared to be Henry's sheeted body over to the coroner's van. They lifted up the gurney into the open double doors and secured it. As they closed up, the coroner got inside and drove away.

Otis and another tall, broad-shouldered man exited Henry's house. Engaged in deep conversation, they motioned vividly with their hands, no doubt discussing the mechanics of how Henry's murder had probably come about.

When the men began walking toward Fran and Lucy, Fran stood, preparing herself mentally for their inevitable questions.

"Detective Stevenson, this is my wife Lucy Parnell, and her sister, Fran Lightfoot," Otis told the man standing beside him. "They own the Saucy Lucy Café here in town. If you're ever hungry and need a bite to eat, I highly recommend their food."

Fran and Lucy said, "Hello," at the same time.

"Pleased to make your acquaintance, ladies, although I wish it could be under different circumstances," Detective Stevenson responded in a deep, rumbling voice as he shook their hands.

"Gabe is with the Westonville Police Department," Otis said. "He's a recent transplant from New York City, but he's got plenty of experience under his belt."

Detective Stevenson wore jeans, western boots, a worn black leather jacket, and a black Stetson. He had curly brown hair and a healthy tan complexion. A police badge on his belt glinted in the sun. He might hail from back east, but he cut a solid western figure and seemed to fit right into his new role.

He nodded at Fran. "Otis tells me you found the body."

"Yes," she answered in a whisper of a voice. She swallowed, finding her throat dry as the desert.

"How well did you know the victim?" Detective Stevenson asked Fran.

"I only met him yesterday. We went to the fall carnival with some friends of his last night."

Stevenson scribbled in a notebook, then asked, "What time did you return?"

"About 9 p.m. Then I went home."

"Can anyone vouch for your story?"

Fran nodded. "My daughter, Eva."

He jotted down something else, and Fran noticed Otis also took notes. It boosted her confidence to see both lawmen documenting her testimony, which would no doubt come into play as they investigated this case.

"Do you know of any enemies Henry Whitehead might have had?" Stevenson leaned against the house and crossed his long legs. "Someone who would be capable of murder?"

"Again, I barely knew the man," Fran said. "He did say his exwife, Vivian, that's her over there sitting on the planter, was angry at him."

"I see," the detective said.

"Uh, I suppose I should mention this," Fran said. "Something weird happened on my way home from Henry's house last night."

"What?" Otis asked.

"A car rear-ended me at the stop light, then took off."

"Why didn't you call me and report that?" Otis asked.

"I didn't see a license plate and it was too dark to get a clear vehicle description," Fran said. "I figured you couldn't follow up without more evidence."

"That wasn't for you to decide," Otis said, taking more notes.

"Ms. Lightfoot, I understand you're divorced," Detective Stevenson said. "You and your ex-husband having any trouble?"

"Dan lives in California. I haven't heard from him in months, and neither has my daughter."

"How does he behave around you?" Stevenson's brows raised. "For example, does he have a temper?"

Fran went cold. "What are you implying?"

The detective shrugged. "Could be he's the jealous type. I have to ask."

"He's remarried . . ." Fran trailed off, as if that answered the detective's question. There was a dark part of her life with Dan she chose to keep dead and buried. She didn't want to talk about it, especially not with the inquisitive detective from Westonville. Besides, she didn't believe Dan's behavior in this case was relevant.

Stevenson took more notes, as did Otis.

"Stay around town, Ms. Lightfoot," Stevenson asked. "We don't consider you a suspect, not yet anyway. There may be more questions we need to ask you, especially since as far as we know, you were the last person to see Henry Whitehead alive."

"Of course," Fran emphasized, considering it most unlucky to be in that role.

"Let me know what your crime lab finds out, Stevenson," Otis said. "I'll ask around town and try to come up with some leads, too."

"Much appreciated." Stevenson took long strides over to Vivian Whitehead, who was still weeping and blowing her nose into a crumbling tissue, and began talking to her.

"Man, oh man." Otis rubbed his neck. "Our small corner of the world doesn't see many murders."

"You can say that again," Lucy added.

"I'm just sick about this," Fran muttered. "It's frightening to think there's a murderer running loose. For some reason, it doesn't seem real."

"You gals can head home now," Otis said. "Try to stay clear of those hack reporters. Okay?"

Both Fran and Lucy nodded.

Once Otis had joined Stevenson in questioning Vivian, Lucy shook her head. "What is this world coming to?"

"I don't know, but it sure isn't good," Fran said. "All I want to do right now is go home and be with my daughter."

"I don't blame you for being upset, Fran. Who wouldn't be?" Lucy patted her arm. "Let's close the café today so we can get our thoughts in order."

"That's a good idea," Fran said. "I've got a splitting headache anyway, and I don't think I'd do a good job of handling orders."

"Take it easy," Lucy said. "I know the outlook seems terrible right now, but things will eventually settle down."

"I hope so," Fran said.

"I have faith that Otis and that new detective from Westonville will solve this murder," Lucy said, then headed toward her car, got in, and drove away.

With an empty sensation in the pit of her stomach, Fran walked over and climbed into her truck. She revved up the engine, and rattled home.

FIVE

BACK AT THE HOUSE, FRAN PUT UP THE CLOSED SIGN in the café window and turned to Eva. "I have some bad news, honey."

"It must be awful if you and Aunt Lucy are closing the café," Eva said. She came out from behind the order counter and sat down at one of the tables, clutching her cell phone in its pink sparkly case.

Fran slid into the seat beside Eva, dropped her purse on the floor, and patted the back of her hand. Fortunately, most of her daughter's classes were online this semester, so she'd been able to help staff the café. Today, however, after the recent unsettling events, everyone deserved a break.

"It's about Henry Whitehead, the man I went out with last night."

"Okay," Eva said slowly. "What gives?"

"He was murdered."

"OMG!" Eva's eyes opened wide. "What happened?"

"When I went over to get my purse this morning, I found him, er, his body. The police and Uncle Otis are investigating."

"How awful." Eva bit her lower lip, then continued speaking. "You're not in trouble, are you?"

"No, no," Fran reassured her. "After I called 911 and the police arrived, they had questions. That's all. They may have more as time goes on, but it depends on how their investigation goes."

"What did Uncle Otis say?"

"He reassured me he'd handle the investigation, along with the Westonville Police Department, and that I shouldn't talk to the media."

"That's good. I didn't know him well before we moved here, but I like him, Mom. I feel certain he'll get to the bottom of this."

"I'm sure he will, too. Meanwhile, Aunt Lucy thought we should all take the day off so we can process what happened."

"That's a good idea," Eva said. "Hey, do you mind if I go up to my room? I need to work on a project."

"Go right ahead," Fran told her. "I'm wound pretty tight, as you can imagine. I've got to find some way to relax."

"I get it," Eva said as she left the room.

Fran leaned over and folded her arms on the table so she could pillow her head. She thought about Henry's murder. Her stomach churned as she envisioned seeing him on his kitchen floor surrounded by blood.

The car that had run into her last night also weighed on her mind. Who had been driving? Had they run into her on purpose?

Unbidden, thoughts about Dan crowded into her consciousness. Dan and Davina were married now, and the two of them continued to reside in California, occupying the same home she'd shared with her ex-husband. She recalled Detective Stevenson's suggestion that Dan might have returned to Moose Creek to cause trouble.

Could Dan be stalking her? Was he responsible not only for ramming into her truck, but for Henry's murder?

A shiver danced up her spine.

Her reality had turned topsy turvy. Thank goodness for Otis, Lucy, and Eva, who she knew would stand by her through anything. Good Lord, what if the police decided all the evidence pointed to her as the killer? What would she do then?

Better get a good attorney.

She had money in her savings account. Nevertheless, she disliked the idea of spending any of it for an expensive trial lawyer to save her neck from the gallows.

Don't borrow trouble, she heard her mother's firm counsel.

Good advice, of course. No one had said anything about charging Fran with murder. Just further questioning. That thought improved her state of mind.

A knock on the front door of the café startled her. She had put up the CLOSED sign, right? Considering her unsettled state of mind, perhaps she hadn't. Pulling herself up from the table, she crossed the room and opened up.

"Sorry, we're closed," she said, giving the man on the stoop an apologetic smile. She recognized Barnard Scott, a reporter for the Moose Creek Chronicle, standing there.

There was no doubt in her mind that he had come to grill her.

Probably in his fifties, he wore a gray wool fedora with a feather in the hat band and a rumpled suit that appeared too large for his lithe figure. In his hands, he carried a notebook and a stubby pencil. Wetting the writing instrument with the tip of his tongue, he held it above the paper and said, "Fran Lightfoot?"

"That's me," she answered, her heart skipping a beat.

"What was your relationship with Henry Whitehead?"

Warning bells clanged in Fran's mind. She remembered Otis warning her not to talk with the media.

"Ahem . . . No comment."

"Had you known Mr. Whitehead long?"

"No comment," she insisted as perspiration dotted her upper lip.

"Why were you at his home when the police arrived this morning?"

"Please leave," Fran said, her blood starting to boil.

"Do the police consider you a suspect?" Barnard raised his shaggy eyebrows and studied her with intensity.

"The café is closed today, sir, so I'm going inside now." Fran closed the door and leaned against it. To her frustration, Barnard knocked again. She ignored him. She'd heard from others that once Barnard Scott was onto a good story, he persisted like a chronic cold you couldn't shake.

THAT NIGHT FRAN WENT TO BED EARLY. Her dreams were fitful. She tossed and turned, unable to sleep a wink. By two a.m. her bed looked like a battlefield. She shoved her tousled hair into a head-band and padded downstairs in her slippers to the kitchen. Once her coffee began brewing, she brought up her checking account online and paid bills.

After getting dressed and drinking a large cup of coffee, she swept the kitchen floor, then got down on her hands and knees and scrubbed it with a vengeance, even though it was spic and span after the dishwasher escapade.

It was barely light when she went outside and began hoeing the remains of her garden. The second she started hacking at the dusty weeds, she knew she was going to be sorry. Her muscles, still stiff and sore from getting rear ended in her truck, wouldn't appreciate how she took out her frustration on the good earth. Oh well. Maybe she'd be in so much pain she could keep her mind off the murder.

The sun had nearly melted her into a puddle and she was breathing heavily by the time Eva came out and grabbed her by the shoulder.

"Mom, Mom!"

Fran dropped her hoe and swung around to face her daughter. "What?"

"You're going at those weeds like a madwoman."

Fran put a hand over her heart, feeling it hammer under her palm. "I am mad. Mad at life."

"Well, you're gonna keel over if you don't knock it off."

Fran followed her daughter over to an ancient picnic table and sat down. Eva took a seat across from her, poured a glass of lemon-ade from a pitcher she must have brought out, and slid it over the splintered wood.

"Drink," she commanded. "I thought you might be thirsty by now, so I made this."

Fran swallowed the cool, tart liquid. "Thanks."

"What's up?" Eva asked.

"I can't stop thinking about Henry Whitehead and who could have murdered him. It creeps me out because we'd just been on a date together."

"So?" Eva shrugged. "It's not like you're the black widow or anything. It's bad luck is all."

Ah, the simplicity of youth. So untainted by the real world. Then Fran remembered Madame Evangeline's warnings. Should she give them any consideration? Did someone wish her ill?

For goodness' sake. How ridiculous of her to even take that fortune-telling nonsense into consideration.

"Mom?"

Fran pulled herself together. "Yes, honey?"

"Have you heard from Dad lately?"

"No. Have you?"

Eva shook her head, her eyes, the color of her father's, sad.

"He's probably caught up in his work," Fran reassured her.

"And with Davina and their new baby, I bet. I'm sure she's had him or her by now."

"No doubt," Fran said. "Unless she has the gestation period of an elephant."

"I could have a half brother or sister and I don't even know their name," Eva said as she flew back into the house.

Fran took another drink of lemonade. Her heart fractured as she thought of her daughter's pain. She wished she could bear the sorrow in her place.

Shaking off her unease, she focused on her current concern—who had killed Henry Whitehead. Someone in this town had answers. While Fran knew very little about him, other people must know more.

Thank goodness Otis would be investigating the homicide, as would Detective Gabe Stevenson.

She trusted Otis to ask the right people the right questions. Detective Stevenson looked capable enough, but he'd only recently moved here. To top it off, he lived over in Westonville.

What did he know about anyone in Moose Creek?

As she swatted at a fly buzzing around her face, she realized that was an unfair assessment. The detective seemed competent and professional. She doubted this was the first murder case he'd worked on, especially since Otis had vouched for his law enforcement background.

Nevertheless, Fran decided there was only one person who knew this town and its citizens like the back of her hand. Her sister. If Moose Creek had a pulse, Lucy had her finger on it.

Fran glanced at her watch, noting she had an hour before the café opened. She pulled her cell phone from her pocket and punched in Lucy's number. When Lucy answered, Fran said, "I need your help."

"What's going on?" Lucy asked.

"I'm worried."

"About what?"

"The murder investigation. I have faith that Otis will handle everything correctly, but what do we really know about Detective Stevenson? How can we trust him?"

"I'm sure he's good at what he does," Lucy said. "He's single, by the way. Actually, he's a widower."

"Lucy, concentrate. I don't care about the man's marital status. But I do care about his investigation abilities. What if he decides I killed Henry?"

"That would be impossible. The Westonville coroner will determine Henry's time of death, and I'm sure it will be hours after you went home."

Fran thought about her truck getting rear ended. "I know it's a stretch, but what if somebody has it in for me? What if I'm next?"

Lucy was silent a moment. "I never thought of it that way."

"I think the two of us should try to find out who killed Henry."

"I don't think that's too smart," Lucy cautioned. "It could be dangerous."

"We'll be careful."

"I'm not so sure that's a good idea."

"Picture me in an orange jumpsuit if Johnny Law tries to pin the murder on me," Fran insisted. "Or, worse yet, pushing up daisies if somebody comes after me." When Lucy didn't respond, Fran added, "I know I sound crazy, so I understand why you don't want to get involved. I'll do this myself."

"Oh, stop. You are not going to jail and you are not going to die," Lucy said. "You win. I don't think we'll find the murderer, but we could ask around to see what people know."

"Yes! Where do you think we should start? You know this town better than I do. I've been away too long."

The line was silent a moment while Lucy seemed to mull over Fran's question. "At Nailed to the Wall, of course," Lucy said. "Women are as loose-lipped over at Carma Leone's beauty parlor as teenage girls at a sleepover. We have to open the café shortly, but tomorrow morning, we'll have our nails done while we listen to shoptalk."

"You do your own nails, right?" Fran asked.

"Yes, I do, so I don't give a fig about having fancy manicures. But we are, after all, on a mission to try and ferret out a murderer."

SIX

W HEN FRAN AND LUCY WALKED INSIDE Nailed to the Wall the next day, the shop bell tinkled on the door. Bright sunlight slanted across the walls, imbuing the place with a comfortable vibe.

The cow-shaped clock above the checkout desk revealed it was only eight in the morning. Fran reassured herself that she and Lucy had plenty of time to get manicures before they opened the café at noon.

She glanced at the ivy-stenciled walls, which held floral wreaths and posters displaying models dressed in fabulous clothes. Advertising the latest nail designs, they beamed with confidence. On the floor, thick rose-colored carpet spread out beneath everyone's feet. Gilt-edged mirrors offered customers the chance to observe the reflection of their freshly coiffed and shining appearances.

Upon Fran and Lucy's entrance, everyone froze in the various stations of beauty treatment—massage, pedicure, manicure, and hairdressing—and looked up. Before long, low, tittering comments drifted across the room.

"Welcome," Carma Leone said as she walked in their direction. "It's good to see you both today."

"Hello, Carma," Fran said, recognizing her former classmate from high school. "Nice to see you, too. It's been a long time."

Carma had graduated from Moose Creek High School the same year as Fran. But her looks had changed over the years—for the better.

Back in high school, Carma had been tall and plain. She'd worn unflattering glasses, too. Now she'd blossomed into a lovely woman with dark, exotic good looks and mysterious green eyes. Her black smock and black slacks emphasized her sleek, sophisticated appearance.

Carma's dark brows arched into an expression of curiosity, and she folded her arms across her chest. "What brings you ladies here today?"

"Would you have time to do our nails this morning?" Fran held up her ragged paws.

Carma smiled. "We sure do. Let me know if there are any other services we can provide—bikini waxing, eyebrow plucking, facials, you name it."

"Thanks, Carma," Lucy said. "We're only interested in manicures today."

"Of course." Carma tucked her hair behind her ears. "Actually, I have a cancellation this morning and so does Georgia. We'd be more than happy to take care of you."

"Great," Fran said, anticipating the latest gossip.

"Georgia will do your nails, Lucy. Go ahead and have a seat at her station and she'll be right back. She's just powdering her nose." Carma pointed toward a desk adjacent to hers and Lucy lowered into a chair.

"You're looking good," Fran said Carma as she sat down. "Your business seems quite successful."

Carma shrugged. "It helps when you run the only beauty shop in town."

"I understand completely," Fran said. "It's like that with my café. Still, you must be doing something right."

"I try my best," Carma said, then added, "I'm so sorry to hear about your parents passing away."

"Losing a loved one is a huge loss," Fran said, her heart twinging.

"And I was also surprised to hear that you and Dan broke up," Carma continued. "You two always seemed meant for each other."

"Things change," Fran said.

"And your daughter? How is she doing?" Carma began buffing Fran's short nails.

"It was rough at first, of course. She's fine now and is a freshman at Westonville University."

"I hear that you serve excellent food at your place," Carma emphasized. "I needed to stop by sometime and try it for myself."

"You should," Fran said. "I make a mean huckleberry pie I'm sure you'd love."

Carma chuckled. "Like I need those kinds of calories."

"We'll make it a very small piece," Fran suggested. "By the way, how's your grandfather doing these days?"

"He died a couple of years ago."

"Oh, gosh, I'm so sorry. I always enjoyed talking with him when I was a kid. Loved his army stories."

"Pops always told the same tales over and over, but my mom and I pretended we were hearing them for the first time. I do miss him, and I miss my mom since she's gone, too. I don't have anyone except my aunt and . . ." She cleared her throat. "Do you have any idea what color of polish you want?"

"Red, I guess. And I'm sorry for your loss." Fran felt a stab of sadness. Even though she and Carma hadn't run in the same circles as teenagers, she empathized with her.

About that time Georgia made an appearance. She sashayed into the room, her long, flowered muumuu flowing, her long blonde hair falling over her shoulders.

"Thanks for being so patient, honey," she said to Lucy in a heavy southern accent. She sat down in her chair and reached for Lucy's hand.

"Poor thing," Georgia exclaimed. "Your skin is all red and chafed and those nails . . ." She shook her head.

"They are dishpan red," Lucy admitted.

"It's downright good you came when you did, honey. Why, if these nails of yours had gotten any shorter or drier, I'd have had a tussle taking care of them." Georgia pulled out a buffer and ran it across the nails on Lucy's right hand, then her left.

Fran listened to the low buzz of voices in the shop while Carma worked on her nails, then heard Lucy pipe up. "Isn't it a shame about Henry Whitehead?"

"Ain't it, though?" Georgia shook her head. "I wonder what kind of shenanigans are happening in Moose Creek. A genuine murder. Just think of it."

"There's no excuse for killing another human being. However, I understand Henry didn't endear himself to a lot of people," Carma said.

"Why, I was talking to his poor wife Vivian just last week," Georgia said. "She told me about some of the things that went on in that marriage of theirs. Do you know Henry wanted them to participate in swapping?"

A lady under a hairdryer leaned forward, a few pink rollers peeking from beneath the hood. "Did you say shopping? What's so bad about that?"

"No, swapping," Georgia emphasized. "They do it in Denver and a lot of big cities. It's where husbands and wives go to parties with each other. They size each other up as bedroom partners. Then the spouses agree to trade with each other for a night of . . . well, you can only imagine."

"Why, I think that's crazy," the hairdryer lady said. "No wonder poor Vivian left him. What a deadbeat. Of course, that's no reason for someone to do away with him." Shaking her head, she slid back under the hairdryer and resumed reading a hairstyle magazine.

"How well do you know Vivian?" Fran asked Georgia.

"She's been my neighbor for ten years."

Lucy and Fran exchanged a glance, silently acknowledging they had chosen a good place to come for gossip.

"Are you and Vivian good friends?" Lucy asked.

"Good enough," Georgia drawled.

"Would Vivian have gotten angry enough at Henry to do something desperate?" Fran asked.

Georgia offered a questioning look. "Like murder him?"

Fran shrugged. "Maybe."

Georgia shook head. "No ma'am, I don't think so. Not Vivian. She just ain't the type."

Carma piped up, "You never know what people can be capable of when they are pushed too far."

Lucy nodded. "I've heard it can cause them to do terrible things."

"True. But not poor Vivian. She'd have been more likely to go into a convent than to kill someone," Georgia said.

Fran wondered about that. She recalled Henry stating that Vivian had been following him like a stalker. Vivian had also spoken poorly of Henry before discovering his body. Obviously, Vivian and Henry did not have high opinions of each other.

"What about these swapping parties?" Fran asked. "Did Henry ever get Vivian to go to any of them?"

"Vivian claims it never got that far before she filed for divorce," Georgia said. "But she did mention Henry was living a wild single life."

"Henry Whitehead had women parading in and out of his house day and night," Carma said. "He was a womanizer."

"Yes siree-Bob," Georgia said. "Henry Whitehead had become the Casanova of Moose Creek. That's why Vivian went for the jugular when they got divorced. Since she'd already gotten her revenge with a good divorce settlement, she didn't have any reason to do him in."

"Maybe it wasn't as good a settlement as it seemed," Lucy said.

"Vivian gave me the impression that it was," Georgia said.

Carma produced a fat pink file and began the final buff on Fran's nails. "I've seen Henry hanging out at MacGreggor's Pub. Maybe he got involved with a married woman. Could be a jealous husband found out and decided to teach him a lesson."

"That's one theory," Fran said.

"Now, enough with the cross examination," Carma said. "If I didn't know better, I'd say you two were trying to do your own police work."

A short while later, as Fran and Lucy sat under the nail dryers with nearly identical red nail polish on their fingers, Lucy turned to her younger sister. No one else was nearby, and they could talk freely.

"What do you think about all this, Fran?

"We have to become a couple of bar flies."

Lucy groaned. "I suppose you're right, but I'm not a fan of bars."

"Come on," Fran said. "How could it hurt to wander around and listen to people talk for a while?"

Lucy frowned.

"That's okay, you can stay home," Fran said. "Since it's Friday, and lots of people will be there, I'm going to check it out tonight."

"Over my dead body," Lucy said. "I'll be right there with you."

SEVEN

FRAN AND LUCY RETURNED TO THE CAFÉ and prepared the daily soups by lunchtime. Before long, the crowd began to shuffle in. Fran put on her best customer-service face, despite her preoccupation with Henry's murder.

She nodded to her regulars which included old Ian Fletcher, a retired army veteran who had served in the Vietnam war. His wife Akiko, a tiny Japanese lady whom Ian had married a few years ago, sat at a table with him.

Fran went out to their favorite spot by the large bay window. Most people ordered at the counter, but Akiko and Ian liked the personal touch. Since they were such good customers, Fran waited on them.

Akiko, a small woman in a striped skirt and a red sweater who wore her black hair in a medium length bob hairstyle, looked about ten years younger than her husband. She ordered her usual pot of green tea, an egg salad sandwich on honey oat bread, and a piece of apple pie.

Ian, in his mid-seventies, wore a plaid flannel shirt, frayed jeans, and boots, with his long gray hair tied back by a leather thong. In what seemed an unusually soft-spoken manner for a former sergeant who used to bark orders, he asked for tuna on rye, along with a piece of peach pie, and black coffee.

Akiko had once mentioned to Fran that Ian moved and spoke quietly for a specific reason—his army survival training. The men who'd served tours in Vietnam learned to move stealthily and maintain low voices while they patrolled the thick jungles, praying the Viet Cong wouldn't detect their movements.

When Fran brought out their food and placed it on the table, Akiko commented, "Your eyes are very sad, Fran."

"I'm tired. There's a lot going on."

"Ah, I see." Akiko tilted her head to the side, a lock of black hair sliding across her brow. "We heard about Henry Whitehead being murdered. Read an article in the newspaper about it."

Fran nodded, a lump in her throat. "It's terrible, isn't it?"

"I heard you two were dating," Akiko said as she poked Ian, who was leaning back in his chair reading a magazine. He grunted in response but didn't lower the reading material.

"We only had one date," Fran answered. "I barely knew him."

Akiko narrowed her eyes. "You be careful. People may stop coming here to eat. Maybe they are afraid."

Fran was stunned. What kind of wild gossip was going on in Moose Creek? Would people honestly stop eating here?

She and Lucy's café business, along with their catering option, enjoyed huge popularity in town. So far, things had been running smoothly and customers came and went just like before the murder.

Hopefully Akiko's prediction wouldn't come true.

"I think we'll make out," Fran told Akiko. "So far, no one's mentioned any concerns."

"It's so sad someone took Henry's life," Akiko said. "Who do you think would want to do that?"

"I have no idea," Fran said, not in a mood to discuss the matter any further. "Please, enjoy your meals."

Ian put down his magazine and began eating his food.

Akiko's tiny silver earrings tinkled against her pink cheeks as she said, "Thank you for making our lunch, Fran, it looks delicious, as always."

"It's good to see the two of you," Fran said, then immersed herself in taking care her duties: wiping down tables, clearing away plates and utensils when people were finished with their meals, etc. She returned to the counter to take the order of her next customer, one of the local farmers wearing coveralls and a green John Deere ball cap. He ordered beef stew and cornbread muffins. When Fran had it ready, he picked up his order from her and sat at a bistro table near the soda machine.

After things quieted down out front, Fran headed into the kitchen where her sister stood by the counter mixing more huckleberry muffin batter, one of their most requested items.

"How's it going?" Lucy asked as she ladled a gooey dollop into a floured muffin tin.

Fran didn't mention Akiko's comments. Best not to get Lucy worried that customers would steer clear of their café. There was no proof that would happen, after all.

"All's quiet on the western front," she said.

"Good." Lucy glanced at her watch. "I have to leave for my doctor's appointment soon. You sure you'll be okay working here alone for a couple of hours?"

With Lucy out of pocket and Eva cramming for an exam upstairs in her room, Fran would be left to her own devices.

"Of course." Standing beside the stove, Fran grabbed a large metal spoon and stirred a crock-pot full of golden broth, tender white chicken pieces, vegetables and chunky, homemade noodles. When her cell phone rang, she fished it out of her apron pocket.

"Saucy Lucy Café," she answered. "This is Fran."

"We need to talk."

"Excuse me?" Fran stopped stirring the chicken soup, her spoon poised in mid-air. "Who is this?"

"My apologies. This is Detective Stevenson."

"Hello, how goes the investigation?" she asked eagerly. "Have you found the murderer yet?"

After Fran said that, she wanted to smack herself. Although it would have been spectacular, it also would have been a miracle if Detective Stevenson and Otis had solved Henry's murder that fast.

"We're making progress," Detective Stevenson affirmed. "It appears we've found the murder weapon, though we're still conducting tests."

"That's good," Fran said.

"I need to speak with you ASAP."

Fran tensed, wishing she didn't have to go over the murder anymore. "Why?"

"Don't want to tell you on the phone. Will you meet me at the Westonville Police Station today?"

"I can't, I'm covering the café alone this afternoon."

"I see. Then I'll drive over to Moose Creek. But I won't be able to get there till later." The line was silent a moment. "Have dinner with me."

"I don't know," Fran said with hesitation.

She had to admit, the prospect of Detective Stevenson coming here seemed safer. For some reason, she feared if she went to the police department in Westonville, she'd wind up locked in a dark jail cell.

"How about seven thirty?" the detective pressed.

"I never said yes."

"I'm doing my best to accommodate you," he said. "Cooperate with me, okay?"

"I'm sorry to sound so negative," she said. "As you can imagine, I'm reluctant to keep reliving the morning I found Henry Whitehead's body."

"That's understandable," he said. "And I don't blame you one bit. But I'm just trying to do my job."

Remembering her tryst tonight with Lucy, Fran suggested, "Let's meet at MacGreggor's Pub. You can try a bison burger or maybe a steak."

"You eat bison around here?"

Fran chuckled. "You've never heard of that? Some local ranchers specialize in handling large herds. Thanks to conservation efforts, bison are no longer an endangered species."

"Well, I'll be." He chuckled. "I suppose that's something I haven't considered before. I just might give it a try."

"It's true that you're a long way from home," Fran said. "Which brings me to the question, if I'm not being too nosey, why did you move to Wyoming?"

"No specific reason," he said. "See you at seven thirty." A second later, his phone disconnected.

Fran sensed she'd ventured into the forbidden waters of Detective Stevenson's past, which he wasn't willing to disclose. Curious as to why, she clicked off her cell.

The man had definitely piqued her interest.

EIGHT

"MOM, COULD YOU LEND ME $200?" Eva asked, standing in Fran's bedroom door. She appeared innocent enough wearing her white T-shirt and pink leggings, but Fran had serious doubts about what the money would be used for.

"Hmm, let me think about it a minute." Fran slid on dark pantyhose, then stepped into black high heels. For her dinner with Detective Stevenson, she'd chosen a black, long sleeve lace dress with a flare skirt that she slid over her head and zipped up.

Glancing at her reflection in a floor length mirror, she turned this way and that. The waist felt loose, as if she'd lost weight. She plucked at the seam, frowning.

"You look fantastic, Mom. Quit worrying."

"Thanks, honey. I haven't worn this dress in a while and I wondered if I still look all right in it."

"Your dress is fire, Mom. Seriously."

"Fire?"

"It means great."

"Oh, I see," Fran said, realizing she learned new teen slang on a regular basis since Eva supplied her with plenty of information.

"Where are you going, anyway?" Eva leaned against the doorframe and crossed her arms over her chest.

"Out to dinner with Detective Stevenson. Remember I told you about how he and Uncle Otis are working on Henry Whitehead's murder case?"

"Yeah, I remember," Eva said. "It's a surprise to me that you two are going on a date."

"It's not a date," Fran returned in a defensive tone, then softened her voice. "He has more questions about the morning I found Henry's body. That's all."

"Bummer," Eva said. "Why is he taking you to dinner though?"

Fran shrugged. "He wanted me to go to the Westonville Police Department earlier today, but I couldn't leave because I was the only one working at the café."

"I see," Eva said, nodding. "Sorry to rag on you, Mom, but what about that money I asked for?"

Fran clipped on hoop earrings. Studying her face in her dresser mirror, she began to apply makeup from a basket of cosmetics. First and foremost a mom, she couldn't help but wonder what was up with her daughter's request for money.

"What's it for, hon?"

"Trust me. It's going for a good cause," Eva insisted.

Fran fluffed her ginger locks, then spritzed them with hair spray. "If you need something, let me know and I'll buy it for you."

"I don't need anything, Mom. The money is for something, um, different."

Fran's mind reeled for a minute. She wanted to ask Eva once again what she wanted the money for. Then again, perhaps it would be better if she didn't know what her daughter had planned.

She took a deep breath, then reached into her jewelry box, and withdrew two one-hundred-dollar bills. Handing them to Eva, she said, "Use this wisely, grasshopper."

"Huh?" Eva said, a puzzled look on her face.

"Never mind," Fran said, remembering the line from an old TV show she used to watch as a kid. "It's not important."

"Thanks," Eva said. "Like I said before, it's going for a good cause."

"Have you got big plans this weekend?"

"Zoe and I are going hiking in the mountains with a couple of guys tomorrow. Then on Sunday, we're going to do some research at the library together."

"I'm happy you met someone to hang out with," Fran said, pleased to hear Eva had a new friend.

"I'm spending Saturday night in Zoe's dorm room, too. She's got a futon I can sleep on."

"Sounds like you're all set," Fran said.

"Zoe's great, Mom. You'd like her."

"Invite her over for dinner sometime," Fran said. "And the guys are . . . who?"

"Just college guys, Mom. They live in Zoe's dorm."

"I see." Ah, the joys of watching your little girl seeking her independence.

"Lighten up, Mom. It's not like I'm gonna run away and get married. We want to enjoy the warm fall weather is all."

"You're not dating either of these guys, are you?"

"No way. That's too intense for me. But one of them has a cool truck that I like."

Eva held up the greenbacks. "Thanks, Mom. I promise to pay this back."

"All I want is for you to make sure that cause of yours is worthy," Fran said.

"Oh, it is, Mom. It totally is."

"Just a second, dear," Fran said as Eva turned to leave.

"What's up?" Eva asked, raising her brows.

Fran walked over and gave Eva a hug, then pulled away and said, "You remember my friend Janet, right?"

"Sure," Eva responded.

"I received an email from her today," Fran said. "She told me that she heard your father and Davina had a baby girl this morning."

"I have a little sister." Tears filled Eva's eyes and she blinked. "D-did Janet find out what they named her?"

"Ginger."

"That's pretty," Eva said. "But I'll probably never get to meet her."

Fran patted Eva's arm. "Your dad has gotten caught up in his new life. I'm sure he'll call you soon to share the news."

"Sure," Eva said. "I won't hold my breath while I'm waiting, though."

She headed down the hall. A second later, Fran heard her door slam.

"Poor kid," Fran murmured.

Next semester, her daughter planned to move over to the dorms. With the distance, Fran wouldn't be able to physically see her every day. It was time to loosen the apron strings and trust Eva would make good choices, Fran decided. She'd done her best to instill good values and needed to trust her judgment. Glancing at her watch, she noted she had 10 minutes to make it over to MacGreggor's Pub.

Reaching for a light shawl, she threw it across her shoulders, and headed downstairs. After locking the door, she hustled out to her truck in the garage. As she started up the old pickup, hearing the strange, but familiar, rat-a-tat-tat in the engine, she hoped Otis wasn't patrolling the streets. She'd have to step on it to get to MacGreggor's in time, and she sure didn't need her brother-in-law stopping her for speeding. She needn't have worried. After pulling into the pub's parking lot and getting out of her truck, she checked her watch and realized she wasn't late after all.

"Good evening, Fran."

Startled, she looked up to see Detective Stevenson observing her. He wore jeans again, cowboy boots, a white button-down shirt and a tweed blazer.

"Hello there, you caught me off guard," she said.

"Is that a '69 Ford truck you're driving? I'm kind of an old car fanatic."

Fran smiled. "It is. My father owned it and kept it in pristine condition. These days, though, it's gone downhill. I'm surprised you recognized the make and model."

"I'm cursed with an observant nature," he said, chuckling. "Guess it comes with the job."

"No doubt a good skill for you to have," Fran said.

"That's a fact," he agreed. "By the way, call me Gabe. We might be working together for a while."

"The entrance is on this side of the building," Fran said, walking toward the pub.

In one long stride, Gabe caught up to her and opened the door. "I didn't mean to start off on the wrong foot with you, Fran. I've got a crime to solve, so we might as well get along."

Fran met his gaze. "What makes you think we're not getting along?"

"No reason," he said. "You seem sort of distant toward me, like, like you mistrust me."

"I'm sorry you got that impression," Fran said. "I didn't mean to behave that way. I'm upset about what happened to Henry, and I'm worried about a murderer running around loose in town."

"Well, now, I can't blame you for that," Gabe said. "I promise you, I'm doing all I can to bring the individual responsible for his death to justice. Sooner, than later."

"I appreciate hearing that," Fran said, warming up toward Gabe.

Later, when they'd been seated in the restaurant area and had ordered their dinner, Fran decided she wanted to try and get to know Gabe better. After all, it was up to him and Otis to handle the town's recent unrest. She knew Otis wouldn't rest until it was resolved. Rather than suspect Gabe's law enforcement abilities, she thought she'd find out more.

"Tell me, Gabe. Why did you leave the gritty crimes in New York for wind-blown Wyoming?"

He observed her for a moment, a muscle twitching in his cheek. "Police work in big cities is intense and I've got a daughter to raise."

"A daughter? How old?"

"She's 12. I had her in private boarding school back east but she hated it, so I worked to get a new assignment. I hoped out here we'd have more time together."

Fran's heart went out to him—being a single dad couldn't be easy. She had a good idea of what it was like to wind up playing the role of both parents.

"Moose Creek is a nice, quiet town to raise children," she said. "Just so you know, murders aren't frequent here."

"That's why I wanted to move out west," Gabe said. "I've spent nearly two decades of my life handling tough street crime, and I wanted to work somewhere less stressful than New York City."

"I believe you'll find that lifestyle here," Fran said, while at the same time she realized that Otis had been right about Gabe's wealth of experience. "Westonville is also a sleepy college town, and folks there are pretty laid back, too."

Gabe nodded. "So I've discovered."

"What about your ex-wife?" Fran asked. "I imagine she wasn't happy that your daughter came all the way out to Wyoming to live with you."

When Gabe gave her a blank stare, her mouth went dry. No doubt he realized she'd picked up on the gossip that he was a single dad.

Thanks Lucy, for that juicy morsel, since I managed to put my foot in my mouth.

"My apologies for prying," Fran said. "I heard, um, through the grapevine that you are single."

"My wife, ah," Gabe cleared his throat and his voice tightened, "S-she, she passed a few years ago. Cancer."

"I'm so sorry." Fran instinctively reached to pat the back of Gabe's hand, then pulled back. She didn't know him well enough to do that, despite her desire to comfort him. In an attempt deflect the conversation to a lighter topic, Fran asked, "What's your daughter's name?"

A smile twitched at the corners of Gabe's mouth as he poured Fran a glass of wine from the bottle he'd ordered. "Jade."

"How lovely," Fran said. "You know Wyoming is famous for our precious green jade."

"Fran, I wanted to talk with you about something important," Gabe ventured. "We've confirmed that Henry Whitehead was stabbed to death. We found the murder weapon and the lab confirmed that his blood was on it."

Fran took a sip of wine and felt it warming all the way down the length of her body until it tingled in her toes. Nevertheless, her insides felt frozen at the news she'd just heard.

"It's disturbing that someone was ruthless enough to do that to him, but its progress, right?" Fran said.

He nodded. "Have you noticed any butcher knives missing from your kitchen?"

Fran sipped more of her wine and answered, "No. Why?"

"I'm here to tell you one must be missing. Your fingerprints are on it. Along with those of other people in your household."

Fran sputtered as wine went the wrong way down her throat. She remembered being fingerprinted for a summer life guard job she'd held as a teenager, and assumed that's what the police had used to identify her.

"Are you all right?" Gabe asked, giving her a concerned look.

"I'm fine," she managed. "I'm, well, shocked, to say the least."

"I'm sure you are," he said. "Our crime scene technicians found the knife stuck in a tree trunk in the victim's yard."

"My word," Fran managed. "I can't even begin to understand why my prints and my family's prints are on the knife."

"Normally, I wouldn't share this information, but Otis is certain the knife is from a carving set he uses on your family's annual Thanksgiving turkey."

Fran's heart jumped, as if it had been hit with a bolt of lightning. "We keep that set in the pantry to use for special occasions," she said. "It's one my parents used during holiday meals, so it has sentimental value."

"I see," Gabe said. "Otis stopped by the café early this morning before it opened and had a look. He found the carving fork in the box that holds the set, but not the knife."

"He never mentioned that to me," Fran said. "How in the world did he get inside? I keep the doors locked during the café's off hours. Especially after, well, you know, Henry's murder."

"Otis said you weren't downstairs yet," Gabe said. "That's why he used Lucy's key."

"Oh," Fran said. "That makes sense."

"Since I knew I'd be talking with you tonight, I told him I'd let you know."

"Obviously, someone snuck into our pantry and stole that knife right out from under our noses." Fran's extremities went numb. "Do the police consider us all suspects?

"Not at this point because so many people have access to your café—customers, delivery people, etc."

"That's a relief," Fran said. "You'll be trying to track down who could have stolen the knife, right?"

"That's a fact," Gabe said. "Otis and I have discussed that at length. The tracking down part might take a while, however, I wanted you to be prepared for whatever may come your way."

Goosebumps pimpled Fran's forearms when she recalled the fortune teller's dire predictions. Could this be the storm Madame Evangeline had warned about? Maybe she hadn't been referring to the weather.

"H-how long do you think it will take to find the real murderer?" she asked, realizing that even though she wanted the case solved, no one could predict when it would happen.

"It'll take a while to process everything," Gabe explained. "These things take time."

"Of course," Fran said. "It's like I'm in a nightmare and I'm having trouble waking up."

"Tell me what you know about Henry Whitehead," Gabe encouraged. "Anything at all you think might help."

"Let's see," she said, hating that her emotions were up and down like a roller coaster. "As far as Henry goes, I barely knew him."

"Doesn't matter. Tell me what few things you do know."

A server brought their dinner and they fell silent as he handed out the sizzling platters of buffalo steak and baked potatoes. When they were alone again, Fran told Gabe what few things she knew about Henry.

For example, what he'd mentioned about his ex-wife Vivian, and that he feared she was stalking him. She explained when she'd seen Vivian for the first time, the woman had stared at Henry with hatred in her eyes. Also, when Vivian had shown up at Henry's house after Fran had discovered his body, she'd talked about him with contempt

"Not that Vivian's behavior is unexpected, especially since they were not happily divorced, not that anyone ever is . . ." In order to stop stammering, Fran waited a moment before diving back in. "But I heard from some folks in town that Henry was involved with a swinger's group and he wanted Vivian to join, but she refused. I believe they resented each other."

"Definitely bad blood between those two, from what I understand," Gabe said. "Which gives a clear motive for Vivian wanting him gone."

"That makes her a suspect as well, right?"

Gabe nodded.

After a bite of steak, Fran asked Gabe, "Why you think someone wanted to implicate me or someone else from my family in Henry's murder?"

"To take the heat off themselves," Gabe said. "It seems they dislike your family for some reason and wanted to point the finger your direction."

"I'm more than a little worried that someone has us in their crosshairs," Fran admitted.

Gabe wiped his mouth with a napkin and said, "Do what you're already doing—keep your doors and windows locked and maybe install some dead bolts."

"Good idea," Fran said.

"I'm still wondering if your ex-husband might be behind it," Gabe said. "Or another enemy you might not be aware of."

"I don't have any enemies, and neither does my family," Fran insisted.

"At least none you know of," Gabe said.

"True," she admitted. "But Dan is in California with his wife and new baby, so I can't imagine he's been sneaking around Moose Creek causing trouble."

"Give me his phone number anyway," Gabe said. "I'm going to call him and verify his whereabouts the night of the murder."

He handed her his cell phone and she typed in a new contact with Dan's information.

Gabe looked like he wanted to say something else, but the server arrived to clear dishes away, and he remained silent.

Fran's head swam with unanswered questions. Could Dan have sneaked up to Wyoming to follow her around? Had he stabbed Henry, thinking he was her lover? Was he jealous of her, even though he had pushed for a divorce?

Confusion, disbelief, and something she assumed might be shock and fear washed over Fran. She stared through the window at the dark road outside awash with the pink tinge of streetlights.

Was that a dark she saw over there lurking in the shadows? Her heart skipped a beat, then the figure vanished into the darkened alley as quickly as she'd noticed it. If it had ever really been there.

Not much of a drinker, Fran knew she was either tipsy or on the verge of losing her mind. Sensing Gabe's steady gaze, she turned to see he'd grabbed the check and was concentrating on her.

Fran took another sip of wine and looked him right in the eye. "What?"

His brow wrinkled with concern. "You seem jittery."

"You think?" she gave an uneasy laugh.

"Take it easy, okay?"

"Sure," Fran said.

"Watch your every move and stay aware of who is around you," he cautioned. "Make sure no one follows you when you're driving."

"You're thinking of the person who hit me at the stoplight the night I left Henry's house?"

"Possibly the murderer or an accomplice."

A wave of helplessness wash over Fran. "I feel like a sitting duck."

"Are you certain you don't know who was driving the car that hit you?" Gabe asked.

"No. Not a clue."

Fran felt dizzy. That's what happened when you didn't drink very often. One or two drinks, and poof!

"And you couldn't make out the make or model, right?"

Fran nodded. "It was too dark. I tried, but didn't have any luck."

"That's understandable," he said.

Fran folded her hands on the table. "Which reminds me, I still haven't had a chance to get that dent pulled out of my bumper."

"Good."

Fran looked curiously at Gabe. "Excuse me?"

"I'll take a look at it before I leave tonight. Could be some paint was left by the other car. I'll scrape it off and try to trace the make and model."

"Be my guest. Scrape away." Fran rose. "Thank you for the dinner, and for the warning."

Gabe pushed his chair back and stood. "He reached into his tweed blazer and handed her a business card, one dark brow raised. "Call me if you think of anything that might be pertinent to the case. Or even if you'd like to talk."

"Sure." Fran sensed he might have another interest in her besides the case. With the wine coursing through her blood, she couldn't be certain.

He gave her an assessing look. "Can I give you a ride home?"

"Oh, I'm peachy, detective. Just peachy. I appreciate the offer, though."

"Have a nice evening, then."

Gabe sauntered up to the cash register, paid the bill, then exited the restaurant. Fran walked over to the bar and sat on a padded stool to wait for Lucy. For the life of her, she couldn't think of who would have wanted to implicate her or her family in such a nefarious deed as murder.

"Ice water, please," she asked the bartender, looking forward to a drink that would clear the wine from her senses. It was important she get her wits about her. She had work to do.

"Fran Castleton, is that you?"

Fran realized the bartender had spoken to her. Upon closer inspection, she realized Shane MacGreggor, the bar owner's son, had just served her the ice water.

"Shane! It's so good to see you," Fran said. "And my last name is Lightfoot now."

Shane nodded, and his face lit up. "That's right, you married Dan Lightfoot, right?"

"Yes, but we're no longer together," she added.

"It's been a long time since high school graduation," Shane said. "Amazing how time flies."

"It does, indeed," Shane said. "You missed this place so much, you decided to move back home, huh?"

"It was time," Fran said with a chuckle. "Besides, I got to visit with my parents before they passed away."

Shane winced. "That was rough. Their car hit livestock on the road late at night, didn't it?"

Fran nodded. "A freak accident."

"My whole family was sorry to hear about it. We'd have gone to the funeral, but we'd all come down with a flu bug and didn't want to share with anyone. We sent flowers."

"I remember getting them, thanks," Fran said, recalling the large bouquet of yellow roses—her mother's favorite.

"You are more than welcome," Shane said.

"How are your folks doing?" Fran scanned the room. "I don't see your dad walking around giving orders."

Shane laughed. "He retired a while ago, so it's up to me and my sister to keep the place going. Now, he and my mom are living the good life. In fact, they are on a Mediterranean cruise as we speak."

"Good for them," Fran said. "I'm glad to hear that they're doing well. How is Halley these days?"

"She's off tonight or you could ask her yourself, but she's hale and hearty. She keeps busy with the pub and her work with rescue dogs. She fosters them, then helps the animal shelter find them good homes."

"She always did love pups," Fran said. "And you? How is life treating you?"

"It's great. I married Cara Whitney—she was a couple years behind us at Moose Creek High. We've got two boys now. Seth is 12 and Dusty is 10."

"Ain't it grand being a parent?" Fran asked.

"You got that one right," Shane said. "You have a daughter, right?"

"Yes, Eva is 18 and in her first year of college."

Shane used a cloth to rub the counter for a second. "Hey, I read in the newspaper about Henry Whitehead's death. It said you were with him when it happened. Is that true?"

"Barnard Scott wrote it and he didn't report it exactly right," Fran said, wondering what other community members had seen the article. "I went with Henry to the fall carnival and the next morning, I realized I'd left my purse at his house. When I stopped by to pick it up, I found him and . . . well, he was gone."

"What a bad scene."

"I called 911, and the rest is history, even though people like to twist the truth into wild stories." Fran sipped at her ice water.

"So, you didn't kill him?" Shane lifted a brow.

"Of course not."

"I knew it, I only wanted to give you some guff," Shane said. "There's talk going around, you know."

"I'm sure," she said, uneasy to think of what people were saying.

"Henry used to spend a lot of time in here and he did some serious carousing," Shane said. "He was pretty popular with the ladies, married and single, and I heard he broke a lot of hearts."

"Do you think maybe one of his former flames decided to get even?" Fran asked.

"Methinks it's not a shot in the dark to consider it. In fact . . ." Shane glanced around, then leaned closer to Fran. "I'd bet good money that Dr. Raina Ferguson would have it in her to take him out. I heard that Henry wined and dined her, then dumped her like a hot potato, and went on to another woman. I heard Raina was livid."

"I can imagine," Fran said, tucking that name in her mind. "A woman scorned, you know."

He rapped his knuckles on the counter. "Don't be such a stranger. Stop by once in a while and say hi."

"I'll do that," Fran promised. "Come see me and Lucy at the café, too."

"You got it," Shane said as he wandered back to handle his bar duties.

Thankfully, the jumble in Fran's head settled as she sipped more of her ice water. Minutes ticked by, and she watched as Shane placed decorative globe centerpieces on the tables and lit them. Shortly after that, a country western band stepped onto the stage and began playing.

Searching the sea of faces and bodies, Fran still didn't find Lucy anywhere. Maybe her sister had stood her up. Fran stirred the crushed ice in her water glass with a thin red straw, thinking maybe she'd mingle by herself and see if she could pick up more news about Henry. Shane had already given her a juicy tidbit.

A few seconds later, she felt a touch on her shoulder.

NINE

FRAN WHIRLED AROUND, RELIEVED TO SEE her sister standing there. "Geez, Luce, you scared me half to death."

"Sorry." Lucy was dressed in jeans, cowboy boots, and a western cut blouse with leather fringe. "Didn't mean to frighten you."

"Have a seat," Fran told her.

"How did your dinner with Detective Stevenson go?" Lucy asked as she settled in next to Fran.

"He gave me some disturbing news. Henry was killed with a butcher knife that came from our cafe. It's the blade from Mom and Dad's carving set that we use for special occasions."

"You're kidding!" Lucy gasped.

"Wish I was," Fran said. "Gabe said Otis stopped by the café earlier today and verified that the knife from the set is missing. Of course, our family's fingerprints are all over it."

"Are we to be arrested?"

"No, nothing like that."

Lucy blinked. "This is terrible."

"It seems the murderer got into our pantry and stole it, with the intent to frame one us for the murder."

"Why?"

"That's what we've got to find out."

"Hi Lucy," Shane said as he leaned on the bar beside her.

Lucy placed a hand on his shoulder. "Good to see you, buddy! Can I please have an ice water?"

"Coming right up," he said. He returned with the water, placed it in front of Lucy.

"Thanks," she said.

"It's on the house." He laughed and turned to Fran. "Yours too."

"What a guy," Fran called to him as he headed over to another patron who had bellied up to the bar.

"This is serious business, I think, since Detective Stevenson came all the way over here from Westonville to talk to you," Lucy said.

"It's not that far." Fran looked Lucy right in the eye, suspicious of her sister's insinuation. "Don't go getting any ideas. It was like a business dinner. Nothing more."

"The detective is good looking in a rugged, outdoorsman sort of way," Lucy said.

"Lucy, focus on us solving the murder case. I have absolutely no romantic interest in Gabe."

"But you are now calling him by his first name."

Fran shrugged. "He asked me to. Believe me, I've got enough trouble in my life without having a man around to complicate things."

"Oh, sweetie," Lucy said. "I don't want you to die without ever having a good companion."

"I'll be fine," Fran said. "I'm fulfilled and I'm happy."

From the corner of her eye, Fran noticed a tall man in a cowboy hat step away from the jukebox, and another country song began to blare. He headed back over to a long table covered in a white tablecloth. Above it floated bunch of white balloons, one of which said, ENGAGED TO BE MARRIED. People had crowded around, talking, laughing, and toasting.

"That's Bill Waterstone standing by the table with the balloons, isn't it?" Fran asked Lucy.

Lucy turned to look. "Yep, that's him. I heard his daughter had gotten engaged and I bet that's their family celebrating the happy event."

"Let's go say hi," Fran said. "Someone may bring up the murder, and maybe we'll get another clue or two in the case. Shane, bless his heart, already gave me a lead about Raina Ferguson."

"What about Raina?" Lucy asked.

"Henry dated her, then dumped her, and she was pretty upset," Fran said as they approached the celebration table.

"Hi ya'll," Lucy called out, giving a little wave.

Folks greeted them with boisterous shouts, inviting them to join the party.

"Lookee here!" Sally Renee, Bill's daughter called, holding up her left hand to display a large diamond ring.

"How beautiful," Fran gushed, genuinely impressed with the sparkly rock.

The sisters sat down in a couple of empty chairs and joined the conversation. Introductions and greetings made their way around the crowd.

"My blushing groom, Greg," Sally Renee said, hugging the large, broad-shouldered guy seated next to her. "The wedding's set for April, and we'll actually take a wagon ride from the church afterward. I'll be sending out the invitations before long and you're all invited!"

Whoops and shouts rose in the air.

"Wasn't it a shame about what happened to Henry Whitehead?" Bill eventually said.

"And in our fair little town," Lucy added with a tsk, tsk.

Caleb Reinhart, who sat next to Fran, draped an arm around her shoulders and gave her a friendly squeeze. "Well, my mama always told me if you play with fire, you're gonna get burned."

"What do you mean?" Fran asked.

"Whitehead was an old horndog. I heard tell he practically had a revolving door installed on his house to accommodate the gals comin' and goin'. I heard he preferred women who were disillusioned with the dating scene. Fed 'em the crap they wanted to hear, charmed them shamelessly. They fell lock, stock, and barrel for it." He took a swig of beer and gave a mighty guffaw.

The other men around the table nodded and offered similar comments.

A man named Flynn Knox said, "Some of the gals Whitehead was messing around with were married. I'm sure their husbands eventually got wise to his nonsense. There's no telling how angry they became."

"Angry enough to have killed him?" Crystal Livermore asked.

"No doubt," Flynn responded. "You don't mess around with another man's gal, unless you want a black eye or two. Or worse."

A low murmur of agreement rolled through the group.

"I heard that Ernie Howell was pretty hot about his wife Sophie getting messed up with Henry," Caleb said. "Ernie threatened to go after him with a shotgun and a shovel. Swore he'd had enough of Whitehead foolin' with his wife and that he'd kill him with his bare hands if he didn't back off."

An icy sensation shot through Fran. Was this the clue she and Lucy had been looking for? Had this Ernie fellow gone off the deep end? Had he stolen a knife from the cafe and killed Henry, hoping to implicate the sisters and take the heat off of himself, like Gabe had suggested?

"Where does Ernie live?" Fran pressed, and Lucy gave her an encouraging nod.

"I heard he and Sophie moved to Denver," Caleb said.

"Denver, really?" Fran said.

"Ernie planned on opening a business down there," Caleb added.

"Do you know what kind?" Fran asked.

"Not sure exactly." Caleb shrugged. "But I think it had something to do with magic."

Fran folded her arms across her chest. "Lucy and I sure know what it's like running your own business. You have to stay committed to make a go of it."

"Ernie and Sophie's boys got into all those wizard books that gal from England wrote. Ernie liked all that hocus pocus stuff, too," Caleb said. "Come to find out, it seems to draw in the crowds, and I heard their business is a huge success."

"The move to Denver got Sophie far away from Moose Creek and Henry Whitehead," Flynn added. "Ernie hit on a good idea to whisk his family off to Colorado."

So, a potential lead could be in Denver, Fran thought. It was time for a summit meeting with Lucy so they could make plans for their next steps in finding potential suspects.

"Excuse me everyone, I'm off to powder my nose." Fran decided nature's call was a good way to part company with the group. "You coming, Luce?"

"Be right there," Lucy said as she scrambled to grab her purse.

Fran walked toward the ladies' room.

Turning a corner, she headed down a dim hallway, smiling at folks as they passed her. After a fizzle and a pop, the lights went out. Cloying darkness enveloped her like a heavy winter coat.

TEN

"**D**ARN IT," FRAN MUTTERED, groping for the wall. Unable to see anything, she wondered if she should stay where she was, or try to find her way back to the table with the engagement party.

When someone grabbed her arm, she figured it must be Lucy. Obviously not, because the person started to haul her toward the dim outline of the alley door. Fran's heart hammered like a drum as she struggled in the stranger's grasp.

"Hey, let me go! Who are you!"

A meaty hand clamped down hard on Fran's mouth, silencing her shouts. She tried to bite into the flesh, but her assailant pressed so hard, her lips were smashed against her teeth. It was hard to breathe, it was hard to think.

From the bar, Fran heard dismayed howls and shouts. In the midst of the pub blackout, chaos and commotion ruled.

Panic plunged through her as she thrashed, attempting to break free from her attacker's grip. Her efforts were in vain. The individual overpowered her by a seemingly taller and much stronger body.

Fran jammed her elbow into a midsection, and a groan sounded. Despite her struggles, the arms around her tightened. Explosive anger shot through Fran. Someone had glommed onto her like bubblegum to the back of a sneaker.

A surge of adrenaline flowed—the fight or flight syndrome. Loving faces flashed before her eyes: Eva, Lucy, Otis, and Carl.

Do something.

My heels!

A built-in weapon that might just save her butt, she realized. With a grunt, Fran brought her heel down hard on what she sensed was her attacker's instep.

Contact.

The individual gave a surprised, guttural gasp and released Fran as they staggard backward. She fumbled along the wall toward the ladies' room, finally felt a handle, and pushed inside. Moonlight filtered through a small window above one of the stalls. Fran locked the door, leaning against it as she caught her breath.

Someone stomped inside the bathroom. A second later, they slammed against her stall's metal frame with such ferocity, she feared they'd break it. Swallowing panic, she stood on top of the toilet lid, reached up, and tried to shove open the window.

It wouldn't budge.

She slammed her shoulder against the frame, trying to loosen it. An ache radiated through her upper body, but she had to get out of here. At last, the rusty frame cracked, and she wedged it open with a rusty squeak.

"Umph!" a voice complained.

Looking down, Fran spotted a dark form, dressed in what appeared to be a black hooded sweatshirt, attempt to slide beneath the stall door. One thing was for sure, whoever that was down there, they weren't giving up easily. Heart racing, she hoisted herself into the open window, squeezed through, and dropped into the alley below.

The instant she hit the ground, her ankle flared with agony. Biting her lower lip, trying to ignore the pain, she glanced up at the open bathroom window. Relieved not to see anyone, she limped through the gravel and around to the front of the building.

She had to find Lucy and get out of here. Someone had rammed into her truck, and now she'd been attacked. No doubt about it, she'd pissed off somebody. Was it because she'd seen something she wasn't supposed to? Or was it because she and Lucy were checking into Henry's death?

A shiver of contempt raced through her. Either way, how dare they go after her! And who were they, anyway? Suddenly, she realized it wasn't a matter of daring. This person had been desperate enough to kill Henry, which meant they'd have no compunction about trying to prevent their identity from being discovered.

Even if they had to commit a second murder.

Digesting that unsettling thought, Fran ran smack into another large body. After the recent brush that crazy person inside, she started to panic. Gasping, she stumbled backward, ready to defend herself again. Leaning over, she yanked the shoe from her throbbing right foot and held the spike heel out like a weapon.

"Take a hike, bucko," she cried. "I've had enough of your crap!"

Pub lights flashed on, illuminating the person standing in front of her. It was Gabe. In all his lawman's glory. And he looked worried.

Fran tucked the shoe behind her back, feeling like a complete dork. "Man, I'm sorry, Gabe." She wet her dry lips with her equally dry tongue. "I thought you were someone else."

"Don't tell me it's a Wyoming custom to greet everyone you meet by shoving a spiked heel in their face?" He sent her a crooked smile.

"Uh, no, it's not." Warmth crept into Fran's cheeks, causing them to tingle.

Gabe folded his arms across his broad chest and gave her a concerned look. "Are you all right?"

She shook her head. "No, er, well, I'm okay now."

"What happened?"

"Either Shane MacGreggor forgot to pay his utility bill or somebody got hammered and flipped off the main power breaker," Fran said.

"I noticed the lights went out while I was over scraping the paint on your truck," Gabe said. "But why are you ready to launch World War III against me?"

"Someone grabbed me in the hallway," Fran said. "I tried to break free, but they wouldn't let go."

"I didn't hear any screaming," Gabe said.

"Believe me, I'd have hollered for help, but they clamped their hand over my mouth," Fran said. "So I couldn't."

"Shit, that's concerning," Gabe said, narrowing his gaze and looking around. "How did you get away?"

"I stomped my high heel on their foot and ducked into the ladies' room," Fran explained. "They followed me, but I escaped through the window."

"I was afraid something like this might happen," Gabe said, frowning. "Since there's a murderer on the loose who is unhappy with you and your family, you need to keep a low profile. I know I asked you to dinner tonight, but from now on, stay home where it's safe."

Fran felt as trapped as a bug pinned on a science project board. Keeping a low profile would be difficult since she and Lucy were determined to help solve Henry's murder.

"You're right," she told Gabe, then added, "I thought you'd be back in Westonville by now."

"I took in a bit of the night life around here," Gabe said, inclining his head toward the pub.

By now, customers streamed outside and walked past them, still buzzing about the lights going out. Apparently, they'd had enough fun for a Friday evening.

"Really? I didn't see you inside." Fran leaned against the porch railing to take the weight off her throbbing foot.

A muscle twitched along Gabe's whiskered jaw. "I didn't hang out too long. Then I went outside to check out the dent in your truck and do a little paint scraping. Remember I mentioned I was going to do that?"

"Yes, I do remember you saying that," Fran acknowledged.

"If I didn't know better, I'd say you were snooping around and asking questions about Henry Whitehead's murder."

"This is a small town and people will talk," Fran said in a defensive tone. "Especially about a murder."

Gabe nodded. "That's a fact.

Fran put her shoe back on her throbbing foot, then straightened. She tried to put her full weight on it, but it still felt too tender to do that. "Henry had plenty of enemies around here, just so you know."

"I gathered that from questioning we've conducted so far," he said, raising one brow. "I promise, you can leave the murder investigation to me and your brother-in-law, Fran. We'll chase the bad guys, okay?"

She nodded.

Gabe glanced down at her foot. "Go on home now and ice that ankle. Hopefully it'll feel better in the morning."

Fran intended to deny that her foot hurt. But the front door to the pub swung open and Lucy hustled out, a concerned expression on her face.

"Fran, where have you been?" her sister asked. "You disappeared on me."

"I got held up in the hallway outside the ladies' room," Fran explained again. "Somebody grabbed me and wouldn't let go. I managed to get away."

"Oh my gosh!" Lucy said. "Did they hurt you?"

"Scared me for sure," Fran admitted.

"This is alarming," Lucy said. "Do you think somebody is following Fran, Detective Stevenson?"

"I'm not ruling that out," he said.

"What are you going to do?" Lucy asked, her gaze expectant.

"The only thing I can do," he said. "I'll note what happened in my investigation. Fran didn't recognize her assailant, so I can't arrest anyone. And please, call me Gabe."

Lucy nodded. "Sure, thanks . . . Gabe."

"Gabe suggests we stick closer to home," Fran said. "So, let's head that way."

"I'm in total agreement," Lucy added.

"I'll walk you ladies to your cars," Gabe offered. He placed his hands on the small of their backs and accompanied them to the parking lot.

As soon as Fran returned home, she checked the locks on all the doors and windows, left a night light burning, and went upstairs to her room. It happened to be the same one she'd had as a girl, and her parents hadn't changed anything, except for installing updated carpet. Tiny yellow daisies decorated the familiar wallpaper and she slept in the old-fashioned iron bedstead passed down from her grandmother.

Right now, she sat wide awake in bed with her throbbing foot iced and propped on a pillow. As the pain reliever she'd taken kicked in, lessening the ache, she fished her cell from her purse and called her sister.

"Hello?" Lucy answered.

"I think we should drive to Denver and talk to Ernie and Sophie Howell," Fran said.

"It's a bad idea," Lucy shot right back. "Especially after you were attacked tonight."

"How can we pass up the chance to talk with the Howells after what we heard at the pub?"

"Fran—"

"This is important. We have to find out who killed Henry. Whoever did it is targeting our family. Any one of us might be next to be attacked or worse."

"Don't you think you're blowing things out of proportion?" Lucy asked.

"No, I don't." Fran said. "No offense to Otis or the Westonville Police, but they've got so many other cases to handle, how can we trust they'll ever bring Henry's murderer to justice? They have no reason to be in a hurry, but we do."

"I don't know . . ."

"When Akiko and Ian Fletcher came in for lunch today, she mentioned that people are talking about what went on between Henry and me. She didn't say it in so many words, but she insinuated that some might think that I had a reason to hurt him."

"The community members know you better than that," Lucy protested.

"I sure hope so," Fran said. "Nevertheless, Akiko thinks people might stop eating at our café."

"I never considered that," Lucy said. "After all of our hard work, I'd hate it if we had to close the place."

"What do you say? Will you take a field trip with me to Denver to visit the Howell's magic shop?"

"Do I have a choice?"

Fran shrugged. "I could go on my own."

"Over my dead body," Lucy returned.

When Fran finally nodded off that evening, she dreamed of being chased by black-hooded phantoms clutching large butcher knives. It was a relief when the harsh jangling of the telephone jolted her awake.

Despite the pain reliever she'd taken last night, her head pounded. Smacking her dry lips together and blinking in the gray morning light filtering through her lacy bedroom curtains, Fran sat up and reached for her cell phone on the nightstand.

"Hullo?" she managed, wondering who could be calling so early.

"Fran? Hi, this is Bruce."

"Bruce?" she repeated like a parrot, the throbbing in her head slowly taking on jackhammer proportions.

"Cousin Bruce," he said with a little irritation. "Aunt Gladys' son."

"Oh, that Bruce. Sorry. I've got a headache today. Maybe I'm getting the flu."

"Ah, the good old flu. I just got over a bad case of it myself a couple of weeks ago. A real killer."

Fran's mind swam as she tried to recount the genealogy in her muddled mind. Aunt Gladys was her father's sister and Bruce was her son. Ever since he'd put a frog down Fran's shirt at the Fourth of July family picnic when she was ten, she'd never been too fond of him. To her knowledge, he only contacted Aunt Gladys' side of the family when he needed something.

Did he want something from her now?

"How long has it been since we talked?" Fran asked. "About two years?"

"Something like that," Bruce said.

Fran yawned. "What's the occasion?"

"I need to ask you a favor."

Fran did not like the way the conversation was going. "What kind of favor?"

"I'm headquartered in Singapore right now. My company is working with some major investors over there. As district manager of the Far East division, it's crucial for me to be available for all final business transactions. Those won't be complete for about six more months."

"Okay, what's that got to do with me?"

"I flew to Denver about a week ago to visit Mother. She's in a nursing home there and, unfortunately, she's gotten herself into a patch of trouble."

Alarms sounded in Fran's brain. "Tell me already. I'm dying to know. How much trouble can a 70-year-old woman in a nursing home get herself into?"

Bruce cleared his throat. "Plenty. A nurse found her in a, shall we say, compromising situation with one of the male patients."

"Compromising?" Fran questioned as several possibilities crossed her mind.

"You know, they made it to home base."

"Seriously?" Fran laughed. "Means they must be darn healthy. The medical staff should be pleased."

"Well, they weren't," Bruce informed her dolefully. "The nursing home rules prohibit intimate relations between patients. Mother's been given the boot."

"They kicked her out?"

Aunt Gladys had always been eccentric, Fran recalled. Despite seven husbands, she'd never been able to settle down for long. The family attributed her unpredictable nature to the fact she'd been a Las Vegas showgirl in her younger days and just couldn't quite get the exotic flair out of her blood.

"Mother and her, uh, boyfriend probably wouldn't have been in as much trouble if they'd kept their wild romp confined to the privacy of their rooms. But they got caught in the act on the recreation room pool table."

"Goodness, that is a tad exhibitionist, even for Aunt Gladys. But leave it to her to find an octogenarian Romeo." Fran raked a hand through her mussed hair. "What can I do?"

"The retirement home will only allow Mother to stay another two weeks. After that, she has nowhere to go."

"You're kidding me? Can't you find her another home? Hire a nurse or something?"

"I've tried, but everything's full and I don't have time to interview and hire medical staff. I've got to be back in Singapore in forty-eight hours. I'm in a bind here, Fran. Mother said she'd love to live in the home where she grew up. I'm sure it would be the best for her."

Fran thought about her and Lucy's murder investigation. If Aunt Gladys came to stay, she would need constant care. It would be challenging to have her around, but out of consideration for her father's sister, she knew it would be best.

"C'mon Fran, be a sport. I know it would be a major imposition, but can't you help me out? Otherwise, I don't know what I'll do. I'll lose my job if I don't finish up with the Far East clients, and Mother absolutely can't live alone."

Fran knew she couldn't turn down Bruce, but she had one final question. "It's no imposition, Bruce. She's my aunt, and I love her. But, well, doesn't she have a fondness for starting fires?"

"Uh, hem. I hate to admit this, but when no one's looking, she might slip up and start one. All you have to do is keep matches out of her reach and make sure she takes her medication."

Fran nodded. Poor Aunt Gladys, that sweet menace to society.

"I'd love to have her here, Bruce, but I have no beds to spare. Just my old sofa. I'm sure she'd be uncomfortable sleeping with springs up her butt for the next six months."

Not to be sidetracked, Bruce continued. "Doesn't the old Castleton homestead have an attic?"

"Yes, but it's full of storage."

"Clean it out. I'll foot the bill to have the place renovated into living quarters for my mom. I'll send you the same money for her room and board that I've been paying the retirement home. It'll be more than enough to take care of her. You know your mother would want you to do it."

Ah ha. Leave it to Bruce to use the old guilt trip. It wasn't necessary for him to do that, though. Aunt Gladys was, after all, family.

"This will always be her home, Bruce," Fran told him. "I'll pick her up and bring her here."

"You won't regret it," Bruce responded enthusiastically.

Fran wasn't so sure.

ELEVEN

AFTER TALKING WITH BRUCE, Fran immediately called the Carpinelli brothers, who operated a small construction and design business, to take on her attic renovation project. She paid extra for a rush job, and in three days, after working long hours, the upgrades were complete.

At the moment, Fran, Lucy, and Eva stood in the newly refurbished space evaluating the improvements. Fran had stuffed boxes of Eva's old baby clothes and toys into the garage rafters. The cobwebs and dust bunnies that had formerly graced the small, musty space had been cleared and broken windows had been replaced.

Now, a modest-sized sitting room held a floral-patterned loveseat and a reclining rocker. The lace panels Lucy contributed now covered the windows, allowing in wide beams of bright, October sunshine.

The Carpinellis, who had polished the original hardwood floors until they glowed a warm honey-pine color, had installed a small bathroom with a shower. They'd partitioned off a bedroom Fran decorated with antiques from the Moose Creek antiques store, Old Treasures. She'd acquired a Jenny Lind spool bed, an oval-mirrored dresser with a matching night stand, and a wardrobe which nestled in a corner. For a final touch, Fran had rolled out a large carpet adorned with old-fashioned cabbage roses.

A kitchen nook held a drop-leaf table and two ladder-back chairs. A compact refrigerator, microwave, and coffee pot covered the top of a butcher block. Wooden bladed ceiling fans with antique brass accents spun above.

Deep in thought, Fran chewed her lower lip for a moment, then said, "I hope Aunt Gladys likes this. She's pretty particular where she hangs her feather boa, you know."

"Everything looks lovely, Fran." Lucy placed her hands on her hips, nodding appreciatively as she glanced around. "Aunt Gladys is lucky she has such a nice place to stay after that fiasco at the rest home."

"I hope the décor suits Aunt Gladys' tastes," Fran said.

"Considering she got kicked out of her retirement home, I don't think she'll complain, Mom," Eva said. "Remember the photo album she showed us one time? It had pictures of her wearing all those fancy Las Vegas showgirl costumes that showed her bootie. Oh, and those goofy headdresses and tasseled boob pasties she wore. Oh, my God!"

"Eva, girl, watch your language," Lucy scolded.

Eva darted an irritated glance at her aunt.

"Aunt Gladys made a good living as an entertainer, Eva," Fran said. "She put Cousin Bruce through Harvard Law School. It's nothing to be ashamed of."

"Ashamed?" Eva laughed. "I think she's both beautiful and brave. She's lived her life on her terms, as all women should."

"Exactly," Fran said.

"How long will she stay with us?" Eva asked.

"Fran is only taking Aunt Gladys in for a few months until our cousin Bruce returns from Singapore to take care of her," Lucy commented.

Eva snorted. "Right, like I believe that. Bruce will never come to get her. He's made a life of staying away from his mother."

"Eva, honey, Bruce is a busy man with a demanding career," Fran said. "Aunt Gladys is only here temporarily."

Eva shook her head. "Whatever, Mom. She's a feisty old gal, considering her retirement home kicked her out for doing the nasty."

Lucy frowned. "Doing the what?"

"Remember when I called to tell you about her coming, I mentioned she'd been caught in a compromising act, which is why the retirement home asked her to leave?" Fran asked.

"Oh, right," Lucy said, breaking into a laugh. "I can't believe that slipped my mind."

"She's gonna love it here," Eva said, spinning around and taking in all of the improvements. "This room is sick."

"Sick?" Lucy looked confused for a second, then her eyes lit up. "That means good, right?"

"Right." Eva studied the renovated attic with a shrewd eye. "Although, do you think this place'll be too puritanical for her? I mean, you painted the walls powder blue and there are flowers everywhere. Aunt G takes shots of tequila straight up."

"She can add some leopard print throws and zebra striped lamp shades," Fran suggested.

"I'm headed over to the grocery store for some supplies," Lucy said, easing toward the door. "I'll be back in about an hour."

"Remember to pick up more vanilla," Fran said.

"Will do," Lucy said with a mock salute before she left the room.

Eva grabbed her jeans jacket and put it on, then turned to Fran. "When are you and Aunt Lucy going to pick up Aunt Gladys?"

"Tomorrow. Are you okay working alone at the café while we're gone?"

"Of course, and now I'm going for a drive to the park so I can jog," Eva said. "My jeans are getting too tight, so I decided I'd better work off the flab."

"You're paranoid," Fran said, chuckling. "You look great honey, but getting fresh air and enjoying the great outdoors is never a bad thing."

Mother and daughter walked downstairs and outside to the garage. Eva lifted open the old doors, fished keys out of her purse, and got in her car.

"By the way, I want to take you out for your birthday this Saturday night," she called out of the window. "Dinner and a movie maybe. Will that work or do you have other plans?"

That's right, Fran thought. She'd nearly forgotten her birthday. Before she knew it, AARP would be knocking on her door! Well, that was a stretch, but she realized the years were flying by nonetheless.

"No, I haven't got plans," Fran told Eva. "We need to include Aunt Gladys too, you know."

"Not a problem. She'll get a kick out of what I have arranged. See you later."

Fran waved as Eva drove down the dusty street, wondering why her daughter thought Aunt Gladys would get such a kick out of dinner and a movie. She'd probably done that a million times.

A gust of warm October wind blew dry brown leaves across the porch as Fran walked inside. In the kitchen, she glanced at the clock, noting it was 8 in the morning, so there was plenty of time before she and Lucy would open the café.

Opening the pantry door, she headed toward the shelf where they kept the old carving set. An empty spot resided where it had perched, and Fran realized that Otis had probably taken it for evidence. Considering the possibilities of who may have stolen the knife, and how they'd managed to get in the kitchen without anyone seeing them, Fran shook her head. Contemplating possibilities, she brewed herself some hazelnut coffee, savored a cup, then settled down to work.

Retrieving mixing bowls and utensils out of the dishwasher, she began to assemble the day's café menu. Beef stew and the usual sandwich fillings, apple pie, and huckleberry muffins.

She shifted her mind back to Aunt Gladys, hoping she would be comfortable here and wouldn't get too bored.

Yesterday, after completing a brief search of her aunt's retirement home website, Fran discovered it offered hotel-like amenities that included a restaurant, a pool, a gym, a library, a bar, beauty salons, and much more.

However, like Eva had suggested, Aunt Gladys would no doubt appreciate having more freedom. The trip to collect Aunt Gladys in Denver would also enable she and Lucy to stop by the Howell's magic shop.

After surfing through the retirement home website, Fran had researched further online and found Ernie's store—Houdini's Hideout—which she also called in order to verify the Howells were the owners. What would she and Lucy find out when they went there, she wondered? Hopefully, they would uncover more clues that would help them identify Henry Whitehead's murderer.

THE NEXT MORNING AT THE UNGODLY HOUR of five a.m., Fran—all showered and dressed in jeans and a sweater—tiptoed into Eva's room to tell her good-bye. Then she went downstairs to the kitchen and had her morning coffee, along with a bowl of cornflakes and skim milk.

Since Eva would be handling the cafe today, she had made sure several freshly baked loaves of bread, sandwich fillings, and soups were on hand. Her daughter would only need to keep the crock-pots warm and take customer orders.

Fran watched out of the café's bay window for Lucy. When her sister drove up in the darkness, she slid on a light jacket, scooped up her purse, and hustled out into the frosty dawn air. Since her truck wasn't fit to handle the long trip to Denver, and there wouldn't be room for Aunt Gladys anyway, Lucy's vehicle had been chosen to transport them to Mountain Shadows Rest Home.

A cloud of steam swirled from the tailpipe of Lucy's car as Fran hopped inside. Teeth chattering, she said, "S-s-sure glad your car's warm. You could hang meat outside. Think we'll run into any icebergs on I-25?"

"I doubt it." Lucy said, laughing. She wore dark blue pants, a furry blue vest, and a white turtleneck sweater. Pearl encrusted barrettes enhanced her gleaming red hair, which fell to her shoulders in waves.

"My weather app said it's supposed to warm up in a while," Fran added. "We're supposed to get up seventy degrees today. A regular heat wave, at least for Wyoming."

"That's a fact," Lucy responded. "By the way, did you remember to pack your amateur spy kit?"

"The one with the secret decoder ring?" Fran chuckled.

Lucy grinned.

"Nope. But I did bring Cracker Jack." Fran pulled two boxes out of her purse.

"Mercy, I can't resist that," Lucy said, taking one. "I haven't had that stuff since I was, let's see, maybe ten."

"I figured eating it would bring back childhood memories," Fran said.

Indeed, the sisters talked and laughed all the way down to Colorado as they recalled their childhood selves. Once it was light, the blue sky, covered with wispy clouds, arched overhead like a giant dome. Eventually the temperature warmed. Lucy removed her vest and Fran removed her jacket. She watched the cars on the freeway flying past, appreciating that her home town had a much slower pace.

At last Denver appeared with its skyscraper horizon and Front Range Mountain backdrop. With autumn's warm temperatures, flowers, bushes, and trees still sprouted with brilliance throughout the city.

On her cell phone, Fran studied the highlighted route to Houdini's Hideout. Thank goodness for Google Maps, she thought, otherwise Denver would have remained an asphalt jungle to her.

TWELVE

"WHICH EXIT DO I TAKE?" Vehicles zipped past Lucy's car, rushing to change lanes. "I'd like to know before the next century."

"Exit three-twenty," Fran answered. "It's coming right up."

"Great." Lucy steered her car onto the exit ramp. "Right or left?"

"Right." Fran glanced back at the map. "I mean left! Sorry. Take a left at the light."

Lucy raised her brows. "Are you sure which left you want me to take?"

"The left that goes this way," Fran said, gesturing with her left hand.

Fran gave directions as Lucy threaded her way through the narrow downtown streets until she approached a strip mall near rows of older brick homes. Fran noticed Houdini's Hideout as soon as they pulled into the parking lot.

"There it is," she told Lucy, pointing. "See the black top hat and the magic wand on the sign?"

"Yep, so let's go inside and check it out," Lucy said. "Play it by ear, you know?"

"Sounds like a plan," Fran said.

They got out of the car and walked inside Houdini's Hideout where aisles of magic equipment in fancy packaging was ripe for the picking. There were card tricks, strobe lights, fantasy gear, sweeping black capes, and top hats—you name it. Everything to warm the cockles of an amateur magician's heart.

The establishment wasn't extremely large, however, it wasn't postage-stamp-sized, either. Adding to the mystical atmosphere of Houdini's Hideout were its deep purple walls decorated with spar-kling yellow star, moon, and sun decals.

The checkout counter was located on one side of the store where a small woman with a blonde page-boy hairstyle was waiting on a line of customers, a few of whom were rambunctious little boys with stern mothers trying to keep them under control.

The world of illusion sported some hefty price tags. So hefty that Fran would have never even considered purchasing a small, disappearing coin box.

"Go and talk to the lady at the counter," Fran told her sister. "Let's hope that's Sophie."

Lucy smoothed down her hair. "I hope this is worth our time."

"We'll never know unless we try it," Fran responded.

As Lucy wandered toward the clerk, Fran walked down an aisle, picking up and examining different items until she reached a small raised stage at the back of the store. Several people, both young and old, were gathered around a flaxen-haired man prob-ably in his late thirties, wearing a top hat and cape, performing along to music.

He did the white-rabbit-out-of-a-hat trick, and removed a scarf over a cage to reveal several white doves, which he made disap-pear. Impressed, Fran glanced around to see how he might have engineered the act. Of course, she wasn't able to do it, which was the whole reason people called this magic, she realized.

The crowd clapped after the man's last trick, then a young boy of about ten wearing baggy pants and a baseball cap spoke up. "How did you do that, mister? I mean, that was pretty cool."

"Ah, a great magician never gives away his secrets," the man declared. He tapped a paperback book with his magic wand. "But for fifteen dollars and ninety-five cents, you can buy my book, Ernie the Magnificent's Tricks and Illusions. Guaranteed to give you instant success at being a magician. That is, if you follow all the rules to a T," he added.

"Mom, can I get one? Puh-leese?" The youngster stared up at his mom with a long face and beseeching puppy dog eyes.

Mom clenched her jaw and shook her head at her son, mouthing a silent, emphatic, "No." Despite the boy's requests, she remained firm.

Fran studied Ernie the Magnificent. Was he Ernie Howell? Proprietor of Houdini's Hideout and jaded husband of Sophie? She moved closer to the stage, intent on the activities.

"I need an assistant," Ernie declared, his gaze searching the crowd. Immediately, a dozen hands shot in the air. "How refreshing. A crowd of eager apprentices. But for this particular trick, I need a grownup. You, the young lady with the lovely red hair." He gestured at Fran with a patient smile. "Could I convince you to be Ernie the Magnificent's assistant for his next trick?"

"Me?" Fran froze in place. "I'm afraid I'm no good at magic, Mr. Magnificent."

"You don't need to be," he continued. "Leave the illusions to the master."

With reluctance, Fran stepped onto the stage. "Uh, sure, Mr. Magnificent. Whatever you say."

Ernie rolled out a coffin on legs and gestured at another table laden with wicked-looking saws. He made a grand sweep of his hand, indicating Fran should crawl inside.

She cringed. Not a fan of tight, enclosed spaces, she whispered to the master, "Uh, look, Ernie. Is this safe? I mean, I'm too young to die. Ha, ha."

He didn't laugh at Fran's joke. Instead, he took her arm and guided her firmly toward the coffin. "I assure you, Ernie the Magnificent has never harmed an assistant yet."

Fran took exception to the yet part. What was that all about?

She didn't want to be the yet assistant. Ernie helped her climb up into the coffin and she stretched out. Ernie the Magnificent wouldn't risk his budding reputation by killing a volunteer in his performance, would he?

As Ernie started to close the coffin lid, Fran held up her hand, preventing him. He shot her an annoyed look.

"Did you recently move to Denver from Moose Creek with your wife Sophie and your two boys?" she whispered.

"You're interrupting my magic trick," he growled.

Fran wanted out of this death box. Sooner than later. But curiosity outweighed her discomfort.

"Were you angry at Henry Whitehead for having an affair with your wife?" Fran continued. "Did you murder him to settle a score?"

"You're out of your mind," he told her. "My life is in Denver now, and my wife and I are doing our best to forget that whole sordid affair."

He faced the crowd and said with a flourish, "And now for my magic saw trick. Watch closely, ladies and gentlemen. My powers are second only to the great Harry Houdini himself."

Ernie forced the coffin lid closed.

Surrounded in darkness, Fran realized it probably hadn't been smart to confront Ernie the Magnificent about Henry's murder. At least, not right now. What if one of the razor-sharp saws slipped? What if she became a grisly statistic in this magician's act?

Fran realized she was overreacting, nevertheless, her heart hammered. Perspiration dotted her forehead.

Shhh-thunk. One of the blades fell into place.

Fran didn't feel a thing. Maybe she couldn't. She could be bleeding to death and no one would know. Is this what death felt like? Does death feel like . . . nothing?

Shhh-thunk. Another blade dropped.

She heard Ernie tap on the coffin surface, then felt the centrifugal motion as he rotated it.

"Oh, boy," she murmured.

The coffin came to a complete stop and a there was a loud bang. Claustrophobia made it difficult for Fran to breathe. She wanted out of this moldy crate.

"Ernie, I don't care how Magnificent you think you are," she called out. "My assistant days are over. Ernie!"

"Hey, lady," a male voice shouted, "Ernie unlocked your coffin before he stepped off of the stage. Get out yourself."

Feeling ridiculous, Fran lifted the lid and scrambled down onto the platform. Audience members clapped and some even cheered and whistled. Fran looked around for Ernie, but he was suspiciously absent.

"Uh, I guess Ernie the Magnificent also pulled a disappearing act!" she told the audience.

They chuckled as she gave a weak smile, then stepped off the platform, and headed over to where she saw Lucy standing.

Fran placed a hand on Lucy's arm. "Did you see where Ernie went?"

Lucy shook her head. "He took a bow, then high tailed it behind the stage curtains."

"Figures. I think I spooked him."

"How?" Lucy asked.

"I asked him about Henry, and he looked upset. Said he'd been doing his best to forget about the whole sordid affair involving him."

"It's obvious Henry caused a lot of trouble in the Howell's marriage, so I can't say that I blame him," Lucy said.

Fran nodded. "Did you find Sophie?"

"That was her working at the cash register, so I did talk to her. She acted weird when I told her about Henry's murder."

"What did she do?" Fran pressed.

"She turned white as a ghost and started stammering."

"So, it came as a surprise to her to hear her former lover was dead," Fran surmised.

Lucy pressed her hands on her hips. "I'm assuming since Sophie had that kind of reaction, she didn't have anything to do with Henry's death."

"I'd say you're right," Fran said.

"What about Ernie?" Lucy asked. "Did you get a guilty vibe off of him?"

"I'm no expert investigator," Fran admitted. "However, I'd say his reaction to the mention of Henry's murder was caused by anger, rather than from guilt."

"Heartbreak sometimes causes people to behave recklessly and do things they wouldn't normally do," Lucy suggested.

"Yeah, like taking revenge," Fran said. "I'm sure Otis and Gabe have already checked out Ernie as a suspect, if they know what we do. But I don't get the impression that Ernie would commit murder, though."

"Gut instincts are important," Lucy said. "I guess we're done here. Let's go collect Aunt Gladys."

Arm in arm, the sisters walked toward the exit.

THIRTEEN

SUNLIGHT GLINTED OFF THE PINK STUCCO WALLS of Mountain Shadows Rest Home. Like a giant sand crab, it sprawled across an expanse of drying autumn grass that spread out beneath tall evergreens. Gold and orange leaves attached to towering aspen trees fluttered, framing the campus with their lacy finery.

Standing in the parking lot next to her sister, Fran shaded her eyes from the brightness with one hand and studied the wrought iron fence behind the building. It enclosed a large, tree-filled yard where the residents probably took walks and played pinochle on fair weather afternoons.

A pang of sadness touched Fran's heart, and she hoped Lucy wouldn't see the emotion misting her eyes.

Lucy, of course, all-knowing sister that she was, was not fooled one bit. "What's wrong?"

Fran knew better than to hide what she was feeling. "I was just thinking about Mom and Dad. I miss them. Especially this time of the year."

"Of course, because that's when they had their accident," Lucy added. Her eyes glistened as well. "Who would have thought a cow crossing the road would end it all for them? "

"I know. Daddy would never hurt a fly, so he must have swerved to miss its bony hide. If only their seatbelts and saved them."

"Amen," Lucy said. "Look at it this way; they're at peace now. In a much better place than we are."

"True," Fran added as she collected herself.

"Look at the bright side." Lucy nodded in the direction of the rest home. "We've still got our sweet Aunt Gladys to dote on."

They both laughed.

"You can't stay sad around her for too long," Fran admitted. "She's got a funny bone like no one else. The tales she has from her younger days are always a hoot."

"Indeed," Lucy said.

Fran hefted her purse on her shoulder. "We'd best go spring the grand old dame before she causes any more trouble."

As they walked to the front doors of the retirement home, Fran prepared herself for Hurricane Gladys. Needless to say, none of their lives would be boring with her in residence.

"Why do I feel hesitant?" Fran asked.

"Maybe because the last time we saw Aunt Gladys, she set Mom and Dad's house on fire with sandalwood incense and tried to put it out with the garden hose."

Fran laughed. "That's right. And remember how some of their good silver and crystal disappeared along with a couple of family antiques?"

"Yes, I do," Lucy said.

"Good gravy, Dad was upset," Fran added. "He accused Aunt Gladys of being like a firecracker in a pork barrel."

Lucy tsk, tsked. "We do have good insurance on the place, right?"

"Covers flood and fire," Fran said with a nod. "Hopefully, for all the incidents Aunt Gladys can conjure up. Don't know about petty larceny, though."

"Say your prayers and keep your fingers crossed. Maybe it won't be too long before Cousin Bruce comes to collect her."

"I won't hold my breath," Fran said. "He's over forty and still can't manage to find his way home."

The sisters went inside to the front desk and announced who they were. A young lady named Rita assured them she would have a couple of attendants bring Mrs. Maplethorpe out to them right away.

"Please have a seat in the waiting area," Rita suggested to them in a pleasant tone.

Fran and Lucy walked over and sat on a black leather couch. While they waited, Fran studied the Navajo wall hangings and western art covering the walls.

Time ticked by and finally a man with graying hair and glasses approached them.

"Pardon me, are you ladies Mrs. Maplethorpe's nieces?"

"Yes, we are," Fran informed him.

His mustache twitched. "I'm Dr. Ravenwood, her physician. I'm sorry about the wait. Your aunt is missing."

"Missing? As in gone? How can that be?" Lucy rose to her feet, frowning.

"Dr. Ravenwood," Fran said in a concerned tone, rising to stand beside Lucy, "aren't the residents' whereabouts documented?"

"Yes, they are. But I'm afraid Mrs. Maplethorpe managed to slip past our attendants." He offered an apologetic smile. "This is unacceptable, and I hold myself responsible."

The sisters stared at each other, then at Dr, Ravenwood.

"I can assure the two of you, this type of occurrence is very rare."

Fran folded her arms across her chest. "How long has Aunt Gladys been gone?"

"People saw her at breakfast, which is served at 8 a.m. every morning."

Fran glanced at her watch. "The woman's been missing for two hours, and you just now realized she's gone?"

Ravenwood stiffened "I assure you, we run a reliable, reputable establishment. Despite our best efforts, mishaps occur on occasion."

"What are you doing to find our Aunt Gladys?" Lucy asked.

"Attendants are combing the grounds at this very moment," he said in a reassuring tone.

"What if she's not on the premises?" Lucy's eyes went wide. "What if she's out wandering the streets of Denver? Alone?"

"Ladies, please don't jump to conclusions. Rest assured; your aunt couldn't have gotten far. We have video cameras monitoring the entrance twenty-four hours a day. The attendants at the front desk would certainly have seen her had she tried to slip past them. Right, Rita?" He nodded toward the counter.

"Absolutely," Rita-at-the-front-desk agreed. "Shelly and I would have stopped her from going anywhere."

"Your aunt has done this before," Dr. Ravenwood explained. "I'm sure we'll find her unharmed."

"Seriously?" Fran clenched her fists. "This isn't the first time?"

Dr. Ravenwood nodded. "Your aunt fancies the covered pavilions out on the grounds, and that's where we found her last time. Mrs. Maplethorpe claimed she was having a rehearsal for one of her Las Vegas reviews—"

"Dr. Ravenwood, Dr. Ravenwood!"

Everyone turned to the little old blue-haired lady in a flowered housedress and sneakers who shuffled up to them holding clutching a cane. Her chin quivered and her bright green eyes met the doctor's steady gaze. "Someone's up and died out in the courtyard. It's awful."

Dr. Ravenwood put a hand on the elderly woman's arm. "Hazel, did you take your medication this morning?"

She jerked her head up and down. "I'm not seeing things, doc. Honest. And it wasn't just me who saw 'em. Bea and Norton saw, too. Saw 'em out the game room window. Somebody's layin' by the fountain, dead as a doornail. I swear."

"All right, calm down. You go on back and tell Bea and the others to return to their rooms. I'll take care of everything."

Muttering to herself and shaking her blue curls, Hazel shuffled back down a hallway and disappeared.

"You'll have to excuse poor Hazel," Dr. Ravenwood said. "She has delusional spells on occasion. She's apparently had a setback today."

"Hmm," Fran said.

"Mrs. Maplethorpe's son completed most of the forms necessary to release her, and he's given permission for you two to check her out," Dr. Ravenwood said. "But there is still some final paperwork to be completed before your aunt can leave."

"Shouldn't you find our Aunt Gladys first?" Lucy asked.

He nodded toward a sheaf of papers on the counter. "While you ladies take care of those, I'll check on her."

The doctor walked through a pair of glass doors and out onto a flagstone patio.

"I can't believe this is happening," Fran muttered incredulously. "Bruce was paying out the nose for this place, and they misplace their patients?"

"Excuse me, ladies," Rita said. "I've got a pen handy for you to sign the paperwork."

"I'll go look for Aunt Gladys while you John Henry the sheets in that stack," Fran said to Lucy.

As Lucy walked up to the counter, Fran slipped outside the glass doors. Heading across the patio in the direction Dr. Ravenwood took, she descended a set of wide stone steps. Hearing raised voices, she paused, noting they seemed to be coming from behind an arbor filled with fading roses and vines.

Fran hustled around the decorative yard piece and stopped mid-stride.

Aunt Gladys lay on the ground, her cap of snow-white curly hair pressed against the lawn. She wore a tiger-stripe caftan, pink flowered flip-flops, black beads the size of walnuts, large hoop earrings, and black frame glasses. Her face was still as a corpse's.

Uprooted golden and russet-colored Chrysanthemums lay around her in an oval, coffin-like shape. Stretched out like a mannequin, the old gal clutched a mum-bouquet in her red-nailed grasp, her eyes shut against the warm autumn sun, a mischievous grin tilting her plump, ruby-colored lips.

Dr. Ravenwood folded his arms across his chest, his expression stern. "For the second time, Mrs. Maplethorpe, get up. The ground is wet and you'll catch a cold."

"I'm dead. Leave me alone."

"You can't stay out here. You're upsetting everyone."

She opened one eye and peered at the doctor. "Why? You've killed me with all your stupid rules and regulations. A body can barely breathe here."

"You have got to get up. Your nieces are here to take you home."

"And make me leave my Randy? I'm in love with him, you know. He's the only man I've ever loved," she added theatrically.

Fran couldn't help but grin. Aunt Gladys seemed addicted to falling in love.

"Please, Mrs. Maplethorpe," the doctor said.

"This rotten, flea-bag joint is standing in the way of our happiness," Aunt Gladys said.

Fran walked around Dr. Ravenwood and kneeled beside her aunt. "It's nice to see you, Aunt Gladys. It's been a long time."

Aunt Gladys' eyes opened wide. "Fran, is that you?"

"In the flesh," Fran responded,

Aunt Gladys' painted brows drew together. "My brother's girl? All the way from Moose Creek?"

Fran took her aunt's hand, noting the dry, parchment-like skin covered in brown age spots. About fifteen million gold bracelets rattled on her arm.

"Of course, now why don't you get up and come with me?" Fran suggested. "It's time to take you home."

Aunt Gladys sat up slowly, a grin spreading across her face. "How is my younger brother doing these days? James Evan always was a precocious kid. He drove me crazy, but still . . ."

Fran's stomach twisted. "He and my mother were killed in a car accident. Remember?"

"Ah, yes," Aunt Gladys said in a solemn tone as Fran helped her stand." "It's such a tragedy when we lose good people."

"It is for sure," Fran agreed.

Aunt Gladys craned her neck and looked over Fran's shoulder. "Where's that big sister of yours? Lucy? Dr. Demented here says she came, too."

"She's waiting for us in the lobby," Fran said. "We're taking you home to Moose Creek."

"Oh sure, bury me in the armpit of America again." She shook her head. "Where busybodies rule and normal people drool."

"Really, it's not that bad, Aunt Gladys."

Her eyes snapped. "Oh, I know. Can't ever beat returning to your hometown. But can't we go somewhere fun like Las Vegas? I can dance, you know. I could hire on at the Flamingo. Teach those young ladies a thing or two."

"For now, let's go home," Fran told her.

"Is Randy coming with us, too?" Aunt Gladys pressed a hand over her heart. "Please tell me he is or I'll simply have a coronary."

Dr. Ravenwood firmly told her, "Randy's family picked him up yesterday. He is no longer a resident here."

Gladys shoved her hands on her hips. "He left me? Without even saying goodbye?"

"He went home to his family, Mrs. Maplethorpe. Just like you're going to."

"Well, heckfire." Aunt Gladys jutted out her chin and fixed Dr. Ravenwood with a glare.

"You're upset, madam," Dr. Ravenwood said. He took Aunt Gladys' elbow and steered her back inside. "Let's get you to your room so you can get dressed."

Aunt Gladys smacked Dr. Ravenwood on the back of his head. "I am dressed, you nincompoop!"

Something plopped to the ground and landed by Aunt Gladys's caftan. She looked down and sucked in a breath.

"What's this?" Dr. Ravenwood leaned over to pick up a

diamond-studded watch. "I don't recall you having a watch like this, Mrs. Maplethorpe."

Aunt Gladys pursed her lips. "It's not mine, exactly."

"Where did you get it?" Dr. Ravenwood asked.

"I borrowed it from Minnie. You know, the poor old darling doesn't need timepieces these days. She's loonier than a loon. Thinks it's the Roaring 20s."

"I take it you borrowed the watch without Minnie's knowledge?"

"I resent your implication that I stole it. Really, Dr. Demented. Perhaps you are losing your marbles. Physician, heal thyself."

"I'm sure Aunt Gladys meant no harm," Fran said. She met Aunt Gladys' gaze. "You meant to return the watch, right?"

"Of course." Aunt Gladys lifted a haughty brow. "I was merely polishing it."

"Dr. Ravenwood, will you please return the watch to Minnie for Aunt Gladys?" Fran asked.

"By all means." Ravenwood pocketed the watch and took Aunt Gladys' elbow again. "This way, ladies."

As they walked into the retirement home, Fran was glad that she and Lucy were taking Aunt Gladys with them. She hoped that when they got her home, living near family and friends again would help to clear her mind.

Aunt Gladys jerked away from Dr. Ravenwood. "Take your hands off of me. I can still dress myself." Mums drooping in her hands, she pushed past the doctor, and strutted down the hall to her room.

Dr. Ravenwood looked at Fran and shrugged. "Your aunt keeps everyone in this place on their toes."

"I can imagine," Fran said.

FOURTEEN

WITH AUNT GLADYS SIGNED OUT of the retirement home, Fran and Lucy loaded her bags and suitcases, which filled the trunk and most of the back seat. The three women belted up, took off, and headed north. With the fall temperatures soaring, Lucy's air conditioning blasted away. Aunt Gladys sat in the back seat, talking nonstop, all the while crocheting a purple striped blanket.

When the nursing home stories dried up, Aunt Gladys changed to stories about sweet little Brucie when he was a boy. She rambled all the way home, giving the sisters laughing fits with her capers. At last, she fell asleep, snoring loudly enough to wake King Tut.

They returned home without incident, except that both sisters were tone-deaf, thanks to Princess Runs-At-the-Mouth. Lucy and Fran stopped to talk with Eva to make sure the café had run smoothly in their absence, which it had.

Aunt Gladys ooh'd and ahh'd as she looked around, assessing the customer area and the large commercial kitchen that accommodated the sisters' baking and cooking needs.

"This is a wonderful set up," she said. "I'm proud of you two for running your own shop and keeping the old Castleton home in such tip top shape."

"Thanks," Fran said.

"And BTW," Aunt Gladys added. "Your food smells scrumptious."

Both Fran and Lucy raised their brows at the expression.

"I'm not too far behind the times," Aunt Gladys explained with a chuckle. "I've got a cell phone, I text, and I'm familiar with teenage slang. Well, at least some of it, and I know BTW means by the way."

After the tour, Fran and Lucy both helped settle Aunt Gladys in her new attic apartment. She walked past everything, touching different items, and nodding with obvious approval.

"This place looks slick," Aunt Gladys said as studied the renovations. "Very, very, nice. You two have outdone yourselves."

"Well, the Carpinelli brothers did all the work," Fran explained.

"They did a fantastic job," Aunt Gladys said.

"We hoped you'd like it," Fran said.

"We want you to be comfortable," Lucy added as she removed bags full of makeup from a suitcase and took them into the bathroom.

Aunt Gladys walked over and sat on the mattress, testing it with a couple of bounces. "I believe I will. Thank you for letting me stay here. I was getting tired of the retirement home. The same old stuff happens over and over, you know?"

Fran smiled. "We're all happy to have you home."

"That's right," Lucy said as she walked out of the bathroom. "You've been away for too long, and we missed you."

"What about the stairs?" Fran opened Aunt Gladys' suitcase, picked up pieces of clothing and began hanging them in the wardrobe. "Do you think they'll be too much for you to handle?"

"Oh, my dear," Aunt Gladys said, stretching out her long, shapely legs. "I've never stopped playing tennis or golf, and I've raced in local marathons. I'm in tip-top shape for a woman my age. Believe me, the stairs won't be a problem."

Lucy glanced at her watch. "I need to skedaddle. I promised Carl I'd stop by for an award ceremony at his car dealership. They're giving him a salesman of the month bonus."

"Hey, good for him," Fran said. "Tell my nephew congratulations for me."

"And me, too," Aunt Gladys said as she snatched a gauzy, fringed scarf from her suitcase and draped it over a lamp shade. "I want you both to know that I plan to work around the café, too. I'm sure you could use the help."

"That's nice," Fran said. "But we're fine."

"Pshaw, I don't plan to rest on my laurels, so I'll pitch in and do my part." Humming a tune, Aunt Gladys began folding lacy underthings and putting them in wardrobe drawers.

Fran and Lucy headed downstairs. Across the room, Eva gave a little wave, then focused on taking the order of a young lady who stood at the counter.

At the door, Lucy said, "Aunt Gladys doesn't seem as out of sorts now that we've brought her to Moose Creek."

"Bruce told me she wanted to be home, in the same place where she'd grown up," Fran said. "I hoped that would help settle her down. And I bet she's probably been missing family all this time."

"So far, it looks like you are right on the money," Lucy said.

"Her retirement home antics must have taken a lot of energy out of her, don't you think?" Fran asked.

"Sounds reasonable, but from the way she's talking, I believe she's ready to dive into her new life here," Lucy said.

"True, she's like a ball of energy," Fran said.

"Maybe it's time to throw in the towel on the sleuthing, though," Lucy suggested. "I think Otis and Gabe are more than capable of handling Henry's murder case."

Fran frowned. "I don't want to give it up completely. We've uncovered some interesting clues."

"Hmm," Lucy said. "We'll see."

Lucy started to leave, then turned to say, "I'll see you tomorrow. Remember, it's your birthday."

"Right. Thanks for reminding me. I almost forgot I'll soon be another year older."

"It's a day, like any other," Lucy said as she patted Fran's arm. "You're as young as you feel."

After Lucy left, Fran headed back upstairs to the attic to see if Aunt Gladys needed anything else. The two finished unpacking as Aunt Gladys regaled Fran with memories of her life in Las Vegas showbusiness. When Aunt Gladys produced a candle and a lighter, Fran confiscated the loot.

"No, Aunt Gladys. No candles in the house."

Aunt Gladys batted her eyelashes. "Are you serious?"

Fran pictured her house going up in flames. "Ah, it's not a good idea."

"When may I have my candle back?" Aunt Gladys persisted.

"After I have a smoke alarm installed up here," Fran explained.

"Very well then." Aunt Gladys began to hum another show tune and Fran busied herself picking up plastic bags that had once held pairs of shoes.

After dinner, Aunt Gladys went to bed, claiming she was exhausted. No doubt, Fran thought. Eva headed upstairs to study. Fran cleared away the remains of dinner, started the dishwasher, and went up to her bedroom, feeling like she'd weathered a tornado. Crawling between the sheets, she tried to sleep. Unfortunately, she tossed and turned all night.

At last, she slumbered, dreaming of a shadowy person chasing her with a butcher knife. Like a wild woman, she ran all over Moose Creek, trying to escape. Everywhere she went, the figure stalked her.

How could she get a decent night's sleep? A killer wandered the streets of Moose Creek and it seemed they had evil intentions toward her.

Even counting sheep didn't help.

At 5 a.m., Fran shot out of bed like a bolt of lightning. She showered and dressed, then crept to the attic to check on her aunt. Burrowed in blankets, Aunt Gladys slept soundly, surrounded by piles of suitcases. Fran made a mental note to come up later in the afternoon, collect the luggage, and store everything in her garage rafters.

Heading downstairs, she decided to make plans for she, Eva, and Aunt Gladys to visit different attractions in Westonville, like the museum and the botanic gardens. With the café being closed Sundays and Mondays, they might as well enjoy what this neck of the woods had to offer in the way of entertainment.

In the kitchen, she brewed a pot of coffee—butter rum flavor. She inhaled deeply and sighed; it smelled heavenly. When her cell phone rang, she fished it out of her pocket.

"Hello?"

"Fran. Just called to check up on you. How are things going?"

"Hi Gabe," Fran responded. "Everything's fine."

"Sounds like no one's been bothering you, then, eh?"

"No."

"Good, good," Gabe said.

"What's happening with the murder investigation?" Fran asked.

"There's been a development," he said. "We found out Henry Whitehead was involved with a woman named Sophie Howell. Yesterday afternoon, I called and talked with her husband, Ernie."

"I see." Fran punched the speaker on her phone and set it on the counter. Gabe had come up with the same lead she and Lucy had, so they must be on the right track.

"Ernie and his wife have a store in Denver. He said they wanted to get away from Moose Creek and try to work on their marriage."

"Sounds like a good idea to me," Fran said.

"He mentioned two women with red hair visited his place yesterday, asking lots of questions. He wondered if they were undercover cops. I assured him they weren't."

"Really?" Fran had a good idea what was coming next.

"I figured you and Lucy stopped by their shop for a chat," Gabe said. "What were you doing, exactly?"

"Hold on a sec," Fran said as she removed a roast from the refrigerator and plopped it into a crock-pot. Running water into a Pyrex measuring cup, she added a package of dry onion soup and poured it over the meat. She finished by placing a lid on the pot.

"You know we're on the same side, right?" Gabe asked.

"Of course." Fran wiped her hands on a paper towel and set the crockpot on medium high.

"Are you still there?" Gabe asked.

"Yes, I'm busy cooking," Fran said. "Our special today is pot roast soup."

"Fran," he said in a low voice. "Didn't I tell you to leave the investigation to the police?"

"What makes you think the redheads were me and my sister?"

"Otis mentioned that you and Lucy were in Denver yesterday to pick up your Aunt Gladys."

"All right, we did stop by Houdini's Hideout before we picked her up. We were looking for games, books or puzzles. Something to keep her busy."

"I knew it," he said.

"So what? It's a free country, you know."

"Why were you questioning Ernie and Sophie?" Gabe said.

"We were curious."

"How did you know about Sophie and Henry's affair?"

"We heard rumors at the pub the other night."

"Ah, ha. So, you were snooping, weren't you?" Gabe asked.

"People talk, Gabe. This is a small town."

Just then, Aunt Gladys shuffled into the kitchen wearing fuzzy pink slippers with floppy bunny ears and a silky, zebra stripe robe embellished with a feather collar. Her head, covered in pink sponge rollers, bobbed as she looked around the room.

"Good morning," she said with a yawn. Aunt Gladys fiddled with the large, square topaz ring on her right ring finger, then went over and poured herself a cup of coffee. "This coffee smells amazing."

"What's going on?" Gabe asked.

"It's my aunt; she's staying here with me," Fran told him.

"May I use your blender?" Aunt Gladys asked. "I need to make my fortified breakfast drink. I have it every morning."

"Sure. It's right there on the counter."

Aunt Gladys shuffled toward the refrigerator. Whistling yet another show tune, she dug through the contents, selected the items she wanted, then dumped eggs and milk into the blender. Next, she removed a small packet from her robe pocket and poured it in.

"Fran," Gabe said. "Tell me what you found out when you went to Houdini's Hideout."

At that exact moment, Aunt Gladys flipped on the blender. Between her singing and the blender's whirring, Fran could barely hear herself think.

"Hold on," she told Gabe. When the blender and its operator fell silent, Fran told Gabe, "Sophie seemed surprised to hear that Henry was dead. I believe I annoyed Ernie with my questions, but he seemed to be telling the truth about wanting to move his family away from Moose Creek so they could bond again."

"Thanks for the info," Gabe said. "Please, take care of yourself and leave this investigation to the police. I don't want you stirring up trouble for yourself. Got it?"

"No problem," she said, then disconnected the call. Gabe honestly seemed concerned about her and Lucy, but she couldn't promise not to keep looking for clues in Henry's murder. It hit too close to home, literally.

A strange odor filled her nostrils, and she glanced at her aunt. "What is that stuff?"

"I told you, it's my fortified drink. It makes me feel like I'm 20 again." She poured the liquid into a clear glass, sat down at the table and began to chug-a-lug.

Fran grimaced at the oatmeal-colored concoction. "We're going to go out to dinner tonight after we close the café. Are you all right with that?"

"That sounds splendid. Eva told me all about her plans before I came downstairs. Happy birthday, BTW." She nodded at the crockpot. "What's cooking? It smells great."

Fran refreshed her coffee and sat down beside Aunt Gladys. "Today's café special, pot roast soup."

"Your little Eva has certainly grown up," Aunt Gladys commented. "Last time I saw her, she had two of the cutest strawberry blond pigtails."

"I know, right? And now she's in college. Can you believe it?"

"Hell's bells." Aunt Gladys shook her head. She reached toward the middle of the table and picked up the ceramic salt and pepper shakers shaped like tiny poodles. "She got any beaus?"

"She dates off and on. But there's no one steady." Fran wondered if the poodles were long for this world since Aunt Gladys, who had a slight problem with kleptomania, had taken a fancy to them.

"You are lucky to have such a beautiful daughter." Aunt Gladys sipped her drink. "Bruce told me someone in Moose Creek was recently murdered."

"That's right," Fran said, surprised. "How did he hear about that?"

"You know the guy who runs Remington's Barbershop downtown? He and Bruce went to school together. They stay in touch."

"I see," Fran said.

"Remington told Bruce that you were dating Henry Whitehead. Is that true?"

"One date, is all," Fran said, figuring she'd better explain the rest of what happened, because she had no doubt Aunt Gladys would want to know. "I left my purse at his house and when I went to get it the next morning, I found him dead."

"Boy howdy, I bet that was a shock," Aunt Gladys said.

"Yes, it was."

"No more talk about people dying," Aunt Gladys insisted. "I know what we need."

"What's that?" Fran sipped her coffee, which by now had gone cold.

"A hairdo from Winkie. If he's still in town, that is."

"Winkie? Who's Winkie?"

"Winfield Hightower. He used to cut my hair before I moved

away. He's a true artist and that will be my birthday present to you."

"That's very generous," Fran commented, realizing she hadn't had her hair styled in ages. "Lucy and I don't open the café until noon, so we should have plenty of time, if he's free, of course."

"He may not have his beauty shop downtown anymore, though," Aunt Gladys said as she pulled a cell phone from her pocket and began punching on it. "I'm going to try and find him online . . . ah, here's his number!"

FIFTEEN

A̲unt Gladys punched the speaker button on her cell, and Winkie's deep voice filled the room.

"It's so good to hear from you, Gladys," he said. "You're a doll to want me to do your hair again after all these years."

"I wouldn't have anyone else," Aunt Gladys gushed.

"I'm retired now," he said. But I'm not expired! I'll be right over so I can wield my scissors on one of my favorite customers!"

"My niece, Fran, too, if you don't mind," Aunt Gladys said.

"Of course, doll," Winkie said.

Aunt Gladys went upstairs to get dressed while Fran putzed around in the kitchen, preparing for the customers who would arrive at noon when they opened up. A short while later, the café door opened with the sound of the tinkling bell.

Fran glanced into the eating area where she saw a tall, broad-shouldered man with salt and pepper hair enter. He wore jeans, a tangerine-colored shirt, and a sparkling diamond stud in his ear. In one hand, he carried a large black case emblazoned with the words, SHEAR GENIUS. Tucked under his other arm, he held a tiny Yorkshire terrier.

"You're here," Aunt Gladys said as she hurried toward him and took the dog, holding up the wriggling mass of fur to kiss its nose. The dog squirmed, then settled down, no doubt realizing there wasn't much it could do.

"This is Muffin," Winkie said.

"Well Muffin, you're a cutsy-wootsie, aren't you?" Aunt Gladys told the pooch as she escorted Winkie into the kitchen.

Fran assumed Winkie carried his tools of his trade in his bag. He set it on the kitchen table, patted the leather case, and said, "That was the name of my beauty shop."

"Very clever," Fran said.

"I love what you've done with this place," Winkie said as he looked around. "I've ordered food from here a time or two and had it delivered, but I've never been inside."

"Fran, this is Winkie, one of my dearest friends in the world," Aunt Gladys said.

"Nice to meet you," Fran said as she walked over to shake his hand.

He wrapped Fran in a bear hug, then stood back with a bright smile. "My dear, you look a lot like your Aunt Gladys, you know," he said, narrowing his gaze and holding his chin between his thumb and forefinger. "Indeed, your eye color and cheekbone structure are nearly identical."

Fran took that as a compliment, since the pictures she'd seen of Aunt Gladys in her younger days had shown a lovely, glamorous woman who she'd heard had turned many heads. Even now, Aunt Gladys maintained an ageless beauty.

Aunt Gladys headed upstairs as Fran and Winkie exchanged pleasantries. A few minutes later, she returned with a purple silk pillow, which she placed on the floor. After putting Muffin on top of it, she walked over and stood beside Winkie.

"Let's get to work," Winkie declared, running his fingers through Aunt Gladys' hair. "Your hair is dull as dishwater and is screaming for attention."

Winkie steered Aunt Gladys toward a chair on the other side of the room far from the food preparation, where he had her sit down, covering her shoulders with a black plastic cape. Muttering, he dug around in his bag, fishing out a box of hair color and scissors. He began fussing over Aunt Gladys and as the magic happened, they talked, laughed, and caught up on old times.

Listening to their repartee, Fran chopped, sliced, and cooked ingredients for ham hock soup, chicken pot pie soup, and taco soup. She learned that Aunt Gladys and Winkie had been high school friends, both having attended Moose Creek High.

After graduation, Winkie had enrolled at cosmetology college in Westonville, where he applied his passion for hair styling, eventually opening his own beauty shop. Aunt Gladys, who had performed in local plays and shows from the age of 3, took off for California, where she planned to pursue an entertainment career. Earning roles as a dancer and singer, she'd done some TV, worked on a cruise ship, and then headed for the bright lights of Las Vegas where she'd entered the showgirl profession.

"What's going on here?" Lucy asked when she came in the back door, placing her purse and jacket in a tall cabinet.

"I'm giving your sister a new hairstyle for her birthday," Aunt Gladys explained, as she fluffed her freshly snipped locks of frosty white hair, styled into a pixie cut with fringed bangs.

"You showed up in time to take over the food preparations since it's Fran's turn in the hot seat. A new hairstyle is her birthday present from me."

"Aunt Gladys, what a transformation!" Lucy exclaimed. "Your hair looks adorable."

"Does it, now?" Aunt Gladys spun around, the fringe on her hot pink top flapping. "It's all thanks to my friend Winkie."

"That would be me," Winkie made a saluting gesture.

"Hi Lucy." Seated in Aunt Gladys' recently vacated chair, Fran lifted her arm from beneath the plastic cape to wave at her sister.

"I'll finish up the food while you get beautified," Lucy said to Fran, chuckling.

Winkie used a small brush to apply color to portions of Fran's hair, then folded each piece in aluminum foil. About 30 minutes later, he washed her hair in the sink, then began snip, snipping at the strands. After blow drying the style, he tousled Fran's bouncing strands with his be-ringed fingers.

He handed Fran a mirror, which she rotated from side to side, admiring the marmalade and champagne highlights framing her face.

"Viola!" Arms crossed over his chest, Winkie studied his most recent creation.

"You look marvelous," Aunt Gladys said, clapping.

"Thank you, Winkie," Fran said. "I'm in awe at what you've done. And thanks, Aunt Gladys, for such a special birthday gift."

"Fran, you look radiant," Lucy said as she touched her own hair. "Winkie, can I set up an appointment to have you do my hair, too? It could use a lift."

"Of course, my dear," Winkie said. "Even though I no longer have my own shop, I keep a salon chair in a room of my house that I use for special clients. I'll add the three of you to my list."

"How much do I owe you, my friend?" Aunt Gladys asked Winkie.

He beamed. "Nothing, love. It's fabulous to have your radiance back in town. By the way, didn't you adore Vegas?"

"Sin City will always be in my blood," she admitted. "But I'm more than happy to live a simpler lifestyle these days."

The back door flew open and Muffin began woof-woofing. He jumped off his purple silk pillow and ran up to Eva, who entered the room. She leaned over and patted the little dog, then stood and walked toward Fran, her too long jeans dragging on the floor, her blue top a tad too cropped for Fran's taste.

"Mom, I didn't know you'd gotten a dog," she said. "And your hair, it looks amazing!"

"The dog belongs to Mr. Hightower." Warmed by her daughter's compliment, Fran gestured toward Aunt Gladys' friend. "Winkie, this is my daughter Eva."

"Kudos to you, Mr. Hightower," Eva said in greeting. "You've worked wonders with my mother's hair, and BTW, it's nice to meet you."

"Charmed, I'm sure," he returned.

"Mr. Hightower is a dear, dear friend of mine," Aunt Gladys said as she pointed at her head. "Look what Winkie did with my hair. Isn't it grand?"

"It's totally bad ass," Eva said.

AFTER ANOTHER BUSY DAY AT THE CAFÉ, Fran found herself pleased that their clientele hadn't tapered off as Akiko had suggested it might. It seemed that no one was worried about eating here, after all. And thank goodness for that. After closing up at 8 p.m., Fran hustled upstairs to shower and change into fresh clothes for her birthday dinner with Eva.

First, she applied her makeup, then she pulled a blue maxi dress covered in tiny green leaves over her head. She snapped a silver belt around her waist, then stepped into tan suede boots and glanced at herself in a dresser mirror.

Not bad looking for her mid-thirties, Fran thought.

She found Eva in their front room wearing tight blue jeans with so-called fashionable rips, a black sweater, and combat boots. Aunt Gladys, who sat next to Eva on the couch, wore a silky turquoise blue suit with matching shoes. She'd pinned a bright green frog broach to her lapel. While it wasn't an outfit Fran would wear, Aunt Gladys looked pretty snazzy in it.

In a recliner nearby, Lucy lounged. She wore jeans, a brown sweater, and a bright fringed shawl. Her tall boots matched the sweater.

"Well, I'll be darned," Lucy said, standing as Fran entered the room. "You don't look any older than you did yesterday"

"You look crazy good, Mom," Eva said as she rose.

Aunt Gladys draped her arms over the back of the couch. "Your sister and your daughter are right. You cut a swashbuckling figure, my girl."

"Pirates are swashbuckling," Fran said, laughing.

Aunt Gladys shrugged. "Honey, at my age, I can use the word swashbuckling any time I want to."

"We're going to MacGreggors, right?" Fran asked as everyone trailed downstairs and into the cafe.

"Nope," Eva finally said. She punched a button on her cell phone.

Loud music blared and a tall man wearing a Zorro costume, complete with black mask and cape, slid into the kitchen. Chest muscles rippling, he gyrated around the room, slashing a fake fencing sword in the air.

Winkie, who had returned for the party, stood in a corner holding his little dog. Muffin began barking and Winkie shooshed the pooch.

"Eva!" Fran watched in shock as the male dancer leapt around her. "What is this?"

"Your birthday present, Mom."

"Let the fun begin!" Aunt Gladys clapped in time to the music. "This reminds me of the all-male review at the MGM!"

Fran couldn't help but laugh at Eva's gift. It was such an unexpected surprise!

"This is what you needed for your birthday, Mom," Eva told her.

Lucy laughed and laughed, while playfully poking Fran's shoulder.

The more Fran watched Zorro in his tight, black leather costume, the more she laughed, too. She couldn't help it—it was such an amusing idea that her daughter had thought of this. Not in a million years would she have guessed this was her gift.

No doubt, Zorro had been hired with the extra money she'd given Eva. Better this, than a nose ring or a tongue stud. A trickle of relief passed through Fran. All was not wrong with the world.

Eva took Fran's arm, guided her into the eating area of the café, and sat her in a chair. The table behind her held a pile of brightly wrapped gifts, black balloons, and a two-tiered cake decorated with purple frosting.

Zorro danced seductively in Fran's direction while everyone entered the room. As he gyrated his hips, spicy-cologne sweat flew from his hard, lean body. All the while, he swept his cape theatrically and slashed the air with his sword.

Fran tried to catch her breath, finding the room had become quite warm. She had to admit, the dancer was easy on her eyes. Then she realized he was probably around Eva's age.

Eva grinned from ear to ear, and Aunt Gladys was ecstatic, clapping and whooping, encouraging the young man to, "Take it all off!"

Winkie eyed the male dancer intently, fingering the diamond stud on his ear lobe as he clutched Muffin.

At last Zorro peeled away his cape, mask, and his clothes, piece by piece. He danced around the room, showering each of the women, and Winkie, with equal attention. When he brushed up against Lucy, she snapped her fingers at him.

"Shoo, you naughty boy," she shouted playfully. "Go back to the birthday girl where you belong!"

With a devilish grin, he moved on to Eva for a dose of playful seduction.

With a final flourish, he tore off his belled trousers, tossing them aside. When he swept past Aunt Gladys, she produced a bill and stuffed it in his G-string.

Lucy leaned over, grabbed her knees, and howled with laughter.

Zorro's oiled six-pack rippled as he danced his way over in front of Fran again. Oh, well, Fran thought. You only live once. Aunt Gladys handed her a large bill, which she stuffed into Zorro's G-string.

Leaning over, Zorro handed Fran a business card. He whispered in her ear, his warm, moist breath caressing her cheek.

"Call me later, baby. I love cougars."

Fran giggled. Did he really think she would? Not on her life.

Zorro jumped away, performed a few more twists and twirls. When the music ended, he bowed. While everyone clapped, he grabbed his clothes and blew a kiss. After winking at Fran, he sauntered out of the café door.

"I'll order pizza for dinner if that's okay with everyone," Eva announced.

"That's fine with me," Fran said.

"Pizza's good anytime," Lucy added.

"That's my kind of dinner," Winkie chimed in.

"Splendid," Aunt Gladys said. "I haven't had pizza since Brucie put me in Dr. Demented's castle of torture. They're all crazy there, you know."

Screeching tires, a loud thump, and a hoarse scream drew everyone's attention.

Muffin started barking, jumped out of Winkie's arms and ran up to the front window. He stood on his hind legs, placing his paws on the glass in order to see. The party goers rushed out of the house and onto the porch.

Beneath the dim streetlights, a bruised and battered Zorro lay on his back spread-eagled on the asphalt, his cape spread out behind him. Nearby, tire tracks slashed across the road. In the distance, a dark car zoomed off.

Winkie, who had managed to collect Muffin, clutched the growling mutt to his chest and said, "Oh, my God. The boy's been hurt." He pulled a cell phone from his pocket and added, "I'm calling 911!"

SIXTEEN

"WHO WOULD DO SUCH A TERRIBLE THING?" Fran shouted as she sprinted toward Zorro, with Eva close on her heels. The two of them knelt on the asphalt beside him.

Fran's skin prickled with fear as she looked at the blood pooling beside Zorro's head. She gently lifted his wrist and checked for a pulse. Thankfully, she felt a faint thump, thump. Leaning closer, she held the back of her hand near his mouth and felt puffs of air. Thank God he was breathing.

"He's alive," she told Eva. "Hopefully the ambulance arrives soon."

Lucy eased up beside her sister and niece. "Otis is on his way, too."

"Good," Fran said.

"What is happening around here?" Lucy said. "He didn't deserve this."

"Lucy, can you find Zorro a blanket?"

"Be right back," she said, then hurried back inside the house.

Aunt Gladys and Winkie joined Fran in the street, both appearing agitated as they studied the victim.

"Oh my, he's bleeding!" Aunt Gladys backed away; eyes wide. "My, oh my, oh my. I need my pills. I think I'm going to faint."

Winkie, still holding his growling dog, patted Aunt Gladys on the back. "It's going to be all right, love. Help is on its way."

Aunt Gladys shrieked, then pointed at Fran's bracelet. "I never noticed you were wearing that. Where did it come from?"

"It's a family heirloom, remember?" Fran pointed out.

"Oh, I know the story all too well," Aunt Gladys said. "But that bracelet carries evil. No one should ever wear it."

Lucy dashed out of the house carrying a blanket, which she gently spread across Zorro.

Eva crouched next to Zorro, tears rolling down her cheeks. "This is all m-my fault," she sobbed. I never should have hired him to do this."

"It's the fault of whoever hit him and took off," Lucy said.

"At least he's hanging in there," Fran said.

"What were you all talking about before I got here with the blanket?" Lucy wanted to know as she looked back and forth between Aunt Gladys and Fran.

"The Castleton curse," Aunt Gladys said.

In the distance, a siren began to wail. Thank goodness, Fran thought.

"The Castleton Curse?" Lucy made a sound of contempt. "Everyone in the family knows that's a bunch of hogwash."

"What about it?" Fran asked, surprised she'd never heard the story.

"Etta's bracelet is beautiful, but it's deadly," Aunt Gladys insisted. "The thing caused her nothing but trouble until she discovered the legend. She never wore it again after that."

"Legend?" Winkie asked.

Fran and Lucy exchanged a glance.

"First off, the turquoise stones are bad luck," Aunt Gladys said.

Fran found it difficult to imagine that such gorgeous jewelry could ever be considered bad luck.

"Long ago, a Cheyenne princess fell in love with a young brave of low status," Aunt Gladys said, sounding more and more shaken. "As a gift, he strung the beads into a necklace for her, which her father made her return, because she was promised in marriage to another more prominent member of the tribe. Heartbroken, the young man leapt from a cliff into a river and was never seen again. At some point, the stones were sold to French traders and someone eventually made them into that bracelet you're wearing, Fran.

"Aunt Gladys," Fran said, concerned to see her aunt trembling. "You're getting yourself worked up."

"I'm only telling you the facts," Aunt Gladys said. "You need to remove the bracelet this instant."

Ambulance sirens blared as the vehicle rolled around the corner and steered toward the accident scene, red and blue lights flashing. Otis' sheriff's car, along with two Westonville Police cars, arrived next.

Hoping to calm Aunt Gladys, Fran fumbled with the bracelet, trying to remove it. The clasp seemed to be rusted shut, and she had no luck.

"I'll have to remove this later," Fran told her aunt. "It's not coming off without a fight."

Aunt Gladys shook her head. "That jewelry causes nothing but trouble! I'm sure that's why you've been having nothing but trouble."

"Could you take my aunt inside?" Fran asked Winkie, wondering if the bracelet really might have anything to do with her recent bad luck. "She's upset."

"Of course."

Aunt Gladys complained as Winkie guided her back to the Victorian, talking softly to console her.

"Eva, do you know Zorro's name?" Fran asked.

"Elton Briarhurst. He goes to Westonville University, too." She choked back another sob.

A thought occurred to Fran. "Would Elton be a member of the Dr. and Mrs. Miles Briarhurst family who live in Marble Canyon in that huge mansion on the hill?"

Eva nodded. "He's their son."

Fran groaned inwardly. Dr. Briarhurst was a famous surgeon with a golden pocketbook and tons of influence in the little town of Moose Creek, Westonville, Denver, and probably the Great Beyond.

"Why would a kid whose parents are filthy rich take a job as a stripper?" Fran asked.

"He's majoring in drama, Mom. He figures gigs like this will help him learn how to get into character."

Fran leaned close to the young man again. "Elton, can you hear me? Elton, Elton?"

He moaned, but didn't respond.

Otis walked up to them wearing his tan uniform, his sheriff's badge glinting in the streetlight. Brow knitted with concern; he knelt beside Zorro. "Hit and run, eh?"

"Yep," Fran responded. "He's breathing, but appears to be in bad shape."

Otis mopped his forehead with a crumpled handkerchief, turned to examine the tire tracks, and stood up. "Jumpin' catfish. What happened?"

"We were having a birthday party for Mom, Uncle Otis," Eva said.

"Right, right, Lucy told me that. Happy birthday, Fran."

"Thanks," Fran said.

Otis tilted his head toward Zorro. "Is he your boyfriend, Eva?"

"No," Eva shot back. "He was here to—"

"Ahem." Lucy gave her niece a stern look.

"Ah, he was here to, ah," Eva stood, looking at Fran for help.

"He was here to entertain us," Fran finally said.

"Oh?" Otis raised a brow. "With what? A juggling act?" He shoved a cigar in his mouth and lit up, sending a curious look at them all.

"Otis, I really wish you wouldn't smoke those disgusting things," Lucy said. "Besides, it's not healthy to do that around a wounded person."

Grunting, Otis tossed the cigar on the asphalt and ground it out with his boot heel. "Somebody better tell me what the victim was doing here."

"Exotic dancing," Fran finally said.

"I figured as much considering the way he's dressed, er, not dressed," Otis responded.

Fran put her arm around Eva's quaking shoulders. "It's going to be okay," Fran said, trying to reassure her daughter as much as herself.

Paramedics clustered around Elton. They checked for his vital signs, then started an IV. They moved with efficiency, talking back and forth about how to treat their patient.

An old yellow VW bug drove up and parked by the curb across the street. Barnard Scott, wearing his usual outfit of hat and rumpled suit, jumped from the car. He whipped out a camera with an enormous flash and took several photos. Then he took the pencil stub from behind his ear and jotted notes down on a pad.

As the ambulance team shifted Elton onto a stretcher, Gabe arrived in his dark SUV. He exited his vehicle wearing a tweed jacket, a white button-down shirt, jeans, and a cowboy hat. A concerned expression creased his face as he took long strides toward Scott and spoke with him in a gruff voice. Scott gestured wildly, apparently trying to justify his presence.

Otis strode over beside Gabe and Scott, no doubt adding his two cents to the conversation. He pointed an accusing finger at the reporter.

"Is your patient going to be all right?" Fran asked one of the ambulance attendants standing nearby.

"Can't say for sure," he said. "We're transporting him to the Westonville Hospital. I'm sure they'll do all they can."

The attendants lifted Elton's stretcher and loaded it onto the ambulance. Lights flashing and siren blaring, it headed toward the city on the other side of the mountain pass.

Fran noticed her rubbernecking neighbors were out in force. Standing in bathrobes on their doorsteps, they whispered amongst themselves, craning their necks to see.

"Show's over, folks," Otis called out to them, his face set in hard lines. "You all go on back inside." He turned to Fran, Lucy and Eva. "You three, don't go anywhere. Stay put."

Gabe walked over to his SUV and talked into the microphone of his police radio. Garbled responses and static blared back at him. Next, he put on gloves and walked around the crime scene bagging bits and pieces of evidence.

A couple of crime scene investigators also bagged and tagged items as another one took photographs. They talked amongst themselves and also Gabe.

Otis returned with his notebook and asked the women several questions, scribbling furiously to document the information. He had just finished the grilling session when Gabe walked over.

Fran took an uneven breath. Despite the confusion and shock of the evening, she was glad to see him.

Why were all these terrible things happening? Why were people always getting hurt around her? She glanced at her bracelet, wondering if the darn thing really was cursed.

Gabe nodded toward the ladies. "First off, are you all right?"

"Yes," Fran answered. "Shaken up, but fine."

"Good. Otis told me there was a celebration going on when the incident occurred?"

Eva nodded. "My mom's birthday. And then this happened. It's awful."

"Who all was here?" Gabe asked.

"The three of us," Fran answered. "Also, my Aunt Gladys and her friend Winfield Hightower. He's inside getting her calmed down. She's pretty upset."

"I can imagine," Gabe said. "Did you see anyone or anything out of the ordinary?"

"By the time we all rushed outside, Eva's young man was lying in the road," Lucy said. "We only saw a dark car zooming away. Unfortunately, the make and model weren't visible."

"He's not my young man, Aunt Lucy," Eva said in annoyed tone. "He's just a friend."

"Gabe, what can we do to help?" Fran asked.

"Tell me everything that happened," he said. "Even if it doesn't seem important."

"Do you think the person who hit Elton might be the same person who killed Henry?" Fran asked.

"It's hard to say," Gabe answered.

"We'd have to find a solid connection between the two incidents before we could confirm that," Otis said.

Gabe folded his arms across his chest. "Otis is right. We'll have to do some more investigating before we know that for sure. By the way, I did run the black paint I scraped off of your truck through some databases, Fran. It matches the make and model of an older Buick Regal."

"Mercy," Lucy said. "Maybe the driver that hit Elton and the driver that rammed you, Fran, are also one in the same."

"That's what Otis and I hope to find out," Gabe offered.

"Hopefully you find out soon," Lucy said.

"May I speak with you privately for a minute, Fran?" Gabe asked.

"Sure," she told him. She patted her daughter's arm reassuringly. "I'll be right back, sweetie."

Gabe and Fran walked over and stood beneath an ancient elm tree. Nearby, a patch of rosebushes covered with worn and faded autumn blooms rattled in the breeze.

"I didn't want to say this around your sister and your daughter because I didn't want to concern them," Gabe said.

Fran froze. "Say what?"

"I'm worried. I think you're in danger."

"What am I supposed to do?"

"Quit nosing around about Henry Whitehead's murder. That's the job me and your brother-in-law are doing."

Fran stiffened, irritated that Gabe kept bossing her around. "I've been far too busy with my aunt lately to snoop."

"Good." He lifted a dark brow. "It only complicates things when you put yourself in harm's way."

"Are you insinuating that what happened tonight is somehow my fault?"

"Absolutely not."

"Then what are you saying?" Fran asked.

"Just watch your back and mind your business. It's for your own good."

"I know how to take care of myself, thank you very much," she responded, hearing the curtness in her voice.

"Happy birthday, by the way," he said.

Unimpressed, Fran shoved her hands on her hips. "Are we done talking, detective?"

"Yes."

"Good night, then." Fran hurried back to Lucy and Eva.

SEVENTEEN

IRRITATED BY GABE'S SUGGESTIONS, Fran returned to the circle of family members standing outside of her house.

"Let's get going, Lucy," Otis said.

"What about my car?" she asked.

"I'll drive you over tomorrow to pick it up, Otis said.

"Talk to you later, Sis, and happy birthday again." Lucy lifted her hand in a tired wave and walked with Otis over to his sheriff's car. A few seconds later, they drove away.

Fran gave Eva a big hug. "Thank you for the birthday party, hon, even if it didn't turn out the way we wanted."

"I'm sorry, Mom. I feel so responsible for what happened to Elton."

"You're not. It was a terrible accident. No one was at fault, except for the hit-and-run driver, of course."

"You're right," Eva said, sounding miserable. "I still hate that he got hurt."

"Let's head inside. I don't know about you, but I'm exhausted."

When Fran finally crawled into bed that night, sleep refused to come. She couldn't stop thinking about Elton. And worrying about his condition.

Fitful dreams kept her tossing and turning. She woke several times and stared at the ominous shadows slashing across her bedroom walls. The night was warm, despite the fact that the calendar said it was fall. Finally, she glanced at her alarm clock on the bedside table.

Midnight. What an unholy hour to find herself awake.

A fine sheen of sweat caused her thin nightgown cling to her limbs, so she got up and opened her window wider. A warm breeze caressed her face and body, relieving the sticky sensation. Dry, withered lawns streched like silvery webs beneath the streetlights.

With the West in the grips of a severe drought, Fran wondered if it would ever get cold enough to rain or snow. No doubt they would have another brown, parched Christmas—like last year. She stared up at the moon's luminous, smiling face, imagining it mocked the waterless landscape.

Well, she didn't think it was one bit funny. And it was awfully hard for an avid gardener such as herself to have a decent crop of anything besides weeds in these conditions. Hopefully, the weather cycle would change again, for the better, and the drought would come to an end.

Thump, thump.

Fran looked up at the ceiling. The sounds seemed to have emanated from the attic. Aunt Gladys. What on earth was she doing? Had she fallen out of bed? Or perhaps she'd left her television blaring.

Fran reached for her bathrobe, tossed it around herself, and headed into the hallway, figuring she'd better go upstairs and make sure the old sweetheart was all right. She'd had an upsetting night and maybe she couldn't sleep either.

Creak, creak . . .

The ancient stairs complained as Fran padded barefoot to the attic. At the top, she stepped into a short hallway and reached the door to Aunt Gladys' room. Despite the renovations, her nostrils twitched with the musty odor of century-old walls.

Hearing Aunt Gladys' voice intermingled with Winkie's, she frowned. What were those two doing at this time of night?

Fran rapped on the door. "Aunt Gladys? What's going on?"

No answer. A dog barked.

She raised her hand to knock again. "Aunt Gla—"

More barking—Muffin no doubt—and the door swung open.

It took a couple of moments for Fran's eyes to adjust to the inky blackness. Then she saw Aunt Gladys bathed in candlelight wearing a purple caftan covered in gold stars, golden, curly-toed slippers on her feet, her snowy white hair covered by a purple turban decorated with a tall ostrich feather.

The scent of spicy incense wafted into the hallway and Fran sneezed.

"Shhh, you'll scare them away, Fran."

Fran blinked. "Scare who away, Aunt Gladys?"

"The spirits."

Oh, my. "The spirits? What spirits?"

Winkie pulled the door open farther and scowled at Fran. "The spirits who were telling us what is going on in this wicked, wicked little town."

Muffin, who rested comfortably in his arms, yapped at Fran.

"Okay, you two are busted," Fran announced." I heard weird sounds up here."

"Oh, don't worry," Aunt Gladys said. "It was probably just Winkie moving his chair."

Yap yap.

Ignoring Winkie's tiny dog, Fran pushed her way into the room. She didn't see anything out of order in the cozy quarters. Aunt Gladys' curtained alcove with the four-poster bed looked fine as well as the sitting area with the sofa and overstuffed recliner.

The round cupola nook, however, where Fran had positioned the antique drop-leaf table she'd refinished, along with two ladder-back chairs, looked suspicious. A board game of some sort covered the surface of the table with a thingie-ma-bob overturned on the top of it.

The lacy curtains were drawn, revealing a zillion twinkling stars in the dark autumn sky. Along the windowsill sat several chunky pillar candles, all ablaze with flickering light. The burners nestled next to them were filled with tiny cakes of smoking incense.

Fran whirled toward Winkie and her aunt. "Are you two insane? Do you want to set this house on fire, Aunt Gladys? Put out those candles."

Muffin barked again.

"Oh, pish, posh," Aunt Gladys spoke over the dog's protests. "You're too melodramatic for your own good."

Aunt Gladys stood by the drop-leaf table, her purple silk caftan flowing gracefully around her as she sank into a chair. She frowned at the board game. "We had just gotten to the good part, Fran. Now you've ruined it."

"Winkie, will you please tell me what kind of monkey business you and my aunt have been up to at this time of night? In the dark?"

Winkie stroked Muffie's silky head and the pooch's annoying yap yaps turned into low growls. "You've heard of a Ouija Board, haven't you?"

"A what-gee what?" Fran looked back and forth between Aunt Gladys and Winkie. "I have no idea what you're talking about."

"A Ouija Board," Aunt Gladys said again. "Pronounced wee-gee. Didn't you ever play it when you were a kid?"

"No."

"Of course, you wouldn't have," Aunt Gladys said with a nod. "Your father, the preacher, would never have allowed such a device of the devil in his home."

Fran threw her hands in the air. "Would somebody please tell me what a wee-gee board has to do with anything?"

Winkie took her arm and steered her toward the drop-leaf table. "Sit," he said, gently prodding her into one of the chairs.

Fran studied the strange looking board with the thick black letters and the plastic what-cha-ma-call-it lying on top.

"The Ouija can conjure spirits from the Great Beyond." Winkie plopped Muffin on a pillow. He dragged a stool over and sat beside Aunt Gladys.

Fran wrinkled her nose. "What?"

"Dead people, Fran." Aunt Gladys pressed her lips into a firm line. "In fact, we were just talking to Morris Van Scoy. He told us to call him by his nickname, though."

"Huh?" Fran stared at Aunt Gladys. Good Lord, the old gal had really flipped her lid this time. Fran did not want her to have a mental breakdown on her watch, though.

"Mortie had this house built in 1898," Winkie said. "He was a banker."

"Rich, too," Aunt Gladys said. "He brought his wife and five kids out here from Indiana. The railroad had just arrived and Moose Creek was booming."

"His investments helped him become even wealthier," Winkie said.

"Unfortunately, his wife missed her family back in Indiana," Aunt Gladys said. "She got addicted to laudanum and it drove her crazy."

"She killed herself in 1906," Winkie added. "Poor Mortie was so sad. He had to raise the kids by himself."

"He'd invested a lot in this town," Aunt Gladys said. "But when the railroad pulled up stakes and left, Moose Creek was left with only a few wheat farmers and cattle ranchers."

Winkie templed his fingers on the table. "Mortie lost everything, so he abandoned this house and moved back to Indiana in 1911. People said the house was haunted, so no one would buy it."

"If you ask me, I think Mortie's wife, Hortense, haunted her husband because he'd taken her away from her home," Winkie said. "I think she still haunts this place."

"I've never heard or seen anything unusual," Fran said.

"Hortense originally owned that bracelet you're wearing, Fran," Aunt Gladys continued. "When Howard Castleton bought this house in 1920, he found it and gave it to Etta on their wedding day. Hortense is jealous of anyone who wears it or lives in her home, and she brings disaster to them."

"That's crazy."

"You think?" Aunt Gladys said, lifting a brow.

Fran fingered the bracelet. It felt tight, and the skin beneath it itched. She picked at the clasp in an attempt to take it off, but it wouldn't budge. Yikes! Not that she was superstitious, nevertheless, she decided that as soon as she had the chance, she'd find the pliers and cut it off.

"I've had a few rough patches, sure. And now—"

"Now you're living in Hortense's house," Aunt Gladys reminded her. "And remember how the turquoise stones in the bracelet were obtained."

Fran did not like the turn this conversation was taking.

"As far as the Castleton curse goes, Howard and Etta lost all of their money in the 1929 stock market crash and they eventually died in a fire in the old carriage house," Aunt Gladys said. "None of their children lived to adulthood except for their oldest son, Burkley."

"My grandfather, right?" Fran asked.

"Right," Aunt Gladys said. "He brought your grandmother, my mother, Lucille, who your sister is named for, here to live after they were married. He, too, presented her with Hortense's bracelet. I came along in 1953 and your father in 1960, and theirs was a troubled marriage. In 1980, they drowned in Gun Smoke Lake in a freak boating accident. They left this place to me and your dad, who gave Hortense's bracelet to your mom. And look! They wound up dying in a tragic automobile accident."

"Which is terrible."

"You need to get rid of that bracelet, Fran. I tried to get away from the curse by leaving Moose Creek, but I think it followed me anyway. I've lost seven husbands, after all."

"You divorced some of them, Aunt Gladys," Fran pointed out.

"Four of them did die," she added, staring deeply into her niece's eyes, "Now I'm afraid the curse has come to haunt you. I think that's why Henry Whitehead died and why Zorro was run over."

Fran shook her head. "You're kidding me, right? This is a joke."

"This is no joke, Fran. Mortie told Winkie and I some very interesting things. By the way, he likes what you've done to the house. Figures everyone else would like it, too."

"Everyone else?"

"Everyone who has owned the house, you know. All of our ancestors."

Although Fran didn't buy in to Aunt Gladys' theory, she had to admit it had her spooked. "It's time to put up the board game and call it a night."

"I don't want to," Aunt Gladys complained. "You're such a drag. Would you prefer that I return to that lunatic asylum with Dr. Demented and the panty thief?"

Fran frowned. "Panty thief? What panty thief?"

"It was humiliating." Aunt Gladys harrumphed. "No one could catch him, though we were certain it was one of the attendants sneaking around. When we were out of our rooms exercising or having game night, he'd ransack all the ladies' drawers, pulling out their lingerie. I caught him once. It was disgusting."

"No way," Fran said. "Mountain Shadows is an exclusive retirement home. The staff would never allow such a thing to happen."

"You think they actually cared?" Aunt Gladys tapped a be-ringed finger on the table. "People's jewelry turned up missing. You better believe the panty thief was stealing that, too. I'm sure he gave half of it to the staff so they'd keep their mouths shut."

Fran reached over and patted Aunt Gladys' hand. "Honestly, you've got to quit imagining things. Did you take your medicine this evening?"

"Yes! And I'm telling the truth." Aunt Gladys said, raising her voice. "It sucks being old. People don't take you seriously."

"Now, now, dear, calm down." Winkie clutched Aunt Gladys' hand, and Muffin growled from atop his special silk pillow.

Fran felt awful. "I'm sorry, Aunt Gladys. I'm so busy that it's difficult for me to imagine we are being haunted by the paranormal.

Besides, what will Bruce think about you staying with me if we've been infiltrated by ghosts?"

"Do you think he gives a hoot about his old mother? Pffft." Aunt Gladys flicked her red-nailed fingers at Fran. "All he cares about is making money. Hand over fist. Or whatever way he can. That's all that matters to him. The curse has affected him, too. To my son, I'm a nuisance."

"Can't you and Winkie play parlor games another day?" She asked Aunt Gladys in a more sympathetic tone. "It's awfully late."

Aunt Gladys dabbed her eyes with a lacy handkerchief. "No, actually late at night in the dark is when the spirits—"

"Aunt Gladys," Fran warned. "You need your sleep."

"No, hear me out. This is when you get them to really talk. In fact, you should hear what Mortie has to say. Maybe Fran should play, too?" Aunt Gladys looked up at Winkie.

Winkie smiled and clapped his hands. "Splendid idea. But she has to believe."

"Believe what?"

"That the spirits are real. That they are communicating with us."

Fran rubbed her eyes. She wanted to be back in her warm bed, trying to get some sleep. Even though it had eluded her thus far.

"Please play," Aunt Gladys begged. "At least to humor an old lady."

"Hmm," Fran said, still undecided.

"Then I promise Winkie and I will call it a night."

"Absolutely," Winkie added.

"Fine. If it'll get you two off my back. But not for too long."

"It's a deal," Aunt Gladys agreed.

Aunt Gladys flipped over the plastic thingie-ma-jig on the Ouija board and positioned it just so. "You have to place your fingertips on the planchette," she told Fran.

She watched as Aunt Gladys and Winkie delicately touched it. She copied their movements.

Aunt Gladys said, "We ask only to speak with those spirits from the light."

An eerie chill brushed Fran's cheeks as a breeze came through the open window, rippling the long lace-curtain panels.

"Mortie," Aunt Gladys said in a soft, questioning voice. "Are you there?"

All was quiet in the room for a few moments, except for the sound of the rustling breeze and Muffin's panting. Then the planchette began to move under Fran's fingertips. Ever so slightly. It slid up to the word YES printed at the top of the board.

"You guys are pushing this thing," Fran whispered.

Winkie shook his head, then asked, "Are you a good spirit or a bad spirit?"

The planchette spelled out G-O-O-D.

"What is your name?" Aunt Gladys asked.

M-I-N-K, the planchette spelled out.

"Do you know what is going on in Moose Creek?" Aunt Gladys asked.

YES.

"Tell us," Winkie coaxed.

The planchette spelled, E-V-I-L; J-E-A-L-O-U-S-Y; H-A-T-R-E-D.

"I've had enough," Fran said, not wanting to admit that she was a tad wigged out. "Let's put this thing away."

"How can we put a stop to the problems?" Aunt Gladys asked, ignoring Fran.

C-A-N-T, it spelled out. D-A-N-G-E-R, D-A-N-G-E-R!

EIGHTEEN

"IT'S LATE." FRAN STOOD. "Time for everyone to call it a night." She pressed her lips into a firm line. Despite her questions, she couldn't let Aunt Gladys know her fears and concerns. Someone in this family had to maintain their sanity.

Aunt Gladys reached across the table and gripped Fran's hand. "You heard the Ouija. We're all in danger. What shall we do?"

"First off, we need a good night's sleep," Fran insisted. "I think we're getting ourselves upset for no reason."

Fran recalled recent concerning events. The fortune teller's warnings, Henry's murder, Aunt Gladys and the Castleton curse, Elton getting run over, and now the Ouija board's dire predictions. It was getting downright strange, though she didn't want to admit it and add to her Aunt's concerns.

Fran was worried enough for everyone.

"Seniors don't need so much sleep," Aunt Gladys insisted. "It's a proven fact."

"Well, this old person does." Fran yawned, finally feeling sleep tug at her, and raised a brow at Winkie.

Winkie cleared his throat. "Uh, right. We'll get together again soon, dear," he said to Aunt Gladys, patting her hand. "Old Muffin needs his doggie sleep, you know."

Winkie pushed his stool back into a corner and scooped the

Yorkie off his pillow. Aunt Gladys hugged him, then the three headed downstairs. Winkie rescued his trench coat from the hall tree and put it on, then wrapped a lavender cashmere scarf around his neck.

"I often stop by the Sunrise Center to play bridge with friends," Winkie said. "How about I call you the next time I go, Gladys, so you can join us."

Aunt Gladys scowled. "Really, Winfield. Me? Play bridge? Not likely."

"It'll be such fun. Give you something to do, you know."

Fran breathed a sigh of relief. Aunt Gladys had just arrived. No doubt she'd settle into a routine, then life would return to normal. Until then, it would be nice for her to get out and mingle.

"Oh, hell's bells," Aunt Gladys finally said. "What else have I got to do? Fran will take me. Won't you, kiddo?"

She gave her niece an expectant glance.

"Of course," Fran said, pleased that her aunt had decided to pay a visit to the senior center. It would be good for her to get out and meet people.

"It's all settled then," Aunt Gladys said.

"See you soon," Winkie said.

"Too-da-loo!" Aunt Gladys called as he walked out of the front door and closed it behind himself.

"Good night," Aunt Gladys told Fran, then hugged her. "I appreciate how kind you've been to me by letting me stay here."

"I wouldn't want you anywhere else," Fran insisted.

"I'm not the easiest person to live with," Aunt Gladys admitted. "I'm very set in my ways."

"You love life is all," Fran said. "Nothing wrong with that. You've reminded me that I need to focus on good things in the world."

Aunt Gladys blew her a kiss, then climbed up the stairs.

Fran went into the kitchen and brewed herself a cup of chamomile tea, hoping it would relax her. At this late hour, the house seemed to creak louder than usual and long shadows loomed in corners. She recalled Gabe's suggestion that she beef up her security.

Tomorrow, she'd make an appointment with a home monitoring company in Westonville to get her door and window locks reinforced. In addition, she needed to install a new smoke detector in Aunt Gladys' living quarters.

After she'd drained her cup, Fran climbed the stairs to the attic. Inky darkness surrounded her, except for the nightlight plugged into a hallway outlet. Fighting off her unease and the sense that someone was watching her, Fran peeked into Aunt Gladys's room. Only the small bedside lamp glimmered as the faint aroma of cinnamon-scented wax from the candles tickled Fran's nostrils.

Satisfied that her aunt was safely asleep for the night, Fran went back to her room and sank onto her bed. She squeezed her eyes shut and in her mind's eye, saw Henry's bloody corpse on the floor of his house. She fought off that image, then saw Elton lying broken and bleeding in the middle of the street.

Huddled under the covers, Fran tried to force herself to sleep. It didn't work. She rolled on one side, then the other, then onto her back. Too warm, she kicked off her blankets, only to have the chill of the night prickle her skin. She pulled the covers back up and burrowed herself beneath them.

Finally, sleep came. It wasn't an easy sleep. Once again, phantoms with butcher knives chased her. Somehow, she managed to fight them off. Then a car tried to run her down. She stumbled blindly into a heavy mist, trying to escape. Her legs became heavy, as though they'd been covered with cement.

Stuck to one spot, she watched the car coming, coming—approaching her like a night stalking beast. It looked like the dark sedan that had slammed into her at the light the night Henry died. She tried hard to look inside the vehicle to see who was driving.

All she could discern were flashing eyes in a sea of blackness. They stared death at her. She screamed, yet no sound came out of her mouth. Nevertheless, the silence around her spoke to a deep part of her soul, telling her something she didn't want to know.

Someone wanted her to die.

THE NEXT DAY, CAFÉ BUSINESS CARRIED ON AS BEFORE, and people filled the tables as the hours passed, eating and laughing and going on about their lives. Akiko's concerns that their café business would run into trouble occurred to Fran. Yet, considering their full house of customers today, it appeared that no one seemed worried.

Fran, Lucy and Eva handled the crowd as usual. However, due to lack of sleep the previous night, Fran did not feel like her typical chipper self. Worries about other things like, oh, say Henry Whitehead's murder and Elton Briarhurst's accident wouldn't have anything to do with that, would they?

Doing her best to be a trooper, Fran managed to make it through the long hours. Later in the afternoon, Aunt Gladys joined them. She explained she'd slept in late and had fixed herself coffee and a light snack up in her room.

Rolling up the sleeves of her blue silk blouse, Aunt Gladys pitched in to help during the last few hours the café was open, then joined in with the three women to clean up after they'd closed. As soon as they'd finished and Lucy headed home, Fran explained she was beat, and headed upstairs to bed.

"Sorry I kept you up so late last night," Aunt Gladys said as she and Eva followed.

"It's not your fault," Fran assured her. "I couldn't sleep for some reason."

"I told you, it's the Castleton curse," Aunt Gladys insisted. "You've got to get rid of that blasted bracelet, Fran."

"I didn't know we had a family curse," Eva said as they entered the apartment.

"I don't buy into any of that stuff, honey," Fran told her daughter.

"It's connected to the bracelet your mother is wearing," Aunt Gladys said. "It's an old family heirloom, but it brings bad luck."

"What?" Eva plopped in a chair and plopped her feet on a stool. "That's some heavy stuff."

"In order to put a stop to your crazy imaginings, Aunt Gladys,

I've been trying to remove the bracelet, but it won't budge." Fran demonstrated how the clasp wouldn't open.

"Determined little bugger, isn't it?" Aunt Gladys placed her hands on her hips. "Cut it off then."

In her kitchen, Fran removed a pair of pliers from the junk drawer. No matter how she twisted it, the bracelet refused to break. Not even Eva or Aunt Gladys could manage to do it.

"When I get a chance, I'll drive over to Westonville and find a jewelry shop," Fran said. "I'm sure they will be able to get it off."

"Hopefully so," Aunt Gladys said. "Once that happens, toss the dang bracelet in the river or off of a cliff. This family does not need it bringing anymore trouble."

After taking a nice, hot shower and slipping into her pjs, Fran glanced in her front room to see how Aunt Gladys and Eva were doing. She found the two seated on the couch watching an old black and white movie and eating popcorn.

Warmed by the sight of her daughter and aunt together, Fran said, "Good night, you two."

"G'night," Eva called.

"Sleep well," Aunt Gladys added.

Fran's eyes felt like lead weights, and she started falling asleep as soon as her head hit her pillow. Exhausted, she didn't move an inch. A deep, blissful slumber pulled her into cottony depths for the rest of the night.

Two more days went by, during which nothing out of the ordinary happened. Life seemed to settle into a simple pattern of handling café business, cleaning up after hours, watching a program or two on TV with Eva and Aunt Gladys, then hitting the sack. Fran felt blessed going to bed on Saturday night with nothing but prayers for Elton's recovery on her mind.

The next morning, Fran bolted straight up in bed, blinking in the bright sunlight that filled her bedroom.

"What time is it?" she mumbled, glancing at the cow-shaped alarm clock with the black-and-white Holstein paint scheme Eva had given her when she was in the fourth grade.

Holy mother of pearl. It was 10 a.m.

Flying out of bed, Fran threw on a pair of jeans, Crocs, and a T-shirt. Then she hustled down the stairs, rubbing sleep out of her eyes as she slipped her hair into a ponytail holder.

In the kitchen, the delicious, decadent smell of chocolate drifted into her nostrils. Bowls and spoons cluttered a counter also dusted with sugar and cocoa.

Aunt Gladys stood there in her purple caftan, humming to herself and sliding a pan brimming with crusty brownies from the oven with potholders. She shuffled over in her slippers and set it on a cooling rack.

"Morning, Fran," Aunt Gladys said. "Have some breakfast. I've made plenty."

"You made dessert," Fran pointed out.

"Why not?" Aunt Gladys treated her to a radiant smile.

"Hi, Mom," Eva said without looking up. Sitting at the table, with a plate of gooey decadence in front of her, she was reading Homer's, The Iliad and the Odyssey. She munched on one of the chocolate squares and sipped from a tall glass of milk. "Thanks, Aunt G. These brownies are great."

Aunt G? Fran smiled at the nickname Eva had given her. Her daughter looked like she was about ten, except that back then, her favorite reading material had been much simpler than a world classic.

How had the time gone by so quickly? Now that same little girl was walking the lofty halls of Westonville University. Fran had to be in a time warp—like an episode from the Twilight Zone.

She blinked, bringing herself back to the present. "We've got to get ready for customers, Eva. They'll be here soon."

Eva gave her an annoyed look. "Chill, Mom. It's Sunday, remember? The day of rest? The café is closed."

"Oh, I forgot." Fran rubbed her eyes, trying to focus. "I'm still groggy."

"I'll make you some of my special drink if you'd like, Fran. It keeps me on the straight and narrow." Aunt Gladys tapped her forehead. "No old-timer's disease going on in here."

"No, thanks." Fran went over to her coffee maker and reached into the cupboard above it, producing hazelnut brew and filters. "I just need caffeine."

"You swill too much of that poison," Aunt Gladys said. "No wonder you can't sleep."

"Caffeine's not the problem, Aunt Gladys. Besides, whoever heard of eating brownies for breakfast?"

Aunt Gladys' cell phone rang, and she answered it. "Hello Winkie—oh you're going to the senior center today? Yes, yes. I'll meet you there this afternoon. Thanks for the invite!"

When Aunt Gladys clicked off the call, she performed a high kick. "Guess what, girls? I'm going to break down and play bridge this afternoon. Imagine that!"

Laughing along with Eva, Fran sat next to her at the table. She picked up the newspaper and began to read an article about the city council's recent decisions. Other articles about education and local events kept her attention occupied.

After a while, Eva closed her book and said, "I wonder how Elton's doing."

"We'll keep him in our thoughts, Eva," Fran said as she put down the newspaper. "That's all we can do. Pray and hope. And stay occupied to keep our minds off things we can't change."

"How do we do that?" Eva asked.

Fran went over to grab a mug of coffee. After she'd drained the cup, she tied on an apron. "We clean house."

"Ugh." Eva got up and walked toward the staircase. "I have homework to do upstairs. See you guys later."

Taking her daughter's arm before she escaped, Fran crushed another apron in her hands. "At the moment I could use your help."

Fran put all of them to work, including Aunt Gladys. It not only kept their minds off poor Elton lying in the hospital, but it went much faster with the three of them going at. They scrubbed tables, swept and mopped floors, vacuumed, and dusted. All was going well and the place was starting to sparkle, except Aunt Gladys was full of unwanted advice.

"You and Lucy should put your restaurant tables over there," she said, and proceeded to rearrange everything to her satisfaction.

"Only an owl with a microscope could read your menu," Aunt Gladys added. "The lettering needs to be bigger. She proceeded to rewrite the specials and the prices on the whiteboard with a thick erasable marker.

Fran had to admit it looked better than her uneven writing.

Upstairs in Fran's living quarters, the human whirlwind named Aunt Gladys continued to rearrange and suggest new ways of doing things. For a woman of her age, she was amazingly strong and agile, Fran thought. It was a shame her son kept her in retirement homes. She was capable and strong-willed enough to take care of herself, except for her occasional spells of forgetfulness.

They were cleaning up in Fran's apartment when the grandfather clock bonged out 12 noon.

Aunt Gladys' feather duster froze in space and she said, "Didn't I have something to do today, Fran? I don't remember."

"That's right—Winkie's bridge party is this afternoon," Fran told her.

"Hell's bells, I'd better go get ready." Aunt Gladys hurried over to the steps and headed to her attic bedroom. A short while later, she came back down dressed in bright red slacks and a pink silk blouse. Around her wrinkled column of neck, she'd wrapped a tiger-striped scarf and looped five or six strands of colorful beads.

Her hoop earrings tinkled as she said, "I'm ready to go, Fran."

"Let's hit the road, then," Fran said. "I'll be back in a bit," she told Eva who was on the floor sorting through a plastic box full of nail polish.

Fran fished her keys from her purse and Aunt Gladys followed her down to the garage where she helped her aunt into the old Ford, then climbed in on the driver's side. The ancient truck chugged and clunked its way through the bungalow-lined streets, pitching Aunt Gladys and Fran to and fro.

"What? You can't afford a decent vehicle?" Aunt Gladys commented as she clutched the seat. "Ach, my brains—they're scrambled like eggs. Where in Satan's name are you taking me anyway, girl?"

Fran shifted into a lower gear. "To the Sunrise Center to meet Winkie. Remember the bridge party he invited you to?"

Aunt Gladys snapped her fingers. "That's right. A card game for old people. What fun I'll have," she said dryly. "I guess it's better than rearranging furniture."

She fell silent and watched the passing scenery outside her window.

Glad for the reprieve, Fran glanced outside, too. It was another dry and unusually warm day. The distant mountain range hulked in shades of sienna. Rocky peaks shot up into the air, unforgiving and barren, except for a thin frosting of snow at the top; too far up to do the thirsty landscape any good.

Wind rose and began whipping around the truck; it rarely stopped around these parts. People said there were two seasons in Wyoming. Wind and more wind. And if you ever sighted a Jackalope, a rabbit with horns, it meant you would have good luck. Although if you believed in Jackalopes, maybe Santa Claus still climbed down your chimney, too.

Before long, Fran pulled up to an old cinderblock building that had once been Lubbie's Gas and Grub and still had an ancient red pump displayed in front. In its former glory days, before the Conoco station took up residence, it had been a hub of the small community. People had come from miles around to have Lubbie fill-'er-up and discuss the latest wheat prices and cattle ranching problems.

Lubbie's had still been around when Fran was a kid and she recalled meeting friends there to buy soda and gum. Some of the kids convinced old Lubbie to sell them cigarettes. Fran recalled huddling with classmates behind the station and puffing away on the contraband smokes. She'd really hated the way it burned her throat, but she'd wanted to fit in. And of course, when she got home, her parents could smell the odor on her clothing and she would be grounded.

Fran also recalled that a year or so before she'd graduated from high school, the gas conglomerate had bought out Lubbie's Gas and Grub and built a truck stop outside of town. Lubbie, probably in his seventies or eighties, had retired. In the years since then, the old gas station had been renovated and turned into a meeting place for Moose Creek's senior citizens.

"Thank Zeus we've arrived," Aunt Gladys exclaimed theatrically, waving a hankie in front of her face as she opened the truck door. "The fumes from this beast were about to suffocate me. Any longer and I would have gotten black lung."

She slid from the truck and headed past the Sunrise Center sign, a wooden creation with the letters burned onto it, along with a stagecoach image, mountains, and a sun.

Fran got out of the truck and followed her aunt inside, glancing briefly at the vinyl couches and fake potted ferns. A recreation area with pool tables and shuffleboard was off to the right where a large table where a large group of elderly people sat.

Aunt Gladys and Fran approached an attendant sitting at a desk, a sturdy young man with a head full of cropped blond hair. As he stared at his computer screen, Fran decided he seemed familiar. It was something about his beautiful eyes.

"My aunt's here for the bridge game," she told him. "Does she need to check in?"

"Right here," he said, pointing to a page attached to a clip board.

Aunt Gladys picked up a pen and signed her name with a flourish.

A man in a checkered shirt and worn jeans came out of an office and moved up behind the young man. He had silver spiked hair, military cut style. And though his face had a no-nonsense appearance, he was pleasant and nice looking. He reached across the desk to shake Fran and Aunt Gladys' hands.

"I'm Jack Sturgeon, the director here at Sunrise Center." He nodded at the young man. "This is Danny, our office manager."

Danny smiled. "Welcome, and we hope you have a good time here."

"My name's Fran Lightfoot," she returned. "This is my aunt—"

"Mrs. Gladys Maplethorpe," she said.

"Gladys," Winkie Hightower called as he got up from the table and strode in their direction. Dressed all in black again with his gleaming diamond earring, he addressed the director. "Gladys is a dear friend of mine. I invited her for our afternoon bridge game."

"We're glad you could join us," Jack said.

Winkie led Aunt Gladys over to the table and introduced her. Fran watched her aunt shake hands and greet Winkie's acquaintances. She smiled brightly, and seemed pleased to meet them.

"I'll be back to pick her up my aunt when the game is over, Mr. Sturgeon," Fran told the director.

"Jack—please call me Jack." He smiled. "I'm sure she'll enjoy herself. We have a friendly group of seniors here."

Fran bit her lower lip, hoping Aunt Gladys would indeed fit in with the crowd.

"Don't worry; she's in good hands," Jack added.

Oh, but Fran did worry. She remembered all too well the reason Aunt Gladys had been invited to leave her retirement home. However, once she was back in her truck, she breathed a sigh of relief. Maybe this was going to work. It would be nice to bring Aunt Gladys over here a few times a week.

Back home, Fran prepared chicken soup and beef stew and put them in the refrigerator to be reheated for tomorrow's café menu. Then she went upstairs to her living room and sank into her recliner. She glanced at Eva sitting on the floor in front of the boob tube watching TV, toes separated by cotton balls as she painted the nails shiny black.

"Honestly, Eva. That's a hideous color."

"Whatever," Eva responded.

Fran retrieved her crochet project from a large basket. She'd started the granny square afghan last summer for Eva, hoping to have it ready for her when she moved over to Westonville University's dorms.

She'd carefully chosen yarn in her daughter's favorite colors—a deep ocean blue, a sky blue, and a butter yellow to add contrast. As she stitched the granny squares together, Fran imagined Eva cuddling underneath the blanket's warmth.

Fran's eye lids began to droop, and she caught herself falling asleep with her crochet hook held in mid-air. Leaning back in her chair, placing her hands in her lap, she dozed. When a cell phone rang, her eyes popped open.

"It's yours, Mom," Eva said.

Fran shoved aside yarn and hooks and picked it up. "Hello?"

"Fran?"

"Yes."

"This is Jack. You need to come and pick up your aunt right away."

"Is the bridge game finished so soon?"

"Not exactly."

Fran's heart flip-flopped. She had a bad feeling. "Is there a problem?"

"I'd prefer to discuss it with you in person."

"I'll be right there."

It had only been a couple of hours since she'd dropped off Aunt Gladys. What kind of trouble could she have possibly gotten into in that short amount of time? Fran put on her shoes and gathered up her purse.

Eva stopped blowing on her glossy black toenails and flipped hair out of her face. "What's up, Mom? Where are you going?"

Fran paused at the door. "To rescue the Sunrise Center from Aunt Gladys."

"Oh-mi-God. What's she done now?"

"Who knows?

Eva leaned back over her toes and continued with her manual polish blow-dry.

Fran hurried out to the saggy-roofed garage to climb into the truck. Teenagers. Couldn't live with 'em, couldn't disown 'em.

Now she had Aunt Gladys to stew over.

NINETEEN

FRAN'S TRUCK SPUTTERED AND COMPLAINED all the way to the Sunrise Center. For the millionth time, she prayed the temperamental vehicle would stay spit-glued together for a couple more years until she could get Eva's car paid off, and then buy herself something new. It was rotten to be at the mercy of a heap of metal and rubber.

The second she walked inside the building, she sensed tension rippling through the air. In the recreation area, the elderly folks groused at each other in loud voices and Jack Sturgeon stood nearby, a hand on the shoulder of a woman with short, steel gray hair. Winkie stood nearby, his arm hooked through Aunt Gladys'.

Maybe she should have worn full body armor for the battle, Fran thought as she hurried over.

"Gladys Maplethorpe is a cheat and a liar," the gray-haired lady said, chin quivering.

"Alice, there's no need to be so upset," Jack said. "I'm sure we can straighten this all out."

"What's going on?" Fran asked.

"I'm afraid your aunt convinced everyone to switch from bridge to poker. Things got, well, confused."

"No confusion here," Alice spouted. "The old cow straight up and cheated!"

"Did not!" Aunt Gladys said.

"Did too!" Alice insisted.

"Everyone, calm down," Jack said

"He's right, Alice," Winkie added. "Gladys didn't mean to make anyone angry. Did you, dear?"

Aunt Gladys slowly shook her head, but steam practically emanated from her flared nostrils.

Alice shoved her hands on her hips. "But—"

"I'm so sorry for the misunderstanding," Fran interrupted. She looped her arm through her aunt's. "We're leaving now."

Winkie and Jack talked to the elderly group, calming them down, as Fran dragged her fuming aunt out into the reception area.

"That woman's deranged," Aunt Gladys proclaimed. "She needs to be in a loony bin. Why, all we were doing is playing a good old-fashioned poker game and she doesn't even know what a full house is. In fact, none of them did. It's practically a crime."

"Not everyone spent twenty years in Las Vegas gambling every weekend, Aunt Gladys. And not everyone was married to Marty the card shark like you were. Now, let's go home."

As they went outside, Winkie came up and took one of Aunt Gladys' hands, speaking quietly to her. Then a short, pot-bellied gentleman hurried to her side as well, a grin tilting his lips. He had a cap of curly silver hair that gleamed in the sunlight, and he wore a green suit jacket and slacks with a matching green-striped tie. Though his clothing was obviously of good quality, the colors were bright and Fran decided he looked like a leprechaun straight from the Emerald Isle.

"I know you weren't cheating, honey," he told Aunt Gladys in a cultured accent, eyes twinkling merrily. "You're just good at cards. Alice is only jealous."

"Thank you, Frenchie dear," Aunt Gladys said as she stared him with adoring eyes.

"May I call you sometime?" Frenchie asked, holding up his cell phone. "I'd love to take you to dinner."

Aunt Gladys took it and punched in her phone number. "I'm looking forward to hearing from you," she told him as she handed back his cell.

"Later, then." Frenchie walked back inside.

"Who was that?" Fran asked.

"Ferdinand Duckworth the second," Winkie said. "We all call him Frenchie for short, and Gladys thinks he's simply divine. So do I."

"He's rolling in the dough," Aunt Gladys informed her.

Men with money. Aunt Gladys drew them like magnets. "What's a millionaire like Frenchie doing in Moose Creek?" Fran asked.

"He made big bucks in the perfume industry and has been all over the world, even France, of course," Aunt Gladys said. "He's retired now and decided to settle in Moose Creek for a quiet, simple life."

From the corner of her eye, Fran noticed Donna Roos, the local realtor's wife, striding in their direction amid a whirlwind of dry leaves skittering across the sidewalk. A slobbering boxer at the end of the red leather leash she clung to was walking her, more than she was walking him.

"Hi Donna," Fran called.

Donna, however, merely glanced at her and pressed her lips into a hard line. The dog and Donna kept on walking as though Fran were invisible.

Something clicked in Fran's mind and she remembered reading an article in The Moose Creek Chronicle about the recent frightening drop in the local real estate market. Since the early nineties, when recreational mountain property around Silver City and the Ice Queen Resort skyrocketed, investors had purchased land further south in Moose Creek. But the local sales boom had mysteriously stopped.

Oh my gosh!

Did the local real estate agents fear that no one was buying land because there was a murderer on the loose? A sense of unease washed over her and she tried to ignore it, but to no avail. Did people blame her for the trouble because she'd dated Henry?

Determining that Donna's snub wasn't worth worrying about, she concentrated on helping her aunt get settled into the passenger side of her truck.

Winkie gave Aunt Gladys a peck on the cheek, then closed the door.

"Thank you for your help with Aunt Gladys," Fran said to Winkie.

"Do try to convince the poor dear to get some rest this afternoon," Winkie said. "She's gotten herself into such a dither, and it can't be good for her health."

"I'll see what I can do," Fran said, "but she's pretty hardheaded."

"Just like always." Winkie put his hands on his hips. "I'll call her later to see how she's doing."

As Winkie walked back into the Sunrise Center, Jack left the building and approached Fran.

"I'm so sorry about what happened," he told her, an apologetic expression on his face.

"Don't worry about it. My aunt has a way of creating drama with people and situations. It's what she does."

"Well, for what it's worth, I'm sorry it ended this way." He smiled. "And I know it may not be the best timing, but I'd like to see you again."

Fran fought to keep the surprise out of her tone. "I suppose it could be arranged," she managed to answer.

"How about going to a movie with me tonight?"

Finally, a date Lucy didn't have to set up for her.

"Um, sure. How about I meet you at the old Jefferson Theater for the main feature?"

"Great." Jack walked back into the Sunrise Center.

Fran watched him go, amazed. Miracles can happen, she told herself.

Concerned about what to do with Aunt Gladys, but looking forward to her date with Jack, Fran hopped into her truck and drove home. She barely heard Aunt Gladys' complaints. On a whim, she pulled into the Loose Goose Emporium parking lot underneath a canopy of bare tree branches.

"What are you doing?" Aunt Gladys grabbed onto the cracked dashboard. "You're driving like a maniac. I'd be better off hoofing it around town on a skateboard than letting you play chauffer."

"We need toilet paper. I'll be right back." Fran ignored Aunt Gladys' look of irritation when she got out of the truck.

The Loose Goose Emporium—why Fred and Bertie Creekmore had decided on that name was beyond Fran—was housed in the old red brick DeLacy building originally built in 1885. It sported typical Victorian gingerbread trim, cupolas, a wrap-around porch, balconies, and many beautiful stained-glass windows. The building had survived a vast assortment of incarnations as well as fires, floods, blizzards, and drought, since the present lack of rain wasn't the first dry spell Wyoming had ever suffered.

First built by one of Moose Creek's founding fathers as an upscale home in one of the finer neighborhoods of the time, it had later become a mercantile and dry goods store, then a restaurant, another time a dress shop and for a while, the town library. The DeLacy building's most infamous incarnation by far was when it was called the Saddle Up Saloon.

At the moment, the Loose Goose Emporium, while not having such a notorious reputation as the Saddle Up, filled a niche in Moose Creek society. There was a large grocery store in Westonville if you had the time to make the trip. For quicker errands, one could find plenty at the Loose Goose, milk, bread, eggs, cereal, a small assortment of meats, canned goods, and necessary paper items.

Bertie made it a point to stock a little of everything from personal hygiene items to cosmetics and a small supply of clothing. Since the Loose Goose had gone into business in the early seventies, nobody had an excuse to suffer without the necessities.

Fran glanced at the over-sized wooden goose on the store sign. She remembered staring at it as a little girl and wondering if a real goose lived there. Why that had mattered to her, Fran didn't remember. These days, the goose looked tired and worn from age.

Inside, she took a small plastic cart from the front of the store—then made a beeline for the paper goods and chose a 24-pack of bathroom tissue. Next, she swerved down another aisle to the office and art supplies where she picked up a stack of velvet-backed paint-by-number kits. She headed to the wooden checkout counter that used to be the bar and had a large, ornate mirror from the Saddle Up days hanging behind it.

"Well, as I live and breathe, if it isn't Fran Lightfoot." Vivian Whitehead tossed her brunette head at Fran and grabbed another chocolate from the box sitting next to her, popping it into her mouth. "Stolen anyone else's husband lately?"

Fran didn't know Vivian well, but she didn't have a good impression. "Excuse me?"

"Everyone knows how you entice men. Even poor, stupid Henry got duped."

Fran put her items down on the counter with an emphatic thump. "Last I heard, you and Henry were divorced. Why do you care who he dated?"

Vivian glared at her.

"Look, Vivian, I didn't come here to chit-chat with you. I needed a few things."

"I needed a few things," Vivian mimicked. "Well, I'm so freakin' glad I got to wait on you I could just croak. If it weren't for you, my Henry would still be alive and paying his child support. I wouldn't have to be working here."

"Hey, I work for a living, too, Vivian. Most of us around here do."

Bertie exited from a back room, her expression dour. She wore black from head to toe on her skeletal frame and sadness surrounded her like a wreath.

She tapped the ancient cash register with a long finger. "What's going on? It sounds like a wrestling match out here with all the shouting."

"Sorry," Fran said. "I'm just trying to buy a couple of things."

"What did I tell you about confronting the customers?" Bertie said to Vivian.

Vivian, properly chastised, hung her head. "That you'd let me go if I mouthed off."

"Shall I give you notice, then? Hmm?"

Vivian's face turned red.

Fran was irritated, but she really didn't want to be a part of Vivian's job loss. "I think Vivian's just having a bad day."

"Fran's right," Vivian said. "I need this job."

Bertie frowned. "I'll give you one more chance. Otherwise—"

"I know, I know," Vivian said. "I'll behave myself. I promise."

Vivian rang up Fran's items and Bertie said, "I don't know why you're still so defensive about that ex-husband of yours anyway, Vivian. He was a no-good and I knew that boy was going to get himself in trouble. I saw all the women he had parading in and out, day and night, night and day."

Fran glanced outside, noting that the Loose Goose Emporium was right across the street from Henry's pumpkin-colored house. Bertie and Fred had downsized from their home and now lived above the store in the small apartment Fran had once rented. Even with the bird's-eye view, Bertie needed good eyesight or a pair of binoculars to see much. Fran placed a bet on the binoculars.

"You saw Henry a lot?" Fran asked.

"Oh, yes. I imagine he was dead on his feet at work with all the nonsense he had going on at his place. Loud music and goings on till all hours of the morning almost every day. He constantly left his curtains wide open and I could see . . ." she trailed off and cleared her throat, obviously rethinking her choice of words. "People told me they saw all manner of wild parties and, well, unusual activities going on. Why, he was a regular neighborhood nuisance. It's funny his landlord didn't kick him out long before somebody offed him. If you ask me, it's good riddance to have him gone."

"Not for me," Vivian protested. "Don't get me wrong, I hated what he'd become, but I didn't wish him dead. His death ended his child support, so I'll be raising the kids on my own, along with feeding his moose of a dog, Tiny. It's amazing how much he eats."

"I realize it's not nice to speak ill of the dead, but I agree that Henry Whitehead had become an unpleasant person," Bertie said.

"That's the truth," Vivian chimed in.

"Why, I bet it was one of the neighbors hereabouts who did him in," Bertie added.

Vivian rang up Fran's items and she paid with a credit card. After Vivian deposited everything in a brown paper bag, Fran took it, wondering if Bertie had become angry, stolen a butcher knife from the café in order to blame the murder on Fran's family, then attacked him? It would put an end to his unneighborly conduct.

Fran mulled it over a moment. That theory was pretty far-fetched, although it remained a possibility.

"Bertie, did you see anything unusual the night of Henry's murder?" Fran asked.

"Nothing more unusual than the usual." Bertie tapped her sallow cheek. "Except for that old black car. That was definitely not usual. I've never seen it before and I haven't seen it since. I told the police all about that. And then them reporters called like crazy askin' questions. 'Bout ripped the phone off the wall, I did."

Fran's radar flicked on. Could the car Bertie had seen be the same dark vehicle that had rammed into her truck the same night Henry was murdered? The very same one that Gabe had traced back to the black paint marks on her truck?

The car that had hit Elton was dark, too. Could it be the same car as well? Fran decided she needed to mention that to Gabe.

"Did you get a license plate number off of the car, Bertie?"

"Good gracious, no, Fran. It was too far away," Bertie said, shaking her head.

"You ladies have a good afternoon," Fran said, turning to leave.

Carma was entering the store as Fran left, sleek, smooth, and cosmopolitan as ever. Her black designer jeans, green silk blouse, and snakeskin boots definitely did not fit in with the flowered housedresses and red, windblown complexions of most of the women in this town.

She gave a brief, "Hello," and narrowed her eyes at Fran.

"Nice seeing you again," Fran returned.

"Please come to the next book club meeting with your sister, Fran," Carma said. "We read the most fabulous books; the next one we're diving into is that new murder mystery everyone's talking about."

"I'll think about it," Fran said.

"Elections are coming up soon. If you join, you can vote for Lucy as the new president. She would be fabulous."

"I didn't even know she was running," Fran said.

"That's because she doesn't know herself. But she will, you can be sure." Carma laughed. "There's no one else who can fill Susannah Averill's shoes when she resigns this year."

"I'll let you know if I can make it," Fran said, thinking that joining the book club might be a good way to get out more. She also wondered what Lucy would think about being involuntarily elected.

Fran told Carma good-bye and hustled back outside, an odd sensation washing over her. Maybe she was coming down with a cold. Inside the truck, she handed the bag to Aunt Gladys.

"You've been gone about a million years," Aunt Gladys complained.

Fran buckled up and started the truck. "I got you a present. Not the toilet paper."

Aunt Gladys glanced inside the bag and pulled out the painting kits. "What are these silly things for?"

"They'll keep you busy while you're staying with me. You got a better idea?"

"Hell's bells, paint-by-numbers? I can't even paint my own toenails."

"You'll learn." Fran gripped the steering wheel tighter as she turned a corner. "Here are the rules. You're not allowed anywhere unless one of the family is with you."

Aunt Gladys snorted. "I'm under house arrest?"

"Call it what you like. I'm trying to keep you out of trouble."

Aunt Gladys folded her arms and glared outside.

Fran rolled down her window, thankful for the fresh air. The name of the game was survival. At least tonight, she could enjoy some time with Jack Sturgeon. A movie, any kind of movie, should take her mind off of unpleasant thoughts.

TWENTY

SHOWERED, DRESSED, AND READY FOR THE WORK DAY, Fran went downstairs, basking in the orange and red sunlight pouring into the cafe. Bathed in an ethereal, golden glow, the counters, the table and chairs, and all of the kitchen gadgets, the toaster, the can opener, and even the coffee maker looked idyllic—like illustrations from a child's storybook.

"Probably going to be another hot day," Fran murmured. Pausing in front of a window, she spotted a dark car parked across the street. Her heart thumped uneasily, so she fished her cell phone from a pocket and called Gabe. It was only 6 a.m., but she needed to let him know about the strange vehicle sitting across the street before she got busy and forgot.

"This is Detective Gabe Stevenson," his deep voice said on the recording. "I'm not available right now, so leave a message and I'll get back with you."

After the beep, Fran informed him about Bertie's claim that she'd seen a dark car parked in front of Henry's house the night of his murder. Then she told him about the dark car parked across the street from her house right now.

"It's got tinted windows, so I can't see inside," she added. "I'm going to try and get a closer look, maybe get a license plate number."

She called Otis, hoping he'd pick up, but she only reached his voice mail. She left the same message for him, hoping he or Cleve would get back with her before long.

After disconnecting, she went outside on her porch and studied the vehicle. When it didn't move, she walked toward it, cell phone in her hand, planning to snap a picture.

Suddenly, the engine roared to life and the car took off. Fran managed to snap several photos, however. Disappointment shot through her as it zoomed down the street and she feared her efforts had been for naught. After a quick look through her photos, however, she realized she'd hit the jackpot.

Pinching the photos to make them larger, she noted that the vehicle had a Wyoming license plate and was registered in this county. She could also make out the numbers 22, however the rest were too blurry to identify. The words Buick and Regal were also visible on the bumper.

Excited, Fran texted the best photos to both Otis and Gabe. Back in the kitchen, Fran put on her café apron, set coffee to brew, then rummaged through her larder and produced flour, sugar, spices, and other baking and cooking supplies. At least for the time being, cooking would occupy her mind.

Fingers and flour flew. By the time Fran finished, she had produced six loaves of bread consisting of oatmeal raisin, sourdough, and rye, all set to rise on the counter. She switched on the two large commercial ovens to preheat, and stirred together a big pot of golden colored corn-bacon chowder for the soup special. The chowder smelled heavenly by the time she started to put together apple and peach pies.

Bringing with her a whirl of orange and yellow leaves and a warm breeze, Lucy walked in through the back door. She left it open and latched the screen. "Phew, it's hot in here. We need some air."

"Guess what parked in front of the house earlier?" Fran hurried over to show Lucy the cell phone photos she'd taken of the Buick Regal.

"Do you think it's the same car that's been involved in all of the incidents, Fran?" Lucy placed her purse and jacket in a cupboard and slipped on a white café apron.

"I have a feeling it is," Fran said. "I texted the photos to both Otis and Gabe so they're aware it was here."

"I can't believe whoever is driving that vehicle had the nerve to sit outside and spy on this house," Lucy said. "They must think we're too stupid to realize the car might be connected to all the trouble that's been going on."

"I know, it's crazy, right?"

"For sure," Lucy said. "Otis left pretty early this morning for work, before the sun even came up," Lucy said. "But he'll definitely appreciate the pics."

"I'm sure," Fran said.

"How is Aunt Gladys doing today?" Lucy asked. "She was pretty upset when Elton got hurt."

"She isn't up yet," Fran said. "Yesterday, I took her over to the senior center for a game of bridge with Winkie, but I had to pick her up early."

"Uh, oh, what happened?"

"She convinced everyone to switch from bridge to poker, and Lord only knows what went on, except that I understand it wasn't good."

"Um-hum," Lucy said, nodding. "Par for the course."

"The bottom line, everyone was upset," Fran said. "I don't imagine she'll be welcome to go back there any time soon."

"Who loves ya, baby?" Aunt Gladys, wearing a leopard print caftan and enough beads to sink a ship, entered the kitchen. She danced around and sang, clapping and kicking her long legs in the air.

"Oh my," Lucy said. "Do you suppose she thinks she's back on stage in Vegas?"

"Probably." Fran shook her head. "There's no telling with her."

Exhausted and out of breath, Aunt Gladys stopped and glanced around the kitchen. "Where the heck am I? What kind of bar is this?"

"Aunt Gladys," Fran said firmly. "Remember, you're staying with me."

Aunt Gladys glared at her. "Hell's bells, you could at least put cocktail peanuts and appetizers out for the patrons. I'm hungry as a dog pulling a sled."

"Are you all right?" Fran asked her.

Aunt Gladys playfully punched both Fran and Lucy's arms. "I'm fit as a fiddle, girls. And I'm putting on an act! Fooled you two into thinking I've lost my mind, didn't I?"

Fran and Lucy laughed, admitting that Aunt Gladys had indeed fooled them.

"Do you want me to make you some eggs or pancakes for breakfast?" Fran asked.

Aunt Gladys shook her head. "Good heavens, no. I have to drink my special shake." She tapped her forehead. "Keeps me sharp as a tack up here where it counts."

Aunt Gladys proceeded to bulldoze her way through a few cupboards then bellied up to the counter and mixed eggs, milk, and her drink powder. After pouring everything into the blender, she pushed the on button and it whirred into action. Before long the pale, unappetizing drink came to life and Aunt Gladys seemed happy as a clam as she poured it into a tall glass, humming to herself.

"Is she like this all the time?" Lucy asked.

"Ninety-nine-point-nine percent of it," Fran told her.

"I know you girls are whispering about me again," Aunt Gladys said, shaking a finger at them.

"You look nice today, Aunt Gladys," Lucy said as she turned to face her.

"I hope you aren't upset with me after yesterday's fiasco," Fran added, meeting Aunt Gladys' gaze.

"Heck no," Aunt Gladys said, giving a bright red lipstick smile. "Like I said before, I do have a tendency to be difficult. I hope you're not angry with me, my dear."

Aunt Gladys gave Fran a hug and a peck on the cheek, then she did the same with Lucy.

"Of course not," Fran said, glad there wouldn't be any bad blood between them.

Aunt Gladys rubbed her hands together. "Something smells wonderful. What's on the menu for today and what can I help with? After I have my power drink, that is."

"I'm making carrot soup, Aunt Gladys, so would you be interested in peeling and dicing them for me?" Lucy asked.

"I'd love to," Aunt Gladys said.

When Fran's cell phone rang, she removed it from her jeans pocket and said, "This is Fran."

There was a moment of silence, then she heard a click when the call disconnected. She stared at the phone, puzzled.

"What happened?" Lucy asked. "Wrong number, maybe?"

"Don't know, they hung up without saying a word." Fran plugged in the corn chowder crockpot. She removed the chicken and dumpling soup and beef stew tubs from the refrigerator and poured them into other crockpots to warm.

She went to the pantry, removed another tub and placed it on the counter. From it, she began to remove carrots that had been packed in sawdust, which helped them remain fresh after they'd been harvested.

As she dusted off the orange vegetables and set them aside, she said, "I've been thinking maybe it was one of those telemarketer calls. I've been getting a bunch of those on my cell lately."

"I bet you're right," Lucy said.

"Or maybe it was Barnard Scott," Fran suggested. "He does love to get enough information to spin his stories."

"I've heard he's like a dog with a bone," Lucy said.

When Fran's phone rang again, she frowned. "Sometimes I hate this thing. If it is Barnard Scott, I'm going to give him a piece of my mind."

"You go, girl," Lucy encouraged.

"Hello, this is Fran," she said.

"Fran Lightfoot, go back where you came from or you're going to die," a robot-sounding voice warned.

Fran felt the blood drain from her face. She clicked off the phone and shoved it aside as if it had bit her.

"What?" Lucy asked as she dropped carrots into a bowl.

"It, it was a warning," Fran said. "A voice that sounded like a robot told me to go back where I came from or I'm going to die."

Seated at the table, Aunt Gladys put down her drink. "What in the world is going on"

"Call Otis," Lucy encouraged. He'll know what to do."

Fran picked up her cell again and called her brother-in-law, hoping he'd answer this time.

"Sheriff Otis Parnell," he said.

Fran tapped the speaker button. "Otis, I just received a threatening call."

"Tell me about it," he said.

Fran told him what had happened, and he made encouraging noises as she finished explaining and gave him the caller's phone number.

"I've got your complaint written down, Fran," he told her reassuringly. "Block that number, okay?"

"Thanks, Otis," Fran said.

"We're making progress on Henry's murder," he said. "I promise, all of this nonsense is going to come to an end. Then things will get back to normal."

"I sure hope so," Fran said, then disconnected.

"Let's get back to work," Lucy said. "It'll help us keep our minds off of the call."

The sisters turned their attention back to the pies. After pinching the edges on the crusts, they sprinkled the cream-colored pastry with a mixture of cinnamon and sparkling sugar. The preheat lights had gone out on the ovens and Fran popped pies in one of them. Lucy put the properly risen bread loaves into the other.

Glancing at the teapot-shaped clock on the wall, Fran decided everything should be done about the time customers began to arrive.

"Didn't you tell me you had a date with Jack Sturgeon last night?" Fran asked.

"I did. We went to a movie."

"What I want to know," Lucy said, "is how you managed to get a date with the most eligible town bachelor?"

"He asked me."

"That's nice," Lucy said

"He's a nice guy," Fran said.

"Which is why all the single women in town are after him," Lucy said. "He hasn't dated since his wife left him, so I didn't think he was ready yet."

"I guess he is."

"Think you'll go out again?"

"Maybe," Fran said.

Noon came and went; yet there was no familiar ring-a-ling from the bell on the door to announce customers. An hour went by, then two. Aunt Gladys pulled out her paint-by-numbers and busied herself at the kitchen table dabbing color on a black velvet picture of a mountain stream. Fran and Lucy stirred around the kitchen, waiting and watching for signs of life and trying to be hopeful.

No one came to have soup and sandwiches at the Saucy Lucy Café.

Finally, the front door bell tinkled and Akiko shuffled inside and sat at her usual table by the bay window.

"I'll take her order," Fran told Lucy and hurried out to greet the soft-spoken Japanese woman.

"Good afternoon, Akiko." Fran smiled at her, order pad in hand. "What can I get for you today?"

"Good afternoon," Akiko said with a slight bow. She wore black slacks, a white silk brocade blouse with a Mandarin collar, and diamond stud earrings. "I want your soup special and apple pie."

"And your husband? Is he joining you?"

Akiko shook her head. "Aunt Gladys told him about the Castleton curse the other day. He said he wants to stay away until your trouble blows over."

Fran frowned. "There's no truth to that."

"What do you think Henry Whitehead and Elton Briarhurst would say about the curse?"

Fran clutched the order pad harder. "Please, don't buy into that nonsense."

"I warned you about the curse, Fran," Aunt Gladys said as she walked up to Akiko's table.

"Aunt Gladys, please," Fran said.

A loud crashing sound exploded, then something slammed against Fran's head as glass rained down on the floor.

Pain shot through her temples.

Thick, muffled darkness clogged her mind.

TWENTY-ONE

"**F**RAN..."

As if from a million miles away, Fran heard a voice urgently calling her. Someone shook her shoulder.

"Wh-what?" she asked, her mind foggy as the docks of San Francisco's Fisherman's Wharf at midnight. She couldn't move, couldn't think straight.

An agitated voice shouted, "Aliens! We've been invaded by a bunch of aliens! They've bombarded us with one of their evil offspring!"

That's Aunt Gladys, Fran thought as she struggled to the surface of consciousness.

"Fran, wake up!"

Fran dragged her eyes open to see Lucy crouched beside her holding something to her forehead. The cool, hardness of the cloth revealed it was full of ice. It felt good in a way, but also bad because the ice pack pressure caused such intense pain to radiate through her frontal lobes, she wouldn't have been surprised to see pink elephants in spike heels dancing on the bistro tables.

Pushing herself to a sitting position, Fran took the compress from Lucy. Crimson splotches covered the surface. Blood. Intense throbbing drummed in her brain. Fran groaned and pressed the ice pack against her forehead again. "What happened? What hit me?"

"Good question." Lucy's voice shook and her face was creased with concern. "Thank goodness you're all right. I was worried."

"Look! Look!" Akiko crouched in a corner pointing toward the middle of the room where a round, dark green object covered in yellow paper had landed. Several of the bay windowpanes near her table were broken, making it look like a gaping mouth full of shark's teeth. Chunks of splintered glass scattered across the floor, and a warm breeze filled the room.

Aunt Gladys shook her fist. "You'll never take me alive, you little puke-green lizards! I know Elvis personally. He'll cut off your heads and shove 'em down your throat if you touch a hair on any of our heads!"

Fran rose to her feet with Lucy's assistance, glancing at her customer. "Akiko, are you all right?"

Akiko took a deep breath and stood. "One minute everything was fine, then kerflooey! Something flew in through the window."

Fran moved next to Akiko and patted her on the back. Figure the odds she'd ever come back to the café. She and Lucy had probably lost another customer. Just peachy.

"What is that thing?" Akiko stared at the green object again.

Fran examined it closer. "Oh, my gosh, it looks like a—"

"Grenade, grenade!" Aunt Gladys shoved Fran, Lucy and Akiko toward the door. "Fire in the hole! Retreat! Everyone get moving!"

Outside, standing in the middle of the street, the ladies looked at each other in shock.

"What do we do now?" Lucy asked.

"Call the police." Fran fished the cell phone out of her jeans pocket and punched in 911.

Otis was first to arrive. He parked and jumped out of his sheriff's car with frustration lining his face. Deputy Cleve Harris walked alongside him wearing a rumpled uniform that appeared as if he'd slept in it. Those two were probably very overworked these days, considering the recent incidents in town.

"Otis and Cleve look pretty haggard," Fran commented to Lucy as they stood on the lawn.

"And no wonder," she said. "They've been burning the midnight oil, trying to handle all of their current cases and solve Henry's murder. It's driving them both crazy to know there's a murderer running loose."

"It's troubling to all of us," Fran said. "I appreciate how hard they are working, though."

"I'm going to deliver them a basket of huckleberry muffins to thank them," Lucy said.

"I got your message about the dark car outside of the house this morning," Otis said as he approached them. "And it's been duly noted."

Scratchpad in hand, he questioned Fran and Lucy, while Cleve talked to Aunt Gladys and Akiko who stood nearby.

"The bomb squad should arrive any minute," Otis said. "We call them in when explosives are involved."

"Yeah," Cleve added. "That's not something we're trained to handle."

When an ambulance and a fire truck arrived, sirens blaring and lights flashing, Fran figured the neighbors would take up a petition to have the café closed. It seemed that every couple of days, something was going down over here that drew law enforcement.

Westonville Police Department officers rolled in next, parked their squad cars and took possession of the scene. Without hesitation, one of them cordoned off the area around the café with yellow tape.

Following the WPD was an armored EOD truck that pulled up behind them. Several police department bomb technicians jumped out. Wearing black ball caps and matching T-shirts stamped with the department's logo, they poked through bushes, no doubt making sure there weren't any hidden explosive devices or suspicious wires.

After donning a bulky suit, a helmet and gloves, one of the squad members went inside the café. An expectant hush fell as onlookers watched for his re-emergence. One of the technicians, with a nametag identifying him as Tyler Sampson, sidled up to Otis and they shook hands.

"We're all curious to know what kind of grenade is in there, and why it didn't explode," Tyler said.

"Same here," Otis agreed. "I'll work day and night to find out who had the bright idea to throw it at my wife's café."

"Is everyone okay?" he asked as he glanced at Fran's forehead and Lucy's pale face.

"We're all shaken up, but I believe we'll be fine," Fran said.

"This is the first time someone's thrown a deadly weapon at us," Lucy said. "And hopefully the last."

"Yeah, it's pretty concerning when that happens," Tyler said.

Aunt Gladys, Akiko, and Cleve walked over and stood beside Otis.

"What will happen now?" Aunt Gladys asked.

"Did you see our bomb technician enter the house?" Tyler asked. "Jake Cordova is one of our best. He'll evaluate the explosive threat."

Aunt Gladys placed her hands on her hips. "He looked like an astronaut wearing a space suit."

"Those bomb disposal suits are hot, heavy suckers, I can tell you," Otis said.

"We want our team members to have good protection if there's ever a blast," Tyler explained. "Jake's wearing 85 pounds of Kevlar, steel plates, and ballistic plastic. It can only be worn for about 20 minutes before a body wears out from supporting it."

"Wow," Fran said, deciding that type of job wasn't for her. Thank heavens there were brave souls willing to do it.

"He'll decide whether the grenade is stable enough to transport," Tyler added. "If so, we'll take it and dispose of it."

"Thank goodness," Lucy said. "We'd like it gone ASAP, thank you very much."

"We'll do our best," Tyler said.

Finally, Jake came out of the café carrying a bag, which he placed in a container and stowed in the EOD truck. He said something to his teammates, and they laughed uneasily. After removing his bomb suit and helmet, he walked over to Otis, Tyler, and the rest of the group.

"The grenade was military ordinance, all right," he said in a gravelly voice. "World War II-vintage."

"Too old to detonate, you think?" Cleve asked.

"It appears that way," Jake said. "We see that once in a while when people go through their loved one's things after the family's veteran has passed on. They'll run across stored ammo or guns up in the attic or in the basement."

"Holy cow," Lucy said. "That's frightening."

"What will you do with the grenade?" Akiko asked.

"It's in a containment vessel for now," Jake said. "We'll take it to a bomb range for safe disposal."

"I'll be relieved to see it gone," Fran told him. She touched her forehead, wincing at the slight ache.

"I'm ready to start searching for the idiot who threw that thing," Otis said, determination boosting his voice.

"I have some ideas," Cleve said, his eyes full of resolve.

Producing a handkerchief from his pocket, Jake mopped his brow and the fringe of silver hair on his head. "I wouldn't get too excited yet, Sheriff. This could have been a prank. Maybe played by a disgruntled customer." He pulled a piece of yellow lined paper from his breast pocket. "Take a look at this. It was rubber banded around the grenade."

He handed the paper, splattered with the blood from Fran's wound, to Otis. "Hmm, well I'll be darned."

Otis handed the note to Fran.

"You will pay," she read aloud, her blood running cold as she handed it back to him.

"What the heck is going on?" Lucy blinked several times. "How dare someone threaten us?"

An ambulance paramedic wearing blue scrubs with a stethoscope around her neck approached Fran and touched her arm. A petite woman with flaxen hair and a perky, upturned nose, her nametag identified her as Kari Storm.

"Ma'am, would you like us to look at that cut on your forehead?" she asked.

Fran shook her head. "I'd rather that you examine my aunt first."

"Of course," Kari said.

"I'm fine, Fran," Aunt Gladys protested. "Don't worry about me."

"This stunt upset everyone," Lucy said. "And I think Fran's right. You should be looked at first."

"My blood pressure might be up, but I bet that's all." Aunt Gladys went over to Kari and the two headed toward the paramedics' red and white vehicle.

Tyler and Jake wished everyone well, then walked over to join their bomb squad members. The first responders began to pack up their equipment, and before long, all of the emergency vehicles, except for the ambulance, had left.

"Well, I don't know about you ladies, but I've had enough excitement for the day," Akiko admitted. "Thank goodness everyone's okay."

With a wave, she walked over to her car parked by the curb, got in, and drove off.

"Glad you two weren't hurt," Cleve said.

"No kidding," Otis said. He pecked Lucy's cheek. "I've got to head back to work, but I'll see you at home later."

Otis and Cleve headed over to the sheriff's vehicle, crawled inside, and took off down the street.

The sisters hugged, and Fran sensed they were both relieved to have come out of the situation in one piece.

"I'll go find some cardboard and duct tape to fix the window," Lucy said. "That'll keep it together until we can get it replaced."

"Good idea," Fran said, noticing how tired she sounded.

"Go get yourself looked at by that nice paramedic," Lucy said in a concerned tone. "She needs to assess your head wound."

"I will," Fran promised. "Then I'll be right in to help with the cleanup."

"I think we should close the café for the rest of the day," Lucy suggested.

"Sounds like a good idea." A wave of dizziness swept over Fran. Closing her eyes, she stepped back and leaned against a bird bath to steady herself.

"Fran, are you okay?" Lucy rested a hand on her arm.

"I don't feel so good," Fran admitted.

"Go," Lucy said, pointing toward the ambulance.

Fran walked over to the red and white vehicle and sat down on the tailgate. After wrapping a blanket around Fran's shoulders, Kari took her vital signs, and began to poke and prod on her bruised forehead. Fran winced at her touch.

"Sorry if I hurt you, but I think you may have a slight concussion," Kari said. "Do you have someone to stay with you? You know, so they can keep an eye on you in case you suffer more symptoms and feel like you need to go to the hospital?"

Fran nodded. "My daughter drove over to Westonville University for a class, but she'll be home later."

"Good," Kari said. "By the way, your aunt was right. Her BP was elevated, but she's fine. I gave her something to help her rest and she went inside to lay down."

"That's a relief," Fran said.

Hearing an engine, Fran watched as Gabe parked his SUV along the curb. When he stepped out and sauntered toward the ambulance, Fran smiled. A wave of reassurance passed through her as she assessed his tweed suit jacket, button down shirt, and Levi's. It came to her as a surprise that she'd think of him as more than just the detective working on Henry Whitehead's murder case.

Something about him held her interest. Something that didn't quite register, but it made her heart tremble.

"Sorry I didn't get here earlier, Fran," he said. "I was following up on a lead in Henry's case this morning. When I heard on my police radio about the grenade being thrown through your front window, I hurried back here. I was in Cheyenne, so it took a while."

"No worries, the bomb squad hauled the thing away," Fran said. "It was a World War II vintage, if you can believe it."

"So I heard," Gabe said with a nod, then frowned as he studied her forehead and the paramedic attending to it. "Jeez, you're hurt."

"Kari here is doing a good job of taking care of me," Fran said, then introduced Kari to Gabe.

"Kari assures me I'll live," Fran added. "So, there's that."

"Which is good to hear," he said. "By the way, I also got your text. You did good, Fran, getting those photos. I'm going to search the DMV database for people in the county who own Buick Regals and have license plates starting with the numbers 22. This could give us the break we need."

"Perfect," Fran said. "Lucy and I want this cleared up sooner than later."

"We'll do our best," Gabe said.

"Tell me, how did the grenade tossing event go down?" Gabe asked.

"Some jerk pitched it through the front window." Fran winced as Kari dabbed ointment on her wound, then covered it with a gauze bandage. "Unfortunately, it found me."

"You're lucky it didn't explode."

"I'm thankful it was a dud."

Gabe folded his arms across his chest. "I imagine you and Lucy have closed the café for the rest of the day."

"Yes, that goes without saying," Fran said.

"Do you want anything for the pain?" Kari asked, standing back to examine her handiwork.

Fran put up a hand. "No thanks."

"You might rethink that," Gabe commented. "Shock can do funny things to a person."

Fran thought about it for a minute. "If my head starts hurting worse, I have pain reliever in my medicine cabinet I can take."

A muscle ticked in Gabe's jaw. "Take it easy the rest of the day, okay?"

"Yes, sir," Fran said, appreciating that he'd come to check on her. He really hadn't needed to rush over here, yet he had. She considered that briefly, then dismissed it. No reason to go there, really.

"I'll call later and check in on you, if you don't mind."

"I'd like that," she said.

He touched her hand, sending a stream of sparks up her spine, then strode back to his SUV and drove away.

Fran wondered what it was about Gabe that stirred her blood.

TWENTY-TWO

FRAN HEADED INSIDE THE HOUSE and checked on Aunt Gladys, relieved to find her asleep in her room. Then she sat down to rest in her recliner, waiting for Eva to return from the university. She'd been watching TV, about to doze off, when the bell on the front door to the café tinkled. Hearing someone's muffled footsteps, Fran realized no one had put up the CLOSED sign for the cafe.

Had Barnard Scott dropped by to question her? Maybe he'd decided to ask for a quote about the grenade episode. She hustled downstairs and to her surprise, found a scowling, middle-aged couple.

The tall man wore a black, expensive-looking suit and tie. The woman, whose head barely reached his shoulders, wore a beautiful dress with a fur wrap.

"May I help you?" Fran asked. For some reason, she got the impression they weren't paying The Saucy Lucy Café a visit because they'd heard about her decent coffee.

The man, who towered over Fran, fixed her with a hard stare. "Are you Fran Lightfoot?"

"That's correct," she responded.

"I'm Dr. William Briarhurst and this is my wife, Olivia. I assume you know who we are?"

Elton Briarhurst's very rich and influential and seemingly torqued off parents, she thought.

"Yes," Fran said with a nod. "I feel terrible about Elton's accident. How's he doing, by the way?"

"He's a strong boy," Olivia said.

"That's good to hear," Fran said. "Can I get you anything? Or maybe you'd rather sit down so we can be more comfortable."

Fran gestured toward a room off to the right that she and Lucy had restored to an original old-fashioned parlor, complete with period antiques like a brocade settee, fern stands, statues, and an iron fireplace ensemble. A colorful carpet covered the polished wooden floorboards and replica velvet-flocked paper from the turn of the century adorned the walls along with several old oil paintings.

The couple didn't answer, however they continued to glare at Fran. Her heart sank, dreading the fireworks that might erupt any second now, but she did her best to stay friendly.

"I, ah—," Fran stammered. "Well, the sitting room is a popular feature of our café. Customers like to relax in there with their coffee and newspapers. It's sunny and pleasant . . ."

She hoped the Briarhurst's wouldn't notice her nervousness, but doubted that she was hiding it very well.

"You need to realize, Ms. Lightfoot, that we are not here to pay you a social call," Olivia said in a sharp tone, glancing at the bandage on Fran's forehead.

"Is that so?" Fran folded her arms across her chest, an ominous sensation creeping over her. "Why are you here, then?"

"We're here to talk about our son," Dr. Briarhurst said.

"Again, I'm sorry about what happened," Fran said.

"Elton's finally on the mend, no thanks to you," Olivia said with a sniff.

"I hope you don't believe I had anything to do with the accident."

Dr. Briarhurst shook a finger at her. "How could you run over him? Please, enlighten me."

"Run over him?" Fran was flabbergasted by his accusation. "What are you talking about? It was a hit and run. No one knows who did it."

"Don't lie to us, Ms. Lightfoot," Dr. Briarhurst said. "Elton told us everything once he came out of his coma. Due to your irresponsibility, he will now need weeks of therapy in order to walk again."

Olivia began to sob and took out a flowered hankie to dab at her eyes.

"You have it all wrong," Fran insisted. "You need to talk to Elton again and insist he tell you the truth."

"You, as his employer, should have known better than to have him repair your roof without the proper equipment," Dr. Briarhurst persisted. "Why, it's outlandish and you know you're responsible."

Fran's mouth dropped. "Elton told you he was repairing my roof?"

"Yes," Olivia said with another indignant sniff. "We expect you to pay all his medical expenses."

Stunned didn't even begin to describe how Fran felt. She figured Elton didn't want his upper crust parents to know he was moonlighting as a male stripper. No doubt the Briarhurst's gave their son a large allowance to live on while attending college, so they'd be upset to discover what he'd really been doing that night.

"Mr. and Mrs. Briarhurst, please understand—I hate that Elton got hurt. But you have been misinformed about a couple of things. One of them is that he wasn't here to repair my roof, and the other is that he was run over by a hit-and-run driver."

"Don't try to project blame," Dr. Briarhurst growled. "By the time I'm through with you, you'll be ruined."

"You need to talk with the police to find out what really happened that night," Fran said, becoming more and more irritated by their bullying.

"All you need to know, Ms. Lightfoot," Dr. Briarhurst said, eyes flashing, "is that you will hear from our lawyer."

Dr. Briarhurst escorted his sobbing wife down the hall and out the door, slamming it closed.

Had that just happened or had it been a dream? Fran pinched her arm.

"Ouch!" It was no dream.

Had the Briarhursts thrown the grenade through the front window? No, that didn't seem like their style at all, Fran thought. But they could have hired someone to do it for them.

Another headache drummed in Fran's temples as she approached the door, flipped over the CLOSED sign, then entered the parlor and sat down on the old gold brocade sofa that had belonged to Grandmother Castleton.

The room had once been a favorite family gathering place. During the Christmases of her youth, her favorite time of year, the large stone fireplace had been draped with festive swags and a large decorated fir tree had dominated the northeast corner by another large bay window.

Despite the nostalgic comfort she felt in here, Fran toyed with the idea of running away. She wanted to go somewhere—maybe an island in the middle of the Pacific Ocean—where no one knew her. It would be wonderful to disappear and leave all her troubles behind.

Leaning back, she closed her eyes, fighting tears. Warmth sifted through her limbs, and she relaxed enough to doze.

"Mom, wake up."

Fran's eyes flew open and she readjusted herself. "Oh, good, you're home."

Eva stood in front of her, hands on her hips. "What's with the duct-taped window? And your head!" She winced. "What happened?"

Fran explained about the old grenade being thrown through the window and how she'd managed to get in the way of its trajectory. Or actually, her forehead had.

"Then the Briarhursts showed up, threatening to sue me about Elton's car accident," she added. "For some strange reason, they believe he fell from the roof while repairing it."

"Don't worry about Elton's snobby parents," Eva said, plopping down beside Fran on the couch. "They're only trying to scare you."

"They sure succeeded in making me angry," Fran admitted. "Elton needs to tell his parents the truth so they'll get off my back."

"I'll call him and talk to him," Eva said. "I know he doesn't like them much, but I had no idea that he'd lie about his accident."

"I'm sure he knew they'd be upset with him for working as a male stripper," Fran said.

"Yeah, but that's no excuse for him to blame you and get you in trouble," Eva said. "He needs to man up."

"I'm happy to hear that you're on my side," Fran told her daughter.

"Mom, I know you're going through a rough time right now with Mr. Whitehead's murder and Elton's accident," Eva said in a soothing tone, resting her head on Fran's shoulder. "But it's going to be all right. Wait and see."

Indeed, Fran thought. No doubt Eva enjoyed the fact that for once she was able to give advice to her mother, instead of the other way around. Strange how your kids grow up and the roles reverse.

"Thanks, honey," Fran said. "What would I do without you?"

TWENTY-THREE

EARLY NEXT MORNING, AS THE SISTERS were preparing items for their menu, Fran's cell phone rang. For a moment, she considered shutting it off. However, it wasn't only her personal phone, she used it for business, too.

On the outside chance it might be someone ordering pies, a batch of cinnamon rolls or maybe even setting up an event to be catered, she answered.

"Hello?"

Click.

"Ugg." Fran put the phone back in her pocket.

"Another hang up?" Lucy asked.

Before Fran could say anything, her cell rang again. Hesitantly, she answered it, tensed and ready for someone to threaten her.

"Fran?"

It was Jack.

She breathed a sigh of relief. "Gosh, I'm so sorry if I sounded annoyed when I answered. I've been getting a ton of prank calls. In fact, I got one right before you called."

"Have you told the police?"

"Yes, but they really can't do anything."

"Probably kids playing around," Jack said.

"Maybe," Fran said, glancing at her watch, noting that it was only 6 a.m. "This early, you'd think the sweet little angels would still be in bed."

"Good point," Jack said. "Hey, do you want to go fishing with me this morning? You mentioned last night how you miss dipping your line in the water for a fresh catch."

"Well," Fran said, hesitating to commit since she'd have to leave Lucy to finish their preparations.

"I remember you mentioned the café doesn't open till noon, and I don't have to get to the senior center until nine, so thought we'd get out to the lake early while the fish are still biting."

"Hold on a sec," she said, tapping the mute button. "Lucy, it's Jack, and he's invited me to go fishing this morning, but—"

"Go, skedaddle," Lucy said, making a shooing motion with her hands. "It's still early and you have plenty of time."

"You sure?" Fran asked.

"I'll call about getting the window repaired, and I can handle the rest of the food prep," Lucy said. "You and Jack enjoy yourselves."

Fran took the phone off of mute and told Jack, "I'd love to go."

"Great," Jack said. "I'll pick you up at six-thirty."

Lucy brushed off her apron and grinned at Fran. "Wow, you've had two dates in a row with Jack Sturgeon," she said in a teasing manner. "This sounds serious."

"At least I might catch a few of trout," Fran responded. "I haven't done that in ages, and I'll grill them up for dinner."

Aunt Gladys walked into the kitchen wearing a gold, calf-length skirt, a red top, and an orange brocade jacket. On her head she wore a cap covered in rust-colored silk flowers. "That sounds yummy! But I won't be here to enjoy them."

"Really, where are you going?" Fran asked, intrigued that her aunt had plans.

"I'm spending the day with Frenchie," she said. "And we're going to Westonville for dinner."

"Sounds like your love life is blossoming, too," Lucy said.

Aunt Gladys chuckled. "They may not want me at the Sunrise

Center again, but meeting Frenchie there was a bonus. We get along famously. I must say, he's quite the catch, too."

"That's nice he's taking you out, Aunt Gladys, but I'd like you home at least by 10 p.m.," Fran said.

"Giving me a curfew, eh?" Aunt Gladys raised a brow.

"To be fair, I don't want you rolling in at midnight," Fran said.

"Pish, posh," Aunt Gladys responded. "I doubt the two of us will last past eight-thirty, to be honest. But if it makes you feel better to fuss over me, so be it."

"We look out for each other around here," Fran said.

Aunt Gladys rubbed her hands together. "Lucy, what can I help with this morning? I've got some time before Frenchie arrives. Since Fran's going to be on a hot date with Jack, and our little Eva will be studying her heart out upstairs, I want to pitch in."

"Fantastic," Lucy said, pointing to a pile of potatoes on the counter. "Our special today is cream of spud soup, so guess what?"

"Oh goody, I get to peel again." Aunt Gladys marched over to a drawer, pulled out a paring knife, and held it up like a fencing sword. "En-garde!"

Chuckling, Fran headed upstairs to her bedroom. She already wore jeans, but she put on a pair of hiking boots and changed into an old flannel shirt. Tying her hair back in a ponytail, she went downstairs and poured coffee into a thermos. Then she started a fresh pot so Lucy and Aunt Gladys would have more.

"Hey, have you read the newspaper yet?" Aunt Gladys asked Fran as she passed by the table where her aunt sat next to peelings she'd scraped from the mound of potatoes resting on a dish cloth. "There's a story in here you need to see."

Fran read the article over Aunt Gladys' shoulder. The headlines made her shrink into her shoes. Dying For a Date: Local Woman's Life Shrouded in Mystery.

The story, written by Barnard Scott, went on to document everything that had gone on lately in Fran's life, including her divorce from Dan, Henry Whitehead's demise, and Elton's accident, including the rumor that she'd run over him.

"That man seriously needs to get a life," Fran said.

"Hell's bells." Aunt Gladys patted Fran's arm. "Everyone knows that newspaper is a rag, anyway."

"I don't need more people getting the idea that I had anything to do with Henry's murder or Elton's accident," Fran said.

"Ignore that ridiculous reporter," Lucy said, wiping her hands on a towel. "People love gossip, as we know. And that's all it is: gossip."

"I still don't like it," Fran said.

"Hey, Jack Sturgeon's the guy who asked me to leave the senior citizen's center, isn't he?" Aunt Gladys said as she resumed peeling potatoes.

"He is," Fran said. "But in his defense, he wanted to get everyone calmed down after your poker game."

"I don't blame him, Fran," Aunt Gladys said. "Alice Leone is the old bat responsible for the trouble. She's the one who started calling me a cheat."

"Alice Leone? She any relation to Carma?"

"Her aunt. She lives in Snow Village up by the Ice Queen Resort. Used to work at the resort as a waitress, though I imagine she's got too many varicose veins to sling hash any more. She comes down here to Moose Creek once in a while to visit."

The doorbell rang and both Fran and Aunt Gladys went to answer it. It was Jack, dressed in an orange fleece pullover, camouflage pants, an olive-colored T-shirt, and work boots.

"Mornin' Gladys," he said, nodding at her, then turned to Fran. "Are you ready to go?"

"I am, but give me a second, though." Fran returned to the kitchen and grabbed the thermos, her jacket, and her purse.

"I don't have a fishing pole anymore," Fran told Jack when she joined him at the door. "I hope you have a spare I can borrow."

"Of course," he said, taking her by the elbow. "A fellow can't have too many."

"Have fun, kiddies," Aunt Gladys said.

The autumn warmth, combined with the clear blue sky, made for a pleasant morning. At the curb in front of the house, Jack opened the passenger door of his Blue Ford F-250 and helped Fran inside. The pleasant smell of Irish Spring soap drifted into her nostrils.

"Bet the fish are biting like crazy." Jack winced when he looked at Fran's mottled forehead. "What happened?"

Earlier, Fran had removed the gauze bandage on her forehead. However, she'd forgotten about the giant bruise. "See my front window?"

"What in the world happened?" Jack asked after he turned to look at it.

"Somebody threw an old grenade, a dud, thankfully, through the glass," Fran told him. "Unfortunately, it beaned me on the noggin."

"Dang," Jack said. "You call the police?"

She nodded. "We had a full array of first responders here yesterday. The fire department, the Westonville Police Department, the Sheriff's Department, the bomb squad, an ambulance—you name it. Everything got checked out and we're all in the clear. We'd just like to know who tossed the dang thing."

"Yeah, inquiring minds would like to know who that joker is." Jack closed her door, then walked around and climbed into the driver's side of the truck, turned on the engine, and pulled away from the curb.

Fran hated to broach the subject, but curiosity got the best of her. "Did you read the newspaper this morning?"

"Yes, why?"

"What did you think of Barnard Scott's story?"

"Not much, as a matter of fact," Jack said, turning to grin at her. "Most of his pieces are fluff."

Fran relaxed. "So, you still want me to hang out with you today?"

"Nothing could stop me."

"Sheesh, I dodged that bullet," Fran said.

They both laughed.

It was about a 20-minute drive up to Gun Smoke Lake where Jack had a cabin. The rolling landscape on the way there offered views of tangled underbrush with leaves bearing hues of russet, gold, and burnt-orange. After years of living near seascapes, scrubby gray-green trees, and ice plant-covered sand dunes, Fran found the mountain scenery refreshing. It never got old.

The higher the truck climbed into the foothills, the wilder and more tangled the foliage became. Green pine and blue-green spruce trees carpeted the slopes. Aspen trees with quivering yellow leaves added visual interest. Sunlight refracted sparkling white diamonds off the rippling surface of Crazy Woman Creek that meandered like a serpent alongside the road.

Nature didn't seem to be affected by the drought one bit. It still offered a typical fall display with all the splendor it could muster.

Fran enjoyed her conversation with Jack, discovering his passion for nature conservation.

"We simply can't keep taking our environment for granted." He waved a hand at the forest outside their windows. "The planet's resources will only go so far."

"I agree," Fran said. "I'm doing my part. Like, when I brush my teeth. I always shut off the water until it's time to rinse. It's not much, but I don't want to be wasteful."

One brow raised, Jack glanced at her to see if she was being serious or being a smart aleck, which of course she was.

Laughing, Jack pulled off onto a bumpy gravel road lined with clumps of dusky green sagebrush and yucca. Wildflowers of blue, yellow, red, white, and purple, intermixed with tall prairie grass, twitched in the breeze. Their names peppered Fran's mind: Indian paintbrush, sunflowers, vervain, coneflowers, and Canadian milk vetch. Even this late in the year, they clung tenaciously to life, unaware that according to the calendar, they should be fading.

Gun Smoke Lake appeared in the distance, glimmering like blue jewel with a background of gold, russet, and green trees. Dry brown peaks of mountains rose in the distance beyond the water, craggy and immense as they brushed against the sky.

A small log cabin, nestled amongst thick trees, came into view. Jack pulled up to it and parked in the gravel drive. "This is it," he announced. "Home away from home."

"It's lovely," Fran told him, glancing around. "If I could paint, I'd spend forever up here doing nothing but that."

"Next time we come bring your canvas and oils," Jack said.

Fran's cheeks tingled with warmth as Jack came around, opened her door and guided her toward the log home.

Once inside, Fran looked around. A kitchen with a willow branch table and chairs took up space on the northeast side of the room, and rustic living room furniture filled the opposite side. Navajo wall hangings brightened the area, and sturdy sisal mat carpets covered the worn wooden floors.

A stone fireplace with iron candleholders on the mantle dominated one corner and wooden blinds covered the windows. A collection of antique oil lamps covered a wood table in another corner. Several stuffed wildlife figures were positioned strategically throughout the room, along with a couple of sets of mounted antlers.

"You're a hunter?" Fran asked.

Jack nodded. "Pheasant, elk, deer—nothing earth shattering."

"But you got these?" Fran pointed at the taxidermy items.

"Yep."

"Wow. This is a great place. So relaxing."

"Especially if you turn off your cell phone," Jack said. "Unfortunately, I don't get here as often as I'd like. And it's lonely up here by myself. But I'm planning on making a better effort of visiting."

Fran cleared her throat. "Like you said, fish are early risers. Guess we'd better go sink a line."

"Right on." Jack removed fishing poles from the wall. Outside, he collected a metal box from the back of his truck. Fran assumed it contained bobbers, hooks, bait, and the like. As they walked toward the lake, she breathed in the fresh pine scent and basked in the warm sun caressing her face.

This is the way to live, she told herself.

At the water's edge, Fran noticed crumbling white rings where the water depth had receded over the dry years. It was a shame to see the lake so low.

Jack handed Fran one of the fishing rods. He pulled out a white carton of night crawlers and baited his hook. Fran squished one on her hook, wiped her slimy fingers on her pants, and sailed the line toward the sparkling depths. There was a responding splash as it landed in the water, which gave Fran a thrill she hadn't felt in a long time.

"It's been forever since I've fished," she admitted to Jack.

"How long?" He smiled over at her as he cast out his line, causing ripples to radiate toward the middle of the lake.

"Years. Mom and Dad used to bring my sister Lucy and I up here when we were kids. I loved it, though my dad always baited the hook and gutted any fish we caught. That was not a fun part for little girls."

"You don't seem to mind it now," Jack commented.

"I used to bring Eva to visit Mom and Dad and we'd go fishing. Since I had to bait her hook, I got over my squeamishness. Being a mom does that to you." Memories flooded her mind and she sighed. "Lucy and Otis brought Carl, too, and the cousins would have a blast trying to see who could catch the biggest fish. I miss that."

"Things change," Jack said. "Not always for the worst. We just learn to make new good times."

Fran felt a tug. Feet planted firmly, she jerked the line and began to reel it in. The fish surfaced and splashed, struggling to free itself. Tongue pressed into her cheek, Fran managed to bring it in. Soon, it dangled at the end of her line.

"Whoo, hoo!" she shouted. "I still have the touch!"

Jack pried the hook from its mouth and held it out by its gills. "Good girl. You've earned your supper."

As the morning wore on, the sun rose higher in the sky. Between the two of them, they had caught several fish that were tethered to a sturdy fishing line Jack had staked in the water. Definitely a feast fit for a king or at least a very hungry cat.

Fran pressed her sleeve to her damp forehead. "Man, it's getting warm."

"Sure is." Jack picked up a forked stick and propped his fishing pole on the shore. "Watch this, will you? I'll gut what we've caught so far and put them in the refrigerator."

Slowly he pulled in the line of fish staked in the cool shallows and moved down the shore a short distance. One by one he slit their bellies and cleaned them, tossing the guts into the water.

Seagulls flew past and swooped, their gazes on the delectable fish entrails gleaming in the sun. Once Jack finished the job and moved out of the way, the birds dove down to gobble up the treats. They took to the wing again, crying out their pleasure.

Jack hefted the string of fish over his shoulder. "I'll be back with some sodas," he called.

Tired of standing, Fran sat on a boulder and watched Jack until he disappeared into the tree line. She glanced at her watch, noting it was almost 10:30. The fish weren't biting anymore, so she decided she and Jack ought to head back to town.

A familiar honking drew Fran's attention to the sky. Shading her eyes from the sun, she watched a flock of geese flying south in a V-formation. Her stomach grumbled and she put a hand to her abdomen. The muffin she'd eaten at breakfast wouldn't last much longer. She was more than ready for a fish fry.

Closing her eyes, she let the warm sun relax her. The smell of fresh pine was intoxicating. It would be wonderful to come here when life got overwhelming. Jack was lucky. There was no better place to worship God than the great outdoors.

Jack's angry shouts broke the silence and Fran's eyes flew open.

She dropped her fishing pole, slid off the boulder, and ran toward his cabin.

"Jack," she called. "Jack!"

No answer.

When Fran arrived, she noted the string of fish splayed in the dirt beside a bush. Her heart froze in her chest and she frantically continued to look for Jack. Then she saw him. He was standing against a pine tree, his shoulder pinned to the trunk with an arrow. Blood covered his shirt, jacket, and jeans with a reddish stain.

"My God, Jack—"

"Fran," he managed. He looked at her, eyes glazed and pain-filled. "What happened?"

"Someone sh-shot me," Jack managed, before he passed out.

Frantic, Fran checked for his pulse and felt a faint one.

"No!" Fran cried. She whipped her cell phone from her pocket, tapped in 911, and told the operator where she was. "A man has been shot with an arrow."

"Help is on the way," the operator said in a calm, reassuring tone. "Stay with your friend and keep talking. Can you feel a pulse?"

"Yes," Fran said. "Just barely."

"Who shot him?" the operator asked "Are they still around?

"I don't see anyone," Fran said, but she did notice a folded card in the dirt at Jack's feet.

Leaning over, she picked it up. When leaves rustled, she shoved it in her pocket and glanced around. She spotted a flash of movement behind some large bushes.

"Run," Jack urged her. "They're b-back."

"No, I won't leave you," she insisted, placing a trembling hand on his cheek.

"Is someone else there?" the operator asked.

"Maybe," Fran whispered. "Ah, I don't know."

Another arrow hit a nearby tree with a loud thwacking sound.

"Hide . . . hide in the cabin," Jack told her.

Fran hesitated, hating to leave him.

"What's going on?" the operator asked.

"Someone just shot another arrow," Fran said.

"Take cover, ma'am," the operator insisted.

"But my friend!"

"Take cover."

"Go," Jack said in a raspy tone.

Stumbling backward, Fran tripped and fell, wincing as a sharp rock sliced her palm. She pushed to her feet and scrambled inside of the cabin, locking the door. Every fiber of her being screamed that she shouldn't have left Jack. She cursed herself for doing it, even though she knew she hadn't had a choice.

"God, please keep him safe," she murmured.

A thump sounded on the outside of the door. She stared in horror at the wood, now pierced by a black arrow tip.

TWENTY-FOUR

THE FRONT DOOR RATTLED LIKE IT HAD BEEN HIT by a freight train.

"Open up," a gruff voice demanded.

Someone was out there. Someone menacing—trying to get inside.

Trying to kill me.

Blood hammered in Fran's temples and shot to her fingertips, making them tingle.

"What's going on?" the operator asked.

"I locked myself in a cabin and there's someone pounding on the door," Fran said.

"Help is on the way," the operator assured her.

Fran slid her cell back into her pocket. She spun around, looking for a weapon. A door on the other side of the cabin beckoned her. Get out, she thought, then hesitated. She could run, but what if the killer chased her? She was far from being the world's fastest runner.

Instead, she locked the deadbolts on the doors, then hustled to close and lock the window shutters. More rattling from the front door erupted, then pounding. Finally, it sounded as though someone was heaving themselves against the frame.

Fran's gaze shot to the closet under the stairs. She raced over and inspected the inside. Coats hung from a rod, boots, and shoes were lined up on the floor. Beneath those, she noticed what looked like a framed opening.

Shoving aside a mop and a broom, she lifted up a door and peered inside the small, cramped space. Fran grasped a utility flashlight sitting on a shelf. Flipping it on, she shed illumination into the musty darkness. A small concrete cellar full of crates appeared, along with a wooden ladder.

And lots of gooey spider webs. Chock full of arachnid vermin.

Fran abhorred spiders. Black, brown, white, green, or whatever color, they were squirmy, icky creatures. Small spaces gave her claustrophobia. A shiver of disgust ran up her spine.

No time to worry about creepy crawlies. Or cramped spaces. Setting the flashlight aside, she yanked a long wool coat from the rod and spread it over the top of the trap door. Then she slipped under it and climbed down the ladder. Part way down, she reached around the edge of the opening to make sure the coat concealed the door. The door didn't close all the way, and she could see a shaft of light beneath it.

The front door splintered, and a loud crash shook the floor. Fran tightened her grip on the heavy flashlight as the cold dampness of the cellar seeped into her bones. The concrete walls seemed to close in on her.

Above her, floorboards squeaked with heavy footsteps. Dust sifted down in puffs, tickling Fran's face. She wrinkled her nose, fighting the urge to sneeze.

The footsteps moved closer to the closet. The door creaked open. Fran held her breath as the sound of ragged breathing filled the space. Through the small slit the wool coat didn't cover, she spied two dusty black boots. Army boots, Fran thought.

Her nose began to twitch. She was going to sneeze. And cough. And get herself killed.

No!

Tears stung Fran's eyes. She thought about Eva, dear precious Eva, who still needed her. She wanted to live to see her grandchildren. Clenching her teeth, she forced herself not to think of any more of her loved ones.

Otherwise, it would be her destruction.

A mouse scurried from its hiding spot and skittered beneath her feet. Fran bit her lip and returned her gaze to the black boots. At last, the individual left the closet, and the door banged shut.

Fran took a shaky breath of relief. Now she really had to sneeze and cough. Instead, she took a big gulp of air, held her breath, and prayed. The intruder stomped around Jack's cabin, then the sounds faded.

Fran wanted to go outside and help Jack, but she wasn't sure if it was safe yet. Before long, a siren blared, becoming louder and louder. She tensed. Hopefully the cavalry would arrive soon. Jack was in bad shape.

Heavy footfalls sounded. "Westonville police," a man called. "Is anyone in here?"

"Me," she said. She pushed open the storage space door, and shoved aside the coat. One of the officers took her hand to steady her, helping her climb out.

Guns drawn, several burly uniforms stood near the cabin's gaping door frame. Outside the front window, Fran noticed the flashing lights of an ambulance and a couple of police cars.

"You have to help Jack, he's in the yard," she said in a rush.

At that moment, Gabe strode inside, the detective's star flashing on his belt. "He's in good hands," he reassured her. "The paramedics have everything under control and they'll get him to the hospital ASAP."

"Thank heavens," Fran said, the blood rushing back into her extremities as the officers continued searching the cabin.

"What about you?" Gabe asked her.

"Me, I'm fine," she said, realizing she wasn't. Adrenaline still pumped through her, and she was having trouble catching her breath.

"No, you're not." He took Fran's hand, pulled a white handkerchief from his pocket and wrapped it around her palm. "You're bleeding."

"It's just a scratch." She insisted. Although she'd had a good scare, she didn't want to show any weakness. It was important that she remain strong so that she would withstand whatever may come her way. She started walking, and managed to trip over her toe.

"Whoa there." Gabe grasped her elbow to steady her, and led her over to the leather sofa. Removing his jacket, he placed it over her shoulders.

"I know this isn't the best time," he said. "But I need to ask some questions."

Fran nodded.

"Explain today's events to me."

Fran told him everything from the time she and Jack left the house until now. She did her best to recount even minor occurrences, in case they were important.

"A simple fishing trip turned into a nightmare," she said with a morose tone in her voice. "Something none of us needed."

"Hmm," Gabe said as he began to pace. "Does Jack have any enemies?"

"I don't know him well at all." Fran drummed her fingers on her knees.

"We know you have enemies," Gabe said with concern edging his voice. "I'll bet ten to one that you two were followed. Probably by the individual who has it in for you."

"I feel awful that I put Jack in danger," Fran said, a sick sensation churning in her stomach.

"You didn't know this was going to happen," Gabe said. "And it sounds like Jack's going to be okay."

"I sure hope so," Fran said.

"Meanwhile, let's get you home." Gabe sent her a reassuring smile. "You drive up here?"

"Jack did. That's his truck parked outside."

"Give me a few minutes to talk with my guys," Gabe said. "Then I'll give you a ride."

Later, as Gabe drove Fran back to town, she closed her eyes and leaned against the head rest. She didn't feel like talking. All she wanted to do was wrap up in a quilt and sleep. Sleep until everything returned to normal.

Who knew how long that would take, though?

When the car slowed, Fran opened her eyes and saw they were at her house. She grabbed her purse.

"Thanks," she told Gabe.

He nodded. "I'm going over to Otis' office to talk to him and Deputy Harris. Otis was out on another call and couldn't respond to your 911, but he wants to know what happened."

"Of course, yes, that makes sense," Fran said.

"You need anything, get a hold of me, okay?" Gabe lifted a brow at her.

"Thanks, Gabe." Fran got out and shut the car door, then walked up the sidewalk, feet dragging like sacks of flour. On the porch, she turned to watch Gabe drive away, then went inside. Her phone rang and she didn't answer it, figuring if it was important, the caller would leave a voice mail.

Café customers glanced up as she entered. Some nodded and smiled, others said hello. Fran greeted them in return. Eva was taking orders at the counter, smiling and joking as she wrote down their choices.

In the kitchen, Fran found Lucy stirring a crock pot brimming with chicken tortilla soup.

"Sorry I'm so late," Fran apologized.

"We were fine," Lucy said. "The question is, did you catch any fish?"

Fran had completely forgotten about she and Jack's haul. "We caught a batch of them, but something came up, so I couldn't bring them home."

"What's with the bloody handkerchief around your hand?" Lucy asked, a look of concern on her face.

Fran sat down at the table, fighting an overwhelming sense of failure. "Jack and I were followed up to the lake. Whoever it was shot him in the shoulder with an arrow, and I was nearly the next victim. I managed to call 911."

"Oh my gosh, is Jack okay?" Lucy asked. "And are you okay?"

"Yes, thank goodness." Fran sighed. "The ambulance took him to the hospital, but I think I'm still in shock about how it all went down."

Lucy sat down by Fran at the table, putting an arm around her. "I'm sorry that happened! Can I do anything for you? Get you something?" She went silent. "Sorry, I'm prattling. But I'm so upset to hear about your ordeal."

"I'll be all right," Fran said, her voice trembling. "I think I'm going to take Gabe's advice though and stick close to home for now."

"Tell me everything," she urged.

Fran explained that after Jack had been shot, he insisted that Fran hide in his cabin in so the shooter wouldn't come after her. She mentioned the individual wearing army boots who had come close to finding her in her cellar hiding spot.

"Jack is a true hero."

"I owe him my life." Fran held up her wounded hand. "And I owe Gabe a new white handkerchief."

That evening after dinner, everyone tucked themselves away in their rooms, and Fran headed to her own. She shut the door and flopped on the bed, kicking off her shoes. The carved ceiling patterns seemed to move in front of her eyes, she still felt so keyed up.

Who in the heck had shot Jack? Given the opportunity, would they have shot Fran too? Probably, she thought with a chill that ran up her spine.

Squeak, squeak, squeak.

Fran pushed up on her elbows, straining to hear.

Someone was in the house. *The shooter?* Had they followed her home? She thought about calling Gabe. Or maybe she should call Otis?

What if she was making a big deal of nothing and summoned them over here for no reason?

Uneasy, Fran slipped into the hallway. Tiptoeing, she followed the strange thumping and squeaking up the staircase to Aunt Gladys' living quarters. She paused at the attic door; ear pressed against the wood. The noises became louder. Fran grasped the doorknob, slowly turned it, and poked her head inside.

The curtains were closed around Aunt Gladys' bedroom alcove and the noises had stopped. However, an unusual odor wafted through the room. Fran wrinkled her nose and sniffed. It smelled like marijuana. Knowing Aunt Gladys' penchant for starting fires, she became concerned.

"Aunt Gladys?" She walked inside and looked for signs of mischief. "Are you up here? What's going on?"

The curtains jerked open and Aunt Gladys popped her head out, her cap of white curly hair in disarray. Frenchie was stretched out beside her in bed and they had the top sheet pulled up and tucked beneath their armpits. Both of them clenched what appeared to be joints between their thumbs and forefingers.

Fran planted her hands on her hips. "Who said the two of you could do that up here?"

Aunt Gladys batted her eyelashes, obviously pretending to be innocent. "What, do you mean, dear? Are you upset that Frenchie and I hooked up after spending the day together?"

Fran's face prickled with warmth. "No, it's not that. That's none of my business. It's the smoking I don't approve of."

Frenchie grinned. "My weed is medicinal."

"It's illegal to have it in Wyoming," Fran pointed out.

In her mind, she saw Otis and Cleve doing a drug raid on the café. Barnard Scott would have a real heyday with this scoop.

"Sorry, my dear," Frenchie said. He took the two joints and smashed their ends into an ashtray on the bedside table.

"Party pooper." Aunt Gladys giggled. "By the way, how was your date with Jack?"

"Not so good," Fran said.

"Really, what happened?" Aunt Gladys asked.

"I'll explain later," Fran said. "Right now, I'll leave you two to your evening."

She left the attic and returned to her room. After throwing her clothes on the floor and putting on a T-shirt and shorts to sleep in, she crawled back into bed. She drew the covers over her head and huddled into a fetal position.

Thank goodness there hadn't been an intruder in the house tonight. Nonetheless, it was obvious that somebody wanted her dead.

But why?

TWENTY-FIVE

ANOTHER DAY, ANOTHER DOLLAR, FRAN THOUGHT as she and Lucy prepared to open the café the next day. They sliced bread, mixed sandwich fillings and warmed soups in crockpots, like always. Since Fran had hurt her hand, Eva insisted on pitching in more, which honestly helped. Having the three of them working in the kitchen, while Aunt Gladys took orders, made for a much easier day.

The only thing that could have made things better was if Fran had known how Jack was doing. There had been a brief news report on the evening news last night, and the TV anchor had mentioned that he was in stable condition. For any further updates, Fran realized she'd have to be patient. Hopefully when Jack felt better, he'd call and talk to her.

About mid-morning, the Carpinelli brothers came to fix the front window. Banging hammers and a few swear words filled the air as they completed the job. Before long, they had new glass panes installed and it looked as good as new.

"We'll send you a bill," Larry called in through the front door.

"Thanks," Fran said. "You guys are the best!"

"I'm going to take a break," Lucy said about mid-afternoon. She sat at the table with a cup of coffee, flipped open the newspaper, and began reading.

Fran prepared another order for one of their customers—grilled cheese sandwich and fire roasted tomato soup. The comfort food of all comfort foods, Fran thought, at least in her opinion. She placed everything on a wooden serving tray and took it out to Aunt Gladys, then returned to the kitchen.

"Fran," Lucy said, tapping a page of the newspaper. "There's an announcement in here about a celebration of life for Henry Whitehead tonight."

Stopping by the table, Fran read the article over her sister's shoulder. "It's from six to eight."

"I can handle the customers while you two go," Eva offered as she sprayed water in the sink, then used a towel to dry off her hands.

"Are you sure?" Fran asked. "I hate leaving you alone."

"It's not a biggie," Eva insisted. "You guys go and pay your respects. Aunt Gladys will want to go, too. She knows everyone in town, and I'm sure she knows the Whitehead family."

Fran walked over and hugged Eva. "What are we going to do next semester when you head over to the university to live in the dorms?"

"You'll never get another helper like me, that's for sure," Eva said, snapping Fran playfully with her towel. "I know you'll figure it out, though."

Fran grabbed another towel. Mother and daughter spent a couple of minutes snapping the material at each other.

About an hour later, Lucy went home to get ready for Henry's celebration of life reception. Fran showered, then retrieved a calf-length black lace dress from her closet and put it on. She added dark hose and heels, then freshened her makeup. In the dresser mirror, she noted her clothes from last night in a pile on the floor.

"Gosh, I'm getting messy," she muttered.

Leaning over, she picked up her jeans and spotted the folded card in her back pocket. She pulled it out, remembering she'd found it on the ground by Jack yesterday. Flattening the advertisement, she noted that it was a flyer from the Ice Queen Resort Off Track Betting Club, reminding their patrons about their monthly birthday promotion.

Had Jack's attacker dropped this? Maybe they frequented the club. It wasn't located very far from Moose Creek. Because of the brief distance, many of the locals took vacations at the resort to hike, camp, ski, snowmobile and participate in numerous other outdoor activities.

She folded the flyer again and dropped it into her purse. Otis would be at the celebration with Lucy, and she could give the evidence to him. Or Gabe. Either way, she knew they'd want to have it for their investigation.

Downstairs, she found Aunt Gladys dressed in a subdued Navy-blue dress, matching heels, a bright orange scarf, and orange button earrings. The only two people in the café, Aunt Gladys and Frenchie, sat at one of the tables, talking and laughing. He wore a dark suit and tie and with his jaunty smile, he looked quite dapper.

When Fran approached them, they stood up holding hands. Fran hadn't noticed it before, but Aunt Gladys was a tad taller than Frenchie. She smiled. They looked so cute together.

"You two ready to go?" she asked.

"Frenchie says he'll drive us," Aunt Gladys said. "Where is this shindig going to take place?"

"At the First Community Church," Fran said. "Thanks for the ride, Frenchie."

"My pleasure," Frenchie said. "Ladies, follow me."

"See you all later," Eva said as she eased up beside the counter wearing a fresh white cafe apron over her jeans and T-shirt.

Of course, it stood to reason that Frenchie drove a shiny silver, two door Cadillac, vintage in style. He helped Aunt Gladys into the front and she scooted across the bench seat, landing next to the steering wheel. Since the vehicle had three seatbelts in the front, Fran scooted in next to her aunt as Frenchie closed the door.

When he got in the driver's side, everyone buckled up, and Frenchie said, "Fran, dear, please give me directions. I'm afraid I'm unfamiliar with the church you mentioned."

"Of course," Fran said. When he began driving, she told him what streets to turn down and before long, they'd arrived.

Lines of people filed up the concrete steps to the front door and entered the foyer. Fran, Aunt Gladys, and Frenchie joined them. At the front of the building, flowers provided splashes of color and Fran could smell their sweet perfume. She also recognized the spray of white roses she and Lucy had ordered for the grieving family. A table bore a silver urn, and Henry's framed photograph rested next to it, along with a guest book and a feather pen.

Nearby, a lady in a black and purple dress played soft music on a piano. A laptop attached to a whiteboard mounted on one wall played a video filled with clips of Henry enjoying his family and friends.

The pews brimmed with those who had come to pay their respects. Some were sobbing and dabbing at their eyes, and others murmured with each other. On the front row, a man with similar facial features as Henry, and a woman with chestnut colored hair, sat engaged in conversation. Two young girls sat next to them, one resting her golden-haired head on the other's shoulder.

Across the aisle in the front row sat an elderly bald man, a woman with gray hair, and two teenage boys and a girl.

Lucy and Otis came up beside Fran. She wore a brown silk dress and matching cowboy boots and Otis wore a dark suit and tie. Fran had become so used to seeing him in his sheriff's uniform that she gave him a second look, deciding he did justice to his clothing.

"Rick Whitehead, Henry's brother, his wife Wanda and their two daughters are seated on the right side of the church," Lucy told her. "Henry's father and mother, Clint and Betty Whitehead, along with Henry's two sons and his daughter are on the left. I think the people sitting beside them are probably Clint and Betty's brothers and sisters, but I can't say for certain."

"It's so nice that so many of Henry's family members could attend," Fran said as her gaze roamed across the room to check if she recognized anyone else.

She wondered if Vivian had come, and caught a glance of her seated toward the back of the church. Wearing all black, she kept her head down, probably still upset that she'd no longer receive child support from Henry. At least she'd allowed she and Henry's children to sit with their grandparents at the front of the church.

The Parnells, Fran, Aunt Gladys, and Frenchie walked up and signed the guest book, then turned to offer their condolences to the family members. Walking down the aisle, they found spots to sit in a pew at the back of the church. The air stirred as Gabe walked up to Fran, who was seated at the end.

"Can I squeeze in?" he asked, looking very nice in dark slacks, a leather jacket and a bolo tie with a silver and turquoise clasp.

Pleased to see he had come to sit by her, Fran smiled. She started scooting over, which created a chain reaction, and everyone followed suit.

"Hi Gabe," Otis said.

Everyone else muttered "hello" as he sat down.

"How's it going?" he asked Fran.

"Good enough," Fran said. "It was a quieter day at the café, I'm grateful to report, no more items flying through the front window." She chuckled, then sobered, remembering they were at a funeral. "Oh, by the way, I found something you and Otis would probably like to have."

"Is that so?" Gabe raised his brows.

Fran reached into her purse and fished out the birthday flyer from the Ice Queen Resort Off Track Betting Club. "I found this on the ground beside Jack up at the lake. Maybe the attacker dropped it."

"It's a possibility," Gabe said. "I appreciate you grabbing it."

"Of course. I meant to get it to you or Otis sooner, but in all the confusion I forgot."

Gabe held Fran's chin in his hand and tilted her head in order to study the bruise on her forehead. "It's looking better."

"Well, I cheated some," Fran admitted. "I covered it with foundation."

"Hmm," he said. "By the way, Otis and I have narrowed down our search in the database."

"Really?"

He nodded. "We're down to 10 possibilities of who might own the black Buick Regal we're looking for."

"More good news."

Fran and Gabe exchanged a smile, which lingered as their eyes met. Then Fran returned her gaze to the front of the room. She enjoyed the sensation of Gabe's warmth next to her. Again, she realized how comfortable she felt around him, which made her wonder why.

When Reverend Lincolnway stood at the lectern to speak, everyone fell silent and turned their gazes toward the front of the chapel.

"Friends, we gather here today to celebrate Henry Whitehead's life, and how he made the world a better place by his presence in it . . ." the reverend began.

When he'd finished his eulogy, Reverend Lincolnway handed a microphone to Rick Whitehead, who spoke about his brother and shared stories of their time growing up in Moose Creek and attending local schools. Henry's father and mother accepted the microphone and spoke about their son, along with several other people who explained how they knew Henry and talked about their memories.

Sobs issued from several individuals in the audience, and Fran's eyes grew warm. She hadn't known Henry well, but he deserved better than being stabbed to death. He wouldn't even be able to see his children reach adulthood or hold a grandchild. It wasn't right, and it wasn't fair.

Justice needed to be served, and the guilty party needed to be locked behind bars.

Sniffing as well, Lucy kept her arm around Fran. Even Aunt Gladys had tears in her eyes as Frenchie patted the back of her hand. After the ceremony, Reverend Lincolnway invited everyone in the audience to assemble in the recreation hall for a meal prepared by the ladies of church's aid society.

Fran, Lucy, Aunt Gladys, and the men rose and walked into the hall where round tables covered in white cloths were set with floral centerpieces, napkins and silverware. A large rectangle table in one corner held casseroles, salads, and desserts where people lined up with plates.

"There's Dr. Ferguson standing by the stage in the pink jacket," Lucy said excitedly. "We should go talk to her."

Fran looked over at her, noting she was probably in her early forties, and very beautiful with her long brunette bob, trendy business suit, and matching heels. She recalled Shane MacGreggor mentioning at the pub the other night how upset Raina had been after she dated Henry, and he'd broken up with her. If she was so upset, and had actually killed him, why would she show face at his celebration of life?

Aunt Gladys suggested the men to go get something to eat while the women talked, then stopped to listen to her nieces' conversation.

"What would we say to her?" Fran asked, then mimicked, "By the way, Raina, did you kill Henry Whitehead? And why did you do it?"

"No, we couldn't be that blatant," Lucy said.

"I know Raina and her mother, Arlene, and in fact, I went to school with her," Aunt Gladys said, motioning to them. "Walk over there with me and we can make some small talk."

Holding her head high, Aunt Gladys sashayed toward Raina, with Lucy and Fran trailing alongside of her.

Raina was talking with Reverend Lincolnway, and when the two parted, Aunt Gladys walked up to her.

"Raina Ferguson, as I live and breathe, I haven't seen you in ages," Aunt Gladys said.

Raina turned toward Aunt Gladys and smiled. "Gladys Maplethorpe! It has been quite a while since we've seen each other."

"Indeed," Aunt Gladys said, then introduced Fran and Lucy, who both shook Raina's hand. "How is your lovely mother doing? It's been a month of Sundays since I've seen or talked with her."

"She's doing great. In fact, we're both doing great." Raina pointed toward a table where a woman wearing a burgundy pantsuit, her hair twisted into a silver bun, sat with a small child in her lap. She fed the toddler bits of food, and the little one clapped her chubby hands. "There she is, holding my daughter, Olivia."

Aunt Gladys took one of Raina's hands between her palms. "My dear, your mother told me that you weren't planning to marry or have children. She said you were dedicated to your medical career."

"I don't have a husband," Raina said. "As a matter of fact, I didn't believe I could have children."

"What changed?" Fran said, "That is, if you don't mind my asking."

"Of course not." Raina looked around, as if not wanting anyone else to hear her comments, then lowered her voice. "You might have heard the nasty gossip about me being upset with Henry Whitehead after we broke up. And I was—at first. Then I found out that, at age 42, I was pregnant. I squashed my anger at him because I was so thrilled! I didn't think I wanted children, but I changed my mind knowing I was about to bring life into the world. It truly is a miracle, as they say."

"What did Henry think?" Lucy asked. "I assume you told him about the baby?"

"Of course, but he wanted nothing to do with her, which was fine with me because my mother and I had her all to ourselves. She brings such joy to our lives, and Mom watches her while I'm on shift at the hospital."

"So, it's all worked out for you," Fran said.

"Definitely," Raina said. "I wanted to pay my respects to the family by coming today. I'm not certain I'll ever tell Henry's parents that Olivia is their granddaughter. For right now, she's my little secret. Even though Henry and I ended our relationship on bad terms, he gave me a precious gift."

Fran and Lucy looked at each other, and Fran believed Lucy was thinking the same thing. So much for the theory that Raina Ferguson had killed Henry Whitehead.

TWENTY-SIX

"**D**ID I DO GOOD?" Aunt Gladys asked as the three women walked toward the food table. "Did I help you girls figure out another clue in your murder investigation?"

"How did you know we were conducting one?" Fran asked.

"You two don't give me enough credit," Aunt Gladys said with a chuckle as she picked up two plates, handed them to her nieces, then took one for herself. "I hear things. I see things. And I know things."

"I'm sorry if you feel like we're brushing you off," Fran said, although she sensed deep inside that sometimes she did dismiss Aunt Gladys. She decided she'd better quit taking her for granted.

"Exactly," Lucy said. "We didn't mean to make you feel that way, did we Fran?"

"No, we didn't," Fran seconded. "And yes, you helped us with one of our clues."

"Yipee," Aunt Gladys cheered. "I am definitely not ready for the rocking chair. So don't write me off yet."

"Never," Fran said with a chuckle.

"And you've been a huge help in the café," Lucy added.

The ladies filled their plates, then walked over to the table the men had chosen. Lucy sat by Otis, Aunt Gladys sat by Frenchie, and when Gabe patted the seat beside him, Fran took it without hesitation.

After they'd eaten, everyone walked out to the parking lot toward their cars. Lucy left with Otis, and Fran was ready to climb into Frenchie's Cadillac, when Gabe sauntered up and placed a hand at the small of her back.

"I'd like to take you home, if that's okay," he offered.

"Oh, sure," she said, as a tingle ran up her spine. Leaning into the car, she asked Aunt Gladys, "Do you mind?"

"Heaven's no," she said. "I'll see you in a bit, ah, no later than 10 p.m."

Fran lifted a brow. "A curfew?"

"Of course," Aunt Gladys said, smiling.

Frenchie closed the car door and waved at Fran. "I'll get your aunt home safe and sound."

"Thanks," Fran called, then walked with Gabe over to his SUV. He helped her into the passenger side, then came around to the driver's side, climbed in and drove toward Fran's house. He didn't seem to be in a hurry, although Fran supposed that as a member of a law enforcement agency, he would not speed.

"How are you doing today?" he asked, briefly checking his rear-view mirror.

"Good," Fran said.

"I wanted to let you know that the Briarhursts came talked to Otis the other day, then they came to see me."

"Uh, oh." Fran tensed. "Was it about Elton's accident?"

"Bingo," he said. "Both Otis and I told them evidence proved it was a hit-and-run, and that you were in no way guilty of running him over. I also stressed that we are doing our best to locate the driver."

"I'm relieved, to say the least, that they sought the truth instead of continuing to blame me," Fran said.

"Just doing my job," Gabe said. "They admitted they came to your place and gave you a hard time."

"Yeah, they threatened to sue me. I'm glad that's not going to happen now."

"For what it's worth, they apologized, and asked me to pass it on to you," Gabe said. "And I admit, I'm glad I could help make life a bit easier for you."

Warmth rose in Fran's cheeks. "Well, I sure appreciate it."

"Another thing I wanted to let you know is that based on the evidence we've uncovered during our investigations, Otis and I believe that Henry Whitehead's murder, you getting rear-ended, Elton's hit-and-run accident, and the attack on Jack Sturgeon are all related."

"Oh my gosh," Fran said, gripping the edge of the car seat. She inhaled sharply, her mind swirling with questions.

"And we believe," Gabe continued, "that someone's ultimate goal is to try and murder you."

"Charming," Fran said facetiously, "even though I'm not surprised. Still, what am I supposed to do?"

"Be careful, as I've said before, and be aware at all times of who is around you. Make sure those locks on your doors and windows are secure." He reached into his pocket and removed a small, hot pink cannister on a key chain and handed it to her. "Keep this nearby."

Trying hard not to let her hand tremble, Fran took it and dropped it in her purse. "Just what I always wanted," she said. "Pepper spray. Am I right?"

"Yes, it is pepper spray. Don't hesitate to use it."

"I won't," Fran promised.

"Things are going all right at the café, you said?"

"Right, right," Fran told him. "One day it was pretty quiet, and I worried about people not wanting to come around because of all the trouble. But that didn't last."

Gabe glanced at her briefly, then gazed back at the road. "The Briarhursts said that Elton has left the hospital and is now at home recuperating. He'll make a full recovery, as will Jack Sturgeon, who I heard through the police grapevine is in stable condition."

"That puts things on a more positive note," Fran said. "You just made my day."

"I hoped I would," Gabe said as he pulled into her driveway.

They got out of the SUV and walked together up onto the front porch. After strolling beneath the hanging wooden sign that said, The Saucy Lucy Café, they stopped in front of the door.

"You know, when life settles down some, I'd like to get to know you better," Gabe said slowly.

"Same here," Fran said, her heart pinging with delight.

He leaned forward and placed his lips on hers.

Surprised as heck, Fran wrapped her arms around Gabe's neck and pressed against his muscular body. Her physical response came naturally, and she didn't mind her reaction one bit. Gabe smelled good, he tasted good, and he made her insides simmer with excitement. In fact, she felt like warm, gooey butter right now.

When he stepped back, he said, "Have a good night."

"You, too," she said.

After winking at her, Gabe headed back to his vehicle, got in, and drove away.

Feeling as light as air, Fran walked inside the house.

THE NEXT DAY, BEFORE THE CAFÉ OPENED, the sisters and Aunt Gladys made caramel apples for the Halloween Festival that would be held at the Moose Creek Community House later that afternoon.

Fran and Lucy liked attending the annual affair because they got out to mingle with the public, many of whom were current or potential customers. Also, they labeled their treats with Saucy Lucy Café tags, offering them another subtle form of advertising.

The festival had become the community's unofficial Halloween kickoff event. Along with goodies, organizations handed out free reflective strips and flashlights, reminding little ghosts, goblins, and their parents, to stay safe on the 31st when they went out to trick-or-treat.

When it was time to get ready for the costumed affair, Fran, Lucy, and Aunt Gladys dressed in gauzy yellow, purple, and orange satin tutus complete with matching tights, spotted butterfly wings, and curly black antennae. Once again, they left the café in Eva's capable hands. Fran was relieved that her daughter would only have to handle customers for a couple of hours till the café closed.

The three women loaded the cellophane wrapped sweets into large plastic containers and placed them in the back Fran's truck. Fran also threw in the Halloween decoration box from the garage, a roll of masking tape, and the two pumpkins she and Aunt Gladys had carved earlier.

"Honestly, Fran," Lucy said as they drove to the community house in the bumping and grinding truck, "can't you afford a new vehicle?" She gripped the seat with white knuckles and her antennae slipped askew on her head when the vehicle lurched and backfired.

"Not unless you've won the lottery and want to share," Fran said.

"Ha, ha," Lucy said. "Figure those odds."

"I've kind of gotten used to it." Aunt Gladys adjusted a gossamer wing on her back.

"Aunt Gladys, would you mind if Lucy and I do a little sleuthing while we're at the festival?" Fran asked.

"Fine by me," Aunt Gladys said.

"What are we doing this time?" Lucy asked.

"I thought this would be a good opportunity to talk to folks about Henry's murder," Fran said. "Maybe come up with more leads."

"I suppose it wouldn't hurt," Lucy said. "I wish we really could solve his murder."

"That would be dandy," Aunt Gladys said.

"We'll have to slide our questions into casual conversation," Fran said.

"Yeah, no problem," Lucy said. "Don't want people to think we consider them suspects."

"Nope," Fran said. "But I sure hope they help us come up with one."

It wasn't long before the Community House, a large white clapboard building near the city's small recreational reservoir, Buffalo Lake, came into view. In the parking lot, people walked their excited children to the entrance, guiding them inside.

When Aunt Gladys, Lucy, and Fran arrived, business people were festooning their booths with spooky Halloween paraphernalia. Fran went over to the Chamber of Commerce's check-in desk.

With Aunt Gladys and Lucy right behind her, she approached the president, Morton Frost, a tall man with old-fashioned brown and gray mutton chop whiskers. Standing there in his pin-striped three-piece suit, he reminded Fran of the Wizard of Oz, working his magic behind closed doors and curtains.

"I reserved a booth for the Saucy Lucy Café," she told him.

He nonchalantly flicked lint from his suit and perused a piece of paper on the table. "Hmm, I'm afraid I don't see you here."

"There's got to be some mistake," Fran said. "I made the reservation months ago."

"I'm sure we're on the list." Lucy picked it up. "Ah, there's the Saucy Lucy Cafe. We're assigned to booth G." She tapped a line on the paper with a fingertip.

"Sorry for the confusion, ladies," Mort said with an apologetic smile. "Guess it's about time I order some glasses."

The sisters and Aunt Gladys toted their boxes to the designated booth and set everything down. Fran busied herself hanging up orange and purple crepe paper along with cardboard black cats, spiders, and witches. She displayed the jack-o-lanterns at each end of the table, then placed flickering, battery-operated tealights in them.

In one corner of the room, event organizers had arranged a spook alley, complete with creepy graveyard headstones, cobwebs, and scary creatures of the night. An array of plastic jack-o-lanterns sat on a crooked faux stone fence, their faces flickering.

Finally, it was time. Someone opened the double doors, allowing ghosts, witches, and other characters to enter the main hall, their goody bags at the ready. Squealing with delight, they skipped from booth to booth, chanting trick-or-treat in exchange for sweet or salty snacks. Parents watched from the back of the room, talking amongst themselves and keeping a watchful eye on their little ones.

Aunt Gladys, Lucy, and Fran each had a bowl of caramel apples. As the kiddos stopped by, they handed them out, complimenting them on their costumes. At different times, Fran and Lucy mingled with members of the crowd, talking to them about Henry.

After Fran talked to the mayor, who hadn't known Henry at all, she returned to the Saucy Lucy Café booth.

"I'm ready to throw in the towel," she said to Lucy. "I've talked to so many people my mouth is numb."

"Same here," Lucy said. "Methinks our efforts are for naught."

"I'll give you girls an A for effort," Aunt Gladys said.

Lucy frowned at the pile of caramel apples still filling her bowl. "We don't seem to be as busy as the other booths."

"Probably because the little ones might be missing teeth, which would make it difficult to chomp," Aunt Gladys suggested as she held up her bowl, still mounded with the fruit.

"Oh, boy, I didn't think of that when I suggested we hand out caramel apples," Fran said. "Next year, I'll keep that in mind."

One little boy of about 10, dressed like a vampire, approached their booth. "Tre-e-ek-or-tre-e-e-eat," he muttered through white plastic fangs, his eyes sparkling with mischief.

Fran plopped a caramel apple into his outstretched bag. "Are you Count Dracula?"

"Uh, huh," he murmured.

Fran remembered Eva's comment from the other day. "Your costume is really . . . fire."

"Thanks," he said. "I love caramel apples, too."

"And you've got both of your front teeth to boot." Aunt Gladys settled one hand on her orange, silken hip. "I'd say it's a win-win situation."

"Yep," he said, grinning even wider. "I lost those a long time ago."

Aunt Gladys plopped another caramel apple in his bag. "One for the road."

"Some of the kids don't want to stop by here because of the Castleton curse," Count Dracula added. "Bad things happen around you guys, like when someone threw a bomb through your café window."

Aunt Gladys snorted with laughter, while Fran and Lucy exchanged concerned glances.

"It wasn't a bomb," Fran said.

He pointed at Fran with one of his black-clawed fingers and said, "Us kids are daring each other to come and get your treats."

"That's silly," Fran said. "Don't you think?"

"They're all goofy." He shrugged. "I heard you guys asking people around here about Henry Whitehead."

Fran frowned, hoping she hadn't upset any of the children by reminding them about his murder. She hadn't figured they would pay attention to her and Lucy asking questions.

"Did you know him?" Aunt Gladys asked.

"He's my neighbor, er, was my neighbor," the count said. "Sometimes I'd let his dog Tiny off his chain and take him into my backyard. We'd play ball for a long time."

"How sweet," Fran said, glad to know the pooch had experienced spurts of freedom here and there while he'd lived at Henry's place.

"Sometimes I'd take Tiny up to my bedroom and we'd crawl out of my window to sit on the roof. Once, I saw this dark-haired lady stop by Mr. Whitehead's house. He took her out back to sit on his patio. They talked about their gambling trips to the Ice Queen Resort. I remember she had an animal print purse. Leopard, I think. We studied leopards in school once."

"I found one of the resort's off-track betting club flyers on the ground by Jack the other day when he got hurt," Fran whispered to Lucy behind her hand.

"What did you do with it?" she asked.

"Gave it to Gabe," Fran said.

"The lady told Mr. Whitehead he was supposed to get a date with someone named Fran Lightfoot," little Dracula added. "She told him that once he had Fran reeled in, he needed to kill her, and then she'd pay him. I don't know what reeled in means, but the kill part sounded real bad."

Fran's jaw dropped, and she exchanged a stunned glance with Lucy. She recalled her sister mentioning Henry had been a pest about wanting to meet her. If what the boy had said was true, would Henry have eventually found a way to take her life?

Who wants me dead and why?

"Do you remember what kind of car the lady drove?" Fran asked.

"Hmm, ah, it was black and shiny and big," he said.

"Dang, boy, you've got good hearing," Aunt Gladys commented.

"That's what my mom tells me all the time," he said. "Except she says I have good hearing until she asks me to clean my room."

Laughing, Dracula ran off, cape flapping, and joined the rest of the costumed children in the surging crowd.

Aunt Gladys looked back and forth between Fran and Lucy. "What in the heck was that kid talking about? Do you think he really heard that story he told us, or do you think he was making it up?"

Lucy put down her bowl. "I don't know, but I want to go home. I don't feel so good. Fran, what if, what if . . ."

"Don't say it," Fran suggested. "Nothing happened to me. Who knows if the kid really heard what he did. He was eavesdropping from a long distance."

"That's true," Aunt Gladys said. "But I'm with you guys, let's blow this Popsicle stand."

Fran, along with Lucy and Aunt Gladys, began packing up their things and removing the decorations. It didn't take long, because none of them were in a mood to dawdle.

From across the room, a tall woman in a red and white polka dot clown costume shouted at Aunt Gladys, "Hey lady in the orange butterfly costume, wasn't it you who caused all the trouble at the Sunrise Center the other day?"

"No," Aunt Gladys said. "You're mistaken."

The clown's bulbous red nose twitched. "We don't need you here."

"Stuff it, Bozo," Aunt Gladys snapped back. "Unless you want Elvis to knock your block off."

"Shh, Aunt Gladys," Fran said. "Let's just leave."

The clown's eyes opened wider. "Back off, Gladys whatever-your-last-name-is-this-week."

"I'll get to the bottom of this right now." Aunt Gladys stormed toward the clown and yanked off her orange wig. She glared at the dumbfounded woman, her butterfly wings fluttering. "Why, Mazie Bannister, as I live and breathe. You're the one causing trouble now."

"How dare you speak to me like that?" Mazie sputtered.

Growling, Mazie leapt from her booth onto Aunt Gladys. Aunt Gladys crashed on the floor. Arms and legs tangled as the two women mixed it up, scratching, kicking, and biting.

"Both of you, stop!" Fran shouted. She might as well have been yelling at the wind because they didn't pay one bit of attention.

People stared open mouthed at the brawl. Children jumped up and down, probably thinking it great fun to see two elderly ladies go at it.

"Fight, fight, fight!" they chanted.

Mazie landed on top, her clown's face smeared with red and white paint as she tore at Aunt Gladys' butterfly tutu. As for Aunt Gladys, her wings were already in shreds, her antenna bent beyond repair, and skewed atop her white pixie-style hair. The women's grunts and shrieks filled the air as they knocked over chairs and smashed into tables, spilling candy everywhere.

Fran gripped Mazie's shoulders, trying to yank her off Aunt Gladys. But Mazie swung around and ripped the sleeve on Fran's tutu, then smacked her hard in the face.

She staggered backward, unable to gain her balance, then smashed against a table. It fell over, and a basket of potato chips poured over her.

Stunned, she sat there for a moment, catching her breath. Amazed Mazie could hit that hard, she shook the chips out of her hair and threw them onto the floor, then rubbed her aching cheek.

Lucy grabbed a pitcher of lemonade. Taking careful aim, she sloshed the ladies with the pale-yellow refreshment.

Mazie squealed, jumped off Aunt Gladys and stood, spitting and sputtering. Lemonade dripped down her painted nose and face, leaving behind a flesh-colored trail. She shook loose the silvery ice cubes nestled in her costume.

Aunt Gladys rose up and smoothed her rumpled butterfly costume which was covered in wet spots, bits of hay, and whatever else she'd rolled in. With one wiry black antenna hanging in front of her eye, she took a deep breath.

"Come on Aunt Gladys." Fran took her aunt's arm. "Let's go."

As Fran, Aunt Gladys, and Lucy started to leave, Mazie made another run for Aunt Gladys. Just then, Gabe appeared, catching Mazie by the arm.

"Whoa there," he said as she came to a halt.

Otis and Cleve eased up beside Gabe.

When Mazie looked at the badge on Gabe's belt, she stopped squirming.

"Gabe, what are you doing here?" Fran asked, glancing down at her ripped yellow tutu, which looked stained beyond repair.

Gabe frowned. "Otis, Cleve and I were talking about the upsurge of crime in Moose Creek, when someone called the office to report a brawl over here."

Mazie thrust a wobbling finger at Lucy, Fran, and Aunt Gladys. "They started it. They have disrupted the entire festival."

"Don't care who started it," Otis said as he produced a ring of keys from his belt and rattled it. "I'm ending it, and you're all going to jail."

Aunt Gladys, still sputtering and dripping, asked the burning question for the rest of them. "For what?"

"Disturbing the peace," Gabe said.

Fran closed her eyes and groaned.

TWENTY-SEVEN

"CHIPPIE."

"Hussie."

"Jez-e-beeeel—"

"Stop arguing, you two," Fran said to Aunt Gladys and Mazie.

Tired and sweaty, and smelling of stale caramel, she glared over at them. Seated on metal chairs facing each other, they'd been complaining about the prison breakfast that consisted of scrambled eggs and toast. Now they were back to complaining about each other.

Mazie's clown costume was wrinkled, torn, and covered with blotches of food. Her makeup was completely destroyed and consisted of only of red and white streaks. She kept sniffing and wiping her nose on her droopy sleeve. The more she wiped, the more she streaked.

Aunt Gladys' orange butterfly costume, which had once upon a time graced Las Vegas floor shows in hotels such as the MGM Grand and The Flamingo, looked like Jack the Ripper had shredded it. She'd removed her smashed and tangled antennae headpiece long ago and discarded it in a corner where it lay like a mangled bug.

"Fran's right, stop your fussing," Lucy told the elderly ladies from her seated position on the bunk where she'd slept last night.

She had also removed her antenna, and her outfit was spattered with food stains.

For some reason, Lucy seemed to be taking the incarceration calmly and had barely spoken since they arrived the previous evening. She appeared to be patiently waiting for the moment when they would be released.

Fran wanted this whole episode to end. This place sucked. The whole reason they'd wound up here sucked.

Fran watched closely as Mazie and Aunt Gladys resumed eating, staring daggers at each other over the trays clutched in their fingers. She scratched her head and looked around. Practically everything in the Moose Creek Junction jail, or the "pokey" as Aunt Gladys called it, was the same bland color.

Gray food, gray cups, gray sink and toilet, gray blankets on the gray bunks, and gray walls. Even Otis and Cleve and Gabe seemed to have a creeping gray tinge spreading across their flesh whenever they brought in meals or checked on their "prisoners."

Fran resumed pacing the cell, her crumpled butterfly wings flopping. She refused to eat or sleep, so trays of her food remained untouched and her bunk was barely rumpled. She felt demoralized.

None of them deserved to be in jail.

"Psst, hey you," one of the women from the cell across the way called. Fran looked over at her. Last night she hadn't paid much attention to their neighbors. She'd been too outraged.

"That's right, sister," she said with a toss of her head. "I'm talkin' to you."

Fran walked over to the bars and studied the woman and her *compadre* closer.

The woman who had spoken was dressed in a tight, short, black leather skirt, a tight green blouse, boots, and a fur coat. She had poofy, long blond hair that had been teased into proper submission, but probably housed tons of illicit secrets.

The other woman, who was passed out on one of the bunks with her voluptuous rump covered in tight purple satin Capri slacks, was snoring like a buzz saw. She wore her purple-red hair in a punk rocker style and a tight purple crop top, a feather boa, and a fringed, black suede vest.

The blond placed one hand on her hip. "What are you staring at, girlfriend? These?" She squeezed the ample breasts that were about to bust loose from her top. "I paid an arm and a leg to a doctor in Denver for these."

"I'm not staring at anything," Fran said, her cheeks burning.

"Never mind," the blond continued. "I just wanted to tell you and your girlfriends you'd better not plan on moving in on our territory."

"Territory?" Thanks to Mazie's amazing right hook, Fran's face exploded in pain and she placed a palm gingerly on her swollen cheek.

"Is there an echo in here or are you just deaf?" The blond shook her head. "Bambi and I have been working this town for the last six months. And there's no room for anyone else. Got it?"

"We have no intention of moving in on anybody's territory," Fran assured her.

The blond sat on the edge of the bottom bunk and crossed her long, shapely legs. "That's what they all say, honey." She pointed at herself with a long red nail. "Believe me, Trixie's heard it all."

This was the last straw. Now Fran really wanted out of here. Fran walked over to her tray, grabbed the plate and dumped her food into a trash can. Then she approached the cell's metal bars and scraped the plate across them.

"Fran, what are you doing?" Lucy asked, her expression horrified. "You're going to get us in more trouble."

"No, I'm going to get us out of here," Fran returned. "I'm tired of being a jailbird."

Trixie covered her ears and complained. Aunt Gladys and Mazie did the same. Amazingly, Bambi on the bunk continued to snore.

Gabe sauntered from the sheriff's office into the detainment area. "Hey," he said to Fran, irritation chiseled on his face. "What's the problem?"

"This place." Fran quit scraping the plate across the bars. "We want out. Now."

"You're under a 24-hour lockup."

Fran seriously missed her early morning caffeine fix. She had a headache; her mouth tasted like metal. "Isn't there a fine we can pay to be released?"

"Your daughter already paid it," Gabe told her, folding his arms across his chest.

She gripped the tray harder. "Then why are we still here?"

He shrugged. "It was late last night by the time she got here, and you were all asleep. We didn't want to wake you."

Fran clenched her jaw. "Let us take Aunt Gladys home. She needs her medications."

"I suppose you ladies have learned your lesson," he said with a chuckle. "I'll go talk to Otis."

"This is absolutely not funny," Fran said.

He raised a brow. "Maybe not to you."

"You know, you ought to be out looking for the real criminals terrorizing this town."

"What makes you think I'm not?"

"You're taking your sweet time about it," she said.

"Solving a murder is no piece of cake."

"I imagine it isn't," Fran admitted. "But still . . ."

Gabe eased toward the bars and told her, "We are close to breaking this case, Fran. Hold on a bit longer, okay?"

"I'll try, but it isn't easy," Fran said, then instantly regretted her disrespectful tone. "I'm sorry, Gabe. I'm worried, is all. What do you suggest I do? Hire a bodyguard?"

"I don't blame you for being concerned," Gabe said. "I'm concerned, too. In the meantime, lay low and be careful."

Soul weary, Fran rested her head against the bars. This was terrible. Like a nightmare. It wasn't only being stuck in jail. It was all of the misfortune that had been plaguing her ever since Henry Whitehead had been murdered. Deep down, she feared it may never end.

"Hey."

Miserable, she glanced up at Gabe.

"Remember, I'm your friend. Not the enemy."

Despite her irritation, Fran relaxed at the sound of his smooth, reassuring voice. With her index finger, she rubbed the ache between her brows.

"I'm tired," Fran admitted. "I want to go home."

"I'm sure you do." He smiled. "We'll finish the paperwork and let you go."

"Thanks," Fran said.

"By the way." Gabe's eyes twinkled mischievously as he studied her outfit. "Nice tutu."

EVERYTHING WAS QUIET.

It was nearly midnight and black as ink outside in the crisp October air, except for the bright stars and luminous moon that covered the sleeping neighborhood with a silvery cloak. Dark branches on the old elm tree outside Fran's bedroom window scratched the glass, like the fingernails of a night creature tapping to gain entrance.

Dressed in her comfy flannel pajamas and slippers, sipping chamomile tea, she sat at the desk in her bedroom, contemplating recent events. Namely, the Halloween Festival and subsequent jail fiasco.

She, Lucy, and Aunt Gladys had been released early this morning about three hours before it was time to open the cafe. Lucy had gone home, but Fran and Aunt Gladys showered and dressed, and along with Eva's help, they'd re-heated soups and stews, sliced bread for sandwiches, and were ready by noon. Lucy even showed in time to start the ball rolling. The rest of the day, things had gone smoothly.

Fran leaned back, and let her mind wander. The only light was the small lamp on her desk, an amber glass antique that had been in the family for years. Originally kerosene, someone along the way had wired it so it now burned with electricity. Shadows from furniture danced around the room, creating an eerie atmosphere.

Currently everyone in the house was asleep, except for her. It was good they could rest peacefully, but Fran found it difficult tonight. Someone wanted her dead, which accounted for her inability to catch any Z's.

Fran's nostrils twitched when she smelled something, and she wrinkled her nose.

Smoke?

A smoke alarm's loud, piercing shriek pierced the stillness. It sounded like it was coming from downstairs.

She stood and spotted a curl of gray mist coming in under her door.

Aunt Gladys.

Random thoughts flashed through her mind. Either her aunt had lit candles for another Ouija board ceremony and she'd set something on fire, or Frenchie had snuck upstairs and they were having another medicinal smoke.

She threw on her robe and dropped her cell phone in a pocket, then stepped into a pair of slippers. Grabbing her purse, she hustled to the door, checking to make sure it wasn't hot. Judging it to be okay, she slipped out into the hallway.

Curls of smoke drifted through the air. Holding an arm in front of her mouth and nose, she made it up the night-lit stairs to the attic. Coughing, she flung open Aunt Gladys' door, hurried to the bed, and shook her shoulder.

"Wake up, Aunt Gladys! Fire!"

Aunt Gladys moaned and rolled over to stare at Fran with bleary eyes. "Tired? Yes, of course I'm tired."

"We've got to get out of here," Fran urged. "The house is on fire."

Aunt Gladys sniffed and coughed. She sat up, reached for her robe, and slid on her slippers. She also managed to grab her glasses before Fran threw a protective arm around her shoulders and dragged her down to Eva's room.

Eva was already up and wearing her bathrobe and slippers.

"Is there a fire in the house?" Eva asked.

"There must be," Fran said. "Let's get out ASAP."

They all hustled down the smoky stairs and into the frosty night air. Standing on the sidewalk, Fran shivered as the smoke alarm pierced the chill night like a finely sharpened sword.

Shaken but not so badly that she couldn't take the time to observe what was going on, she noted most of the smoke was billowing from her kitchen, located on the west side of the house. For some insane reason, she thought about her homeowner's insurance, and struggled to recall whether she was paid up.

Shock had taken hold of her, she figured. The smoldering house in front of her wasn't just any house. Generations of Castleton's had lived here. No amount of insurance could replace its sentimental value.

"Mom, this is terrible," Eva said as she shivered in the chilly air.

Another loud shrill pierced the night air—a fire engine. One of the neighbors must have called 911 already.

"Hell's bells. This is all my fault," Aunt Gladys sobbed as she slipped on her robe. "I left a candle burning in my room."

A fit of coughing overtook her and she bent over to wheeze.

"It looks like it started in the kitchen, Aunt Gladys." Fran patted her aunt's shoulder reassuringly. "The important thing is we weren't hurt."

"You mean you two aren't upset at me?"

"It's not your fault, Aunt G," Eva said, squeezing her great aunt's hand.

"Heaven's no," Fran said.

"Good to hear—" Aunt Gladys began to cough again, her shoulders trembling.

Worried, Fran held onto Aunt Gladys until the fit passed. The fire could have been caused by an electrical problem, she thought to herself. Or someone could have started it.

The question was, *who*?

Their neighbor from next door, Al Whitcomb, a tall, elderly, barrel-chested man with a thick black beard hustled out of his house wearing his sweats and a heavy jacket. Fran thought he probably resembled Blackbeard the pirate, and that's who she thought of every time she saw him.

"Are you ladies all right? I saw the smoke when I took out my trash and called the fire department."

"Thanks, Al, we're fine," Fran said. "Good thing you're so quick on your feet."

Fran wondered why Al was taking out the trash at such an ungodly hour of the night. It's good he had been prowling, however, so he could help. When an icy breeze sliced into her, she shivered and curled her cold toes in an attempt to keep them warm. It didn't work. They were beginning to feel like ice cubes.

Fran noticed several people stood on their porch steps talking excitedly. Did one of them set the fire? Was it one of her neighbors who had been plotting against her? Which got her to thinking about the dark-haired woman who told Henry he needed to murder Fran. If the kid in the Count Dracula costume had heard correctly, that is.

Despite her concerns, all Fran could process was that she and Aunt Gladys were safe. Eva was safe. The fire department was on its way. Everything would be all right.

"What in the world do you think started the fire?" Aunt Gladys said. "We didn't leave an appliance on in the kitchen, did we?"

"I really don't think so," Fran said, patting her aunt's shoulder.

Siren blaring, the Moose Creek fire fighters rounded the corner in a ladder truck and barreled toward the house. Within seconds, firefighters in hats, rubber boots, and yellow jackets poured from the rescue vehicle, unleashed long hoses, and headed up to the smoking house.

Like a well-oiled machine, the men doused the licking orange fire, daring it to stay alive under a good wet shower. The stubborn flames lit the sky with an unnatural glow.

Before long, the fire seemed to be under control. A firefighter, his yellow rubber slicker covered with ash, walked up to Fran, Eva,

Aunt Gladys, and Al. He was a tall, burly man with a sandy-colored handlebar mustache. The crinkled lines around his eyes were lined with gritty soot and dirt.

"I'm Chief Robert Plowman," he said sternly as he walked up to them. "Was everyone out of the house?"

"Yes," Fran said.

One of Chief Plowman's eyebrows lifted. "You the owner?"

Fran nodded, "Yes, my sister and I."

"You're lucky," Plowman said. "Fire's out. You weren't cooking at this time of night, were you?"

"No," she said. "Is the house salvageable?"

"Hmm, it appears the damage was contained to the kitchen," he said. "You'll have to hole up somewhere while the fire marshal conducts his investigation. Then you'll need to get with your insurance company about hiring somebody to do the repairs."

Plowman nodded at an ambulance. In her shock, Fran hadn't noticed its arrival. "They'll check you folks out," he said.

One of the paramedics walked over to Fran, a short, rotund fellow with a serious expression. "You all right, ma'am?"

"I'm fine, but my aunt isn't."

Aunt Gladys clutched Fran's arm as another paroxysm of coughing racked her frame.

"Probably smoke inhalation," the attendant said, taking Aunt Gladys' elbow. "Just to be on the safe side, we should check everyone for the same symptoms."

The paramedic led Fran, Eva, and Aunt Gladys to the ambulance.

The bustling EMT crew asked both all of them questions as they sat in the back of the ambulance. They covered them with blankets and took their vital signs. The paramedics weren't concerned with Fran and Eva's symptoms, but Aunt Gladys' cough alerted them.

One of the paramedics had Aunt Gladys lie on a gurney and covered her mouth with an oxygen mask.

Then he approached Fran and said in a low voice, "Your aunt's condition has us concerned. She'll need to go to the hospital in

Westonville for observation for a few days. Her lungs may have been
injured by the smoke. That coupled with her age and high blood
pressure, we'd better be safe than sorry."

"Of course." Fran clasped her blanket more tightly. Eva leaned
over and placed her head on her shoulder and the two of them
watched the EMTs fuss over Aunt Gladys.

"Fran?" Aunt Gladys clawed at her oxygen mask.

Fran held her hand. "Don't worry, Aunt Gladys."

"What's happening?"

"The paramedics are taking you to the hospital for a few days
for observation."

"I don't want to go." Her eyes filled with tears. "I hate hospitals."

"I promise you'll be fine. We'll come and check on you."

"Don't let them keep me there," Aunt Gladys pleaded.

"It's only for a short time, then you can come home," Fran
assured her, though she wondered where home would be until the
house was repaired.

Aunt Gladys gripped her hand tighter. "Promise me, Fran.
Promise me you won't put me away again."

Fran's heart melted. She knew she couldn't let her down. "I
promise. I'll bring you home as soon as you're well enough. Now
you've got to rest."

"Thank you." Aunt Gladys closed her eyes. "That's more than
my son ever offered to do."

After the ambulance had hauled Aunt Gladys off to the hospital, red light atop the vehicle blinking in the swirling night mist,
Plowman approached Fran again.

He removed his hat and wiped the sweat from his brow with
a handkerchief. "You won't be staying here tonight, ma'am. You'll
want to call family or someone to stay with for now."

She nodded.

"Me'n the boys will be working here a while longer checking for hot spots and making sure nothing starts to cook again,"
Plowman explained.

"What happens next?" Fran asked.

"We'll get the county fire marshal over here in the next couple of days to determine the cause of the fire."

"What if it's arson?"

"The fire marshal will file a criminal report and turn it into the police for investigation."

Yet one more upsetting event to add to the growing list of things in Fran's life that had been going wrong.

"Thank you, Chief," Fran said.

He gave a sooty grin. "We're just glad everyone's all right."

TWENTY-EIGHT

"**W**HAT A RELIEF THAT NO ONE WAS HURT," Lucy said the next morning as she, Fran, and Eva discussed the fire.

"I am too," Fran agreed. "But it scared the daylights out of us."

The women sat in Lucy's front room, which was decorated in James and Emma Castleton's hand-me-down furniture, along with Nana McCool's ancient vacuum tube television with a dead spider imprisoned inside the screen.

Of course, the TV no longer worked, but Fran knew Lucy kept it for nostalgic reasons. Her sister had covered it with one of their mother's handmade doilies and placed a plant on it. *A spider plant.* How fitting, Fran thought.

"This literally sucks," Eva said as she sat crossed-legged on the couch. "I forgot to grab my cell phone. What will all my friends think when I don't check in online?"

"You can use mine." Fran, who sat next to her daughter, fished her phone from her robe pocket. "You still remember my password, right?

"Yeah, I do," Eva said as she took the device. "I'm going to announce on Facebook what happened."

"What about your college books?" Fran asked. "Will you be all right without them for a while?"

"I should be, but I'll email my instructor and explain about the fire," Eva said. "Aunt Lucy, can I use your computer for my class-work until we can go back home?"

"Of course," Lucy said from her perch in Grandmother Castleton's antique rocking chair. "Otis and I will help with anything you two might need."

"Thanks, Sis," Fran said. "It'll probably only be a few days before we can move back."

"Meanwhile, I'm anxious to find out what caused the fire," Lucy said.

"Chief Plowman said that after the fire marshal completes his investigation, he'll rule whether it was from something like faulty wiring, or if it was set intentionally," Fran said.

"Do you think Aunt Gladys had an accident with one of her candles?" Lucy asked.

Fran shook her head. "She was upstairs sound asleep. Chief Plowman said the fire started in the kitchen."

"How is Aunt G doing, by the way?" Eva asked. "You said you called the hospital this morning and checked?"

"Yes, and she's coming along fine," Fran said. "I don't think she'll be there very long. While I was at it, I also called Bruce to let him know about his mother's condition."

"Is he coming to get Aunt Gladys?" Lucy asked.

"He offered, but I told him we'll be fine," Fran said. "I didn't want him to have to fly all the way home from Singapore. Besides, Aunt Gladys is happy here, and I promised her a home as long as she wants to stay with us."

"It's pleasant to have her around," Lucy said. "And I wasn't kidding when I said that she's a great help at the café."

"I agree," Fran said.

"By the way, have you heard how Elton and Jack are doing?" Lucy asked.

"Sorry, I forgot to tell you. Gabe mentioned that Elton's back home recuperating, and Jack's in stable condition at the hospital," Fran said. "We should go and visit him when we get a chance."

"We should," Lucy agreed. "I remember you mentioning that Elton's folks thought you were responsible for his accident and wanted to sue you."

"Gabe said he and Otis talked with them and set them straight, thank goodness," Fran said. "They are aware now that Elton's accident wasn't my fault."

"Elton's in a ton of trouble," Eva said. "His parents are not happy about him stripping for extra cash."

"I'm sure they're not," Fran said.

Eva finished with Fran's phone and handed it back to her. "I posted about the fire and told everyone we'll be okay. Right, mom?"

"Of course, sweetie," Fran responded. "When life hands you lemons, you have to soldier on."

"I thought you were supposed to make lemonade?" Eva said.

"Same difference," Fran said as she slipped her cell phone back in her robe pocket. Sometimes, it felt like she was standing in front of a machine gun and the bullets kept firing at her. It wasn't every day that you had to deal with the fallout from a house fire.

Lucy must have noticed Fran's unease. "How about a cup of coffee?" she asked.

"That would be super," she told her sister.

Lucy got up and walked into the kitchen, then returned with a steaming cup, handed it to Fran, then sank back into the rocker.

Hands wrapped around the thick ceramic mug, Fran stared into the steamy brew—not drinking, just thinking.

"Mom, why do you think someone would start a fire at our house?" Eva asked.

"You've been busy with school and helping out at the café and I didn't want to worry you, so I haven't told you everything that's been happening," Fran said. "But Uncle Otis and Detective Stevenson believe I'm being targeted."

Eva's eyes opened wide. "Someone wants to hurt you? But why?"

"It's hard to say," Fran said. "The evidence seems to indicate that Henry Whitehead's murder, me getting rear-ended, Elton's hit-and-run accident, and the attack on Jack Sturgeon are all con-nected. And now, this fire . . . I'm worried. If someone set it, I'm afraid the same individual who wants to hurt me is responsible."

"I can't imagine who would want to cause you harm," Lucy said.

Eva's face drained of color. "Whoever this person is, they don't seem to care who else gets hurt."

"That's why I'm not the happiest camper in the world right now," Fran said. "I'm putting other people in danger and I don't like it one bit."

Fran decided that the fire had put the final nail in the coffin, so to speak. It was important, no, imperative that she discover who was out to ruin her life. Other's lives were at stake.

At the rate things were going, either Fran was going to have to take matters into her own hands, or something far worse than the fire might happen. She refused to wait and see what that might be.

"Hello? Earth calling Fran," Lucy said. "You've got that look in your eyes, like you're planning something."

Fran set her jaw. "I feel like a bump on a log, sitting here doing nothing."

"What can you do?" Lucy asked. "Otis and Gabe are working hard on this case. Let them do their job and we'll stay out of their way."

"It's crappy to be smack in the middle of someone's crosshairs." Fran stood and paced—something she'd been doing a lot of lately. "I feel like I need to take action."

"Fran!" Lucy shook a finger at her. "Don't you even think about doing something crazy."

"Believe me, if I had another choice, I wouldn't," Fran said. "But I intend to find the person who has it in for me."

"Mom! Eva crossed her arms over her chest. "You can't try and hunt down this . . . this person! You could get hurt."

"If I don't find the person who hates me, I could wind up . . . d-dead." She fought back the tremble in her voice.

Lucy stood, her face a mixture of apprehension and anger. "We are not going to let that happen."

"Does that mean you'll help me?" Fran asked.

"You bet," Lucy said. "No one messes with the Castleton sisters and gets away with it."

"What about me?" Eva asked.

"You stay with Aunt Gladys and watch over her," Fran said. "Someone needs to keep her safe."

Eva nodded, but didn't look happy. "I wish I could help you two."

"Oh, but you are," Lucy said. "If Aunt Gladys thinks she's been abandoned, she'd be really upset."

Fran stopped pacing and met Lucy's gaze. "Are you sure you don't want me to do this on my own?"

"I'm in this with you, no matter what," Lucy said. "Where do we start first?"

"Let's make a list of everyone we know and what possible reasons they might have to hate me."

Lucy picked up a pad of paper and pencil from an end table. "We have a population of 1,200. Actually, 1,201 if you count the Greensboro's new baby."

A thought occurred to Fran. "We also need to make a trip up to the Ice Queen Resort Casino."

"What's up there?" Eva asked.

"Lucy, remember I mentioned to you at the festival that after Jack was hurt, I found a birthday club flyer from Ice Queen Resort's off-track betting. I believe the person who shot him must have dropped it."

"That's right!" Lucy exclaimed. "The kid in the Dracula costume was talking about Henry Whitehead and the mystery woman's saying they took trips up there to gamble."

"Right," Fran said. "And that the woman told Henry he needed to kill . . ." Fran stopped talking and she exchanged a knowing glance with Lucy. Her daughter did not need to hear that part. She was upset enough already.

"Anyway," Fran continued. "That's why I think it's a good place to start looking. The sooner the better."

"You guys should head up there today since the café is closed due to the fire," Eva said. "I'll go stay with Aunt Gladys at the hospital, that is, if I can borrow some clothes."

"My stuff will fit loose on you," Lucy said. "But it'll get you in the door."

"Perfect," Eva said.

"Unfortunately, my Volvo's in the shop, and your truck's not trustworthy enough to drive that far," Lucy said, "so I'll check with Carl to see if he has anything we can rent from his car dealership."

"I like it," Fran said, glancing down at the darned bracelet she'd been trying to get off of her wrist for days. "There's one more thing," she added.

"What's that?" Lucy said.

"Help me get this blasted thing off," she said, holding up her arm. "Castleton curse or not, I want it gone."

With a chuckle, Lucy stood. "Aunt Gladys has got you all superstitious about it, hasn't she? Let's go out to the garage and get the tool box. Since Otis is at work and can't show us the best one to use, I'm sure we'll find something that will work."

TWENTY-NINE

S OMEONE ONCE SAID THAT IF THE WIND isn't blowing, you're probably not in Wyoming. The gusts began to pick up speed, knocking around the house like a demon when Fran called Frenchie and asked him to come and pick them up. She explained about the fire last night, and that Aunt Gladys was in the hospital for observation.

"Of course, I'll give Eva a ride to the hospital to be with Gladys," Frenchie said. "I'm worried and I want to see her, too."

"I thought you might," Fran said.

"I want to give you a heads' up Fran, that I'm going to ask Gladys to move in with me when she's feeling better," Frenchie said.

"I see," Fran said, wondering how all of that would work out. She couldn't tell Aunt Gladys that she wasn't allowed to do it, although she figured Bruce might want to weigh in on the idea. Best to wait and see what happens, she thought.

"Are you all right with us living together?" Frenchie asked after her silence.

"That decision is up to my aunt," Fran said. "Oh, and one more favor?"

"Whatever you want, my dear," Frenchie said.

"Lucy and I need a ride to Big Daddy's Used Car Lot," Fran said. "Her son works there."

"Consider it done," Frenchie said.

After the women ate breakfast, they took turns showering. Lucy put on jeans and a red sweater and loaned Fran and Eva two of her jogging suits and two pairs of tennis shoes. By the time Frenchie arrived an hour later, they were ready to go.

Frenchie dropped Fran and Lucy at Big Daddy's first, then drove off with Eva toward the hospital. As the sisters walked toward the office, which was located in a single wide trailer, Fran held up her wrist. "Thanks for helping me break the clasp on the Castleton curse bracelet."

"Sure, no problem," Lucy said. "Whatever happens, we don't need to be worried about that now."

"I know it's silly, but—"

"No big deal," Lucy said. "If you feel better about getting the bracelet off, I do too."

They walked past a sea of vehicles, prices painted across their windshields. Flags of orange, red, and yellow draped from utility poles. Standing guard above it all, a statue of a cowboy wearing enormous chaps clutched a sign that said: Howdy Partner.

Following Lucy up onto a wooden porch, Fran eased by a stone planter bursting with colorful petunias.

"Watch out for Mitzi," Lucy said, gripping the doorknob. "She's touchy."

"Who's she?" Fran asked.

"Big Daddy's daughter. She works in the office. Or rather, she paints her toenails in the office. Also, she and Carl are dating."

"You never mentioned that Carl had a girlfriend," Fran said.

"I hoped they wouldn't stay together that long, but I was wrong," Lucy said. "I know I'm being an overprotective mother, but I don't think she's the best girl for him. They don't seem to have much in common, but what do I know?"

Lucy opened the door and they walked inside. Red carpet covered the floors and Venetian blinds hung at the windows. A young woman with fluffy blond hair and golden hoop earrings sat in the corner at a wooden, L-shaped desk. She had one long leg propped up on the top as she painted her toenails a ruby color.

Taking notice of her visitors, she popped her gum and rose. Black vinyl slacks clung to her youthful thighs and she wore a bright turquoise sweater.

"Big Daddy isn't here, and the assistant manager's busy in his office," she said. "You gals want somethin'?"

"Mitzi, I'm here to see Carl," Lucy said.

"Do you have an appointment?"

"He's my son." Lucy smiled. "And he's expecting me."

"Oh, howdy, Miz Parnell. Long time, no see," Mitzi said. "Sorry I didn't recognize you. You two can have a seat while I go get him."

As Mitzi walked down a hallway, Fran glanced at the dusty black leather sofa sitting along one wall. The coffee table in front of it held the remains of an old doughnut and several dog-eared magazines. Fran decided she'd stand and wait, and Lucy made no move toward the couch, either.

Mitzi returned a few moments later, walking closely beside Carl.

Carl's wavy chestnut hair had same thick texture as his mother's, and he was in his early twenties. He lifted weights, so he'd developed an athletic build that would put Adonis to shame. Fran realized her nephew was a handsome young man, as well as easy going and polite. No wonder Mitzi seemed to adore him.

"Mom," Carl said and walked over to give his mother a hug. "And Aunt Fran." He hugged her also.

"How are you doing, buddy?" Lucy asked.

"Busy, as usual," he said. "Let's go outside and talk."

Outside the trailer office at the feet of the giant cowboy, Lucy said, "Carl, is there a vehicle we can rent today? Mine's in the shop."

"Sure," Carl said as he walked them past rows of vehicles. "What's up?"

"I want to take Fran for a drive so she can take her mind off of the fire last night," Lucy said. "Help her unwind, you know?"

"I get it," Carl said. "Sorry to hear about that, Aunt Fran, and I'm sure glad everyone's safe."

"Thanks, Carl," Fran said.

"Where are you two thinking about going?" Carl asked.

"Up to the Ice Queen Resort to have a look around," Lucy said. "It's so pretty up there this time of year."

"Unfortunately, I only have one vehicle I can rent out," Carl said. "I'm warning you though, it's not the prettiest."

"Doesn't matter," Fran said. "We need wheels."

Carl directed them down another row of cars and into a large, cinderblock garage where the clank of tools and buzzing equipment punctuated the air. Busy mechanics labored over all makes and models of cars, rotating tires, doing bodywork, and changing oil. Carl led them over to a van parked in a stall.

Fran's jaw dropped as she stared at it. The vehicle, originally white, had been painted with murals of cookies, doughnuts, bags of peanuts, popcorn, and every type of junk food imaginable on the planet. On top of the van rested a plastic hot dog nestled in a bun, complete with mustard, ketchup, and relish. It must have been three feet long, she figured.

"Oh, my Lord," Lucy said with a grin. "This vehicle is really something."

"I warned you," Carl said.

"It'll do." Fran shoved her hands on her hips. "How well does it run?"

"She's still in pretty good shape," Carl said. "She'll get you up the mountain to the resort and back."

"That's all we need," Fran said.

THE WIENER-MOBILE WAS THE PITS, but Fran, who had opted to drive, wasn't about to admit it. It could definitely have used more soup, more squirrels or something under the hood. It chugged up the mountain past meadows, spruce and pine trees, and aspen groves dressed in fading autumn hues of russet, orange and brownish yellow. The surrounding russet mountains framed everything with dizzying heights.

Fran ignored the strange stares and glares of fellow travelers when they pulled around and zipped past the hot dog truck.

"Rubberneckers," she said, laughing. When a man in a hunting cap roared past in an old Ram Charger shaking his fist at them, Fran stuck out her tongue.

"You're going to get us in trouble," Lucy said. "You've heard of road rage, right?"

"That guy was going way too fast to worry about us," Fran said.

She was more anxious about the van than anything else right now. Even though Carl had assured them it would get them up to the resort, it sounded like the engine might explode. To keep her mind off of it, she counted sagebrush and antelope. The herds thinned out as the van climbed lofty heights to the Ice Queen Resort, leaving sagebrush the winner in Fran's counting contest.

On the passenger side, Lucy sat ramrod straight, looking neither right nor left.

Fran glanced at her sister. "Are you all right? Do we need to stop so you can stretch your legs?"

"Keep driving. I want to get this over with." Lucy set her mouth in a firm line.

"You look pale," Fran said.

"I feel sick to my stomach," Lucy said. "It smells like stale ketchup and mustard in here."

"We're almost there—"

"Stop!" Lucy shouted, her face white as cauliflower.

"But—"

"Now!"

When Lucy clamped a hand over her mouth, Fran veered onto the shoulder. After the van had rolled to a halt, Lucy jumped out, leaving the door swinging. Fran watched as she hustled through the weeds and leaned over a bush, her shoulders heaving.

Fran winced.

A few minutes later, Lucy climbed back in the van and slammed the door. She pulled a wet wipe from her purse and washed her face and lips, then popped a breath mint onto her mouth. Leaning back, she rested her head against the seat.

"Are you all right?"

"I'll live."

"It's not much farther. Can you hang on?"

"Sure," Lucy said. "By the way, did you call the insurance company about the fire?"

"After I finished getting ready this morning, I talked to them," Fran said. "They told me they'll get everything in order so we can get reimbursed for the damage ASAP."

"Good to hear," Lucy said.

"They understand that we want to get the café up and running as soon as possible," Fran added as she rounded a bend and tooled the van higher up the mountain. She shifted the van into a lower gear. Ignoring the alarming whine and click the engine emitted, she concentrated on the road that climbed past dilapidated mine shafts planted on the reddish-brown hills.

Groves of aspen with sparse, rusty orange leaves dotted the mountain ridges like melted butter, interspersed with spruce and pine trees and old cabins with mossy, caved-in roofs.

Crazy Woman Creek, which crossed Potato Creek further up the gulch, hugged the bottom of the ravine lining the steep, narrow road. Ancient tailings raised mounds along the water's edge. Fran could tell by the old waterline the creek was down, no doubt because of the drought.

Lucy vigorously rubbed her ears with her fingers. "My ears are ringing."

"Mine, too," Fran agreed. "It's the altitude. Swallow hard a few times."

The sisters began a swallowing session during which they both admitted their ears had "popped" and felt better. Lucy retrieved gum from her purse and handed a piece to Fran. Together, they chomped, trying to get their ears to adjust.

While concentrating on pushing her tongue into a gum bubble, Fran noticed the line of vehicles stuck behind them. Too bad, so sad. What was she supposed to do? There was no making this beast of a van go any faster and she couldn't pull over. She did her best to ignore them until the road leveled out.

Fran drove the van into a broad bowl of land where the Ice Queen Resort, a large brick edifice with pine shutters, wooden porches, and railings dominated the grassy meadow. Mountains rose in the distance, ringing the resort with majesty. Fran noted the drought had been just as severe up here.

Dry brown ski runs slashed down the slopes next to areas clotted with dry, scrubby bushes, stands of aspen, and the usual pines and spruce. Only a few dirty patches of snow had accumulated in hollows of ground. It was not a good sign for the economic hopes of the ski resort.

Off in the distance, the rooftops of Snow Village, a small town that had grown up around the Ice Queen Resort, edged the sky. Most of the resort staff and their families lived there in modest clapboard homes and trailers.

Lucy pointed toward the horizon, where purple clouds mounded. "There's a storm brewing."

"We could use the water, but hopefully we can get back home before it hits," Fran said.

When Fran pulled the chugging van off the main road and drove toward the hotel, the line of cars and trucks behind her motored ahead and a few people honked.

"Ah, get over yourselves," Fran complained. "People are always in such a blasted hurry."

She pulled under the wooden awning at the front of the hotel and parked. "We may not have had the fanciest vehicle to drive up here in, but . . ."

Fran trailed off, hardly able to believe what she saw.

"What's wrong?" Lucy asked.

"That black car, doesn't it look like the one that hit Elton?" Fran pointed toward a dark vehicle parked by the curb. Slowing down, she noted it was Buick Regal, that it had a Wyoming license plate number that started with 22, and that it was registered in this county.

"Oh my gosh," Lucy said, narrowing her gaze to peer at it.

Fran's heart skipped a few beats. "I'm sure that's it. Gabe and Otis have been trying to track down the owner. Remember a while back, I told you I took a picture of the dark car that zoomed away from the café?"

"Yes," Lucy said. "I recall that. Do you suppose it belongs to the dark-haired woman that the kid in the Dracula costume saw talking with Henry Whitehead?"

"Could be," Fran said. She parked the van, got out and walked over to the mystery car. Fishing her cell phone out of her pocket, she took pictures of it, specifically the license plate.

She and her sister might not have come up here to gamble, however, maybe they had managed hit a jackpot anyway.

"Let's go check out the casino," Fran suggested.

They walked through heavy wooden double doors into the main part of the historic horse racing area. The sound of bells chiming, music jangling and lights flashing filled the air as customers sat on stools punching the spin buttons. Although the machines looked and functioned like regular slots, they produced winning or losing outcomes based on past horse races.

"There are more games than when I was last up here," Lucy commented.

"Seems that way," Fran said. "And they've expanded the room size."

"Looks pretty popular with the crowd," Lucy said. "At least we know it was with Henry and that dark haired woman little Dracula mentioned."

"That's right," Fran said.

The casino's mining theme had been carried throughout the space. Train tracks lined the periphery of the inside walls. Antique ore cars, along with a couple of narrow-gauge trains, dotted the rails. The walls themselves had been given a *faux* cave-like appearance to replicate the inside of a mine. Rusty looking tin candleholders clung to the rock, giving off dim electric light. Huge wagon wheel chandeliers hung from the ceiling, adding more illumination.

Banks of slot machines, lights flashing, swallowed up the gambling pit. Cocktail servers in black pants and black polo shirts bearing the casino's logo took drink orders. Fran noticed one man in particular sitting in a wheelchair smoking a cigarette. Clear tubes were threaded up into his nose, and a canister of oxygen perched next to him.

Both sisters turned to look at one lady who was sobbing so loudly she could be heard over the casino clamor. She wore a purple silk blouse, a tan leather skirt, and high-heeled boots. She sat in front of a machine with Elvira, Mistress of the Dark depicted on the front.

"Excuse me," Fran said when they walked up to her. "Are you all right?"

The woman moved her hands away. Her eyes were red and swollen from crying, with black mascara smudged beneath. She made a surprised squeak, slid off her stool and stood, knocking over her drink cup onto the plush carpet. Grabbing her purse—a leopard print design—she stumbled past the bank of machines and out of sight.

"That was Carma Leone!" Lucy said.

"Yeah, definitely it was her." Fran planted her hands on her hips. "Did you get a load of her purse? Leopard print. Just like little Dracula said."

"I saw that." Lucy snapped her fingers. "I swear she must be dark-haired woman little Dracula spotted at Henry's house."

"I suppose that's possible," Fran said as a cold sensation swept through her. "If the boy did see Carma with Henry, why would she have told him to kill me?"

"I don't know, but I'm heading to the ladies' room," Lucy said. "I'll meet you right back here."

"I won't go anywhere," Fran said, turning to concentrate on the activity.

An older gentleman wearing black server clothing walked up to Fran, holding a tray. "Ma'am, can I bring you something to drink?"

"No, thank you," she said. "Hey, I had a friend who used to come up here and it's possible you might have met him. His name was Henry Whitehead?"

"Never heard of him," the man said, one of his bushy brows lifted. "I meet lots of people, though. Sorry I can't help you."

"That's okay," Fran told him, wondering what she had thought to accomplish.

"Have a nice day," the server said as he walked away.

Lucy seemed to be taking a long time, Fran thought. She pulled a twenty-dollar bill out of her purse and stuck it in one of the machines, punching in her bet. After a few spins, she decided it had been a waste of time to drag Lucy here in the wiener-mobile, sucking rancid ketchup and mustard fumes all the way.

What made her think they could solve anything?

After about a half hour, Fran headed toward the ladies' room. She entered the facility and began checking the bathroom stalls. All were empty. Fran's heart pounded in her ears. Where would Lucy have gone?

Whack!

Something slammed against the back of Fran's head. Dizzy and in pain, she stumbled forward and landed on the floor. A stabbing ache shot through her temples.

Then there was nothing.

THIRTY

FRAN OPENED HER STICKY EYES and lifted her head. She blinked, attempting to focus. Despite her impaired vision, she realized she sat tied to a chair, thick rope wrapped around her body. She tried to wriggle lose, but her bindings wouldn't budge.

What happened? Is Lucy all right?

She closed her eyes, then opened them, relieved as the room came into view and her mind registered that she was in as a musty old cabin, possibly one of those she'd seen along Crazy Woman Creek while driving up here. Strewn across the dirt floor were musty-smelling leaves and dirty rags. Cobwebs trailed from the ceiling and a crumbling rock fireplace sat at one end of the room.

A wooden table and three chairs occupied a corner. Fran assumed she was seated in the fourth chair to the set. A sagging, broken down iron bed hulked in another corner. Smudged, broken glass lined the frame of a small window.

Glancing outside, Fran stared at the dark, swollen purple sky that spit occasional snowflakes and sent them fluttering to the ground. So much for getting off the mountain before the storm hit.

"Hello?" she called out, wondering if whoever had brought her here might be nearby. As her teeth began to chatter, she realized the temperature had begun to drop. She'd freeze to death if she couldn't free herself.

Struggling within her bonds, she attempted to loosen them. They barely budged. Perspiration coated her brow as she controlled her rising panic. Suddenly, the door flew open and a young man walked in wearing jeans, a sweater, and a plaid winter jacket.

He lifted his sandy blond head and met Fran's gaze. She caught her breath, surprised as heck. It was Jack's assistant from the senior citizen center!

"Danny?" she asked incredulously. "What are you doing here?"

"Helping my mom," he said.

"Helping your mom do what? Fran asked.

"She hit you over the head and had me help her bring you up here," he said.

"Wh-why?"

"Shhh." He pressed an index finger to his lips. "My mom doesn't like you."

"Why?"

He shrugged. "She has some sort of grudge, and I'm not going to cross her. She told me to make sure you don't get loose."

"You should untie me and let me go."

He shook his head. "No way. She'll be back soon and you two can settle your differences. I know better than to get involved in my mother's business."

Fran chewed her lower lip, wondering exactly who Danny's mother was and why she hated her so much. Meanwhile, she had begun to shiver. Her whole body had become a giant ice cube.

She didn't have to think long before she heard car tires crunch on gravel. The door opened and in walked Carma Leone with a blast of cool wind, dressed in one of the Ice Queen Resort's black maid uniforms and a white sweater.

Fran's mouth dropped. "Carma? You're Danny's mother? Her blood ran even colder when she glanced outside and saw the black Buick Regal, the cause of so much heartache, parked by a fallen log. The same one that had rammed her old truck as she was on her way home from Henry's house. The same one that had been parked in front of her house. The same one she and Lucy noticed outside the casino not so long ago.

"Ah, I see you recognize my car. How astute you are." Carma cocked her head to the side.

What was Carma up to? Fran licked her dry, cracked lips as things started to make sense. "D-did you murder Henry Whitehead?"

Carma stood beside her son, setting her purse and a brown paper bag on the table. "You got it right, sweetheart."

Fran gasped. "Why on earth did you do that?"

"He needed money for his divorce settlement with Vivian, so I loaned it to him," Carma said. "I told him he wouldn't have to pay it back if he'd do me a favor."

"Which was?" Fran asked.

"Kill you," Carma seethed. "Henry chickened out in the end and refused to do it. So, I stole one of the butcher knives from your café kitchen and went over to confront him at his house after he took you to the carnival. I was so angry! But Henry said he couldn't kill you no matter what I wanted, and insisted he'd pay back the money he owed me. I didn't want the money, though. I wanted you dead."

Another cold shiver shot through Fran, although this one didn't have anything to do with the dropping temperature. The idea that Carma hated her so much shocked her to the core.

"What do you have against me?"

Carma thoughtfully examined her perfect red nails. "You see, back in high school, I had this boyfriend named Dan Lightfoot. Remember him? Tall blond football player with the cute dimples?"

"I had no idea the two of you were dating," Fran said.

"No one knew we were together because we kept it a secret," Carma said.

"Why?" Fran asked.

"My mother didn't like him, so we weren't allowed to date. But I loved Dan with all my heart." Carma rested a hand on Danny's shoulder. "Dan was my first, you know. Danny is our son."

Danny glared at his mother. "You told me you didn't know who my dad was!"

"You didn't need to know the truth," Carma insisted. "It wouldn't have mattered."

"You lied to me," Danny said.

Fran realized now why Danny had looked so familiar the first time she met him at the senior citizen's center. He had his father's large eyes and square chin. He seemed about as tall, too, and the two of them had a similar stride.

"I never heard rumors you were pregnant, Carma," Fran said, her head reeling with disbelief. "You know high school kids are brutal about gossip."

"My mom and I covered it up pretty good, didn't we?" Carma laughed. "Why do you think I slouched and wore all those big, dumpy sweatshirts when I was a sophomore? At the end of the school year, my mom shipped me off to live with my Aunt Alice. I spent most of the summer before Danny was born ratting around in her tiny little trailer. Let me tell you, that was true murder."

"Did you hurt Lucy?" Fran asked, worried why her sister had never returned to the casino.

"I beaned her pretty hard when I saw her in the bathroom, but left her unconscious in one of the stalls, so she'll probably live," Carma said. "I'm not after her. I'm after you."

"Mom, I think you need to stop this," Danny said. "I thought this was supposed to be a joke and that you were only trying to scare Fran. I think you should stop right—"

Carma slapped him. "Shut up. You don't get to tell me what to do."

Frowning, he rubbed his cheek and backed up a few steps, staring at his mother as if he'd never really known her before.

Fran shifted uneasily in her rope bindings. She had to keep Carma talking. She had to buy time. Before Carma did something desperate. Again.

"You didn't give your baby up for adoption," Fran said, hoping that if she could sympathize with Carma and make friends with her, she might relent and untie her. "You kept him with you, which isn't easy. I admire that."

"He is the only part of Dan I got to keep," Carma said wistfully. "My aunt raised him up here on the mountain, away from prying eyes. I came up to visit as much as I could. No one in Moose Creek ever found out that he was mine."

"So that's why you never lived up here with me and Aunt Alice," Danny said. "All these years, I've wondered why not. I thought you hated me."

"Danny, I've told you over and over how much I love you." Carma pointed at Fran. "It's her I hate."

"But why?" Fran asked. "What did I ever do to you?"

"I always believed once Dan and I graduated from high school, we could get married and the three of us would be together," Carma said. "I'd be eighteen and it wouldn't matter what my mom thought. But you came along. You bitch. He fell for you, then you got knocked up with Eva. That was the end of my dreams. You stole Dan from me. Eva got everything my Danny deserved."

"How could I steal him from you when I never even knew you two were together? It doesn't make sense. You should have told Dan you were pregnant. You should have made him take care of things properly. Maybe he would have married you if he'd known. Don't you see?"

Carma blinked, seemingly contemplating the idea as she began to pace. "Don't confuse the issue. It was plain and simple. You stole Dan away from me and ran off to California with him. You had everything. Nice clothes, a home, and a car. Your daughter got everything my son should have had."

"That's not my fault, Carma. Don't fool yourself into thinking my life with Dan Lightfoot was all wine and roses. In the end, he left me for another woman. Do you see the pattern? He can't commit to anyone. He doesn't love people; he only uses them."

Carma started to tremble. "It wasn't his fault. It couldn't have been. You were the one who changed him, made him think he loved you and not me. If he would have stayed with me, I would have been the only woman for him. He'd have loved me forever."

"You don't know that."

Carma's nostrils flared. "You ruined it all, Fran. You don't deserve to live."

It shocked Fran to realize how desperate Carma had become. Now it was all clear. The woman had harbored this hatred for a long time.

Fran met Carma's gaze. "I understand what you went through. And I'm sorry."

"I don't believe you," Carma said.

"Did you shoot Jack with the arrow, too?" Fran asked, realizing just how far Carma would go to have her revenge.

"I'm a good shot, aren't I." Carma's eyes narrowed into angry slits. "I planned to kill you both, of course."

"Why?" Fran asked.

Carma shrugged. "Jack is a nice guy, and I couldn't allow you to be happy with him. It wouldn't be fair since you ruined my life."

"Mom, this is too much," Danny said, alarm threading his voice. "I thought this was a prank—that you only wanted to scare Fran."

"You should know me better than that," Carma told him.

Danny shook his head. "You shouldn't be doing this. They'll put you in jail."

"If no one finds out, it's not a problem," Carma said. "Or will you tell the police?"

Danny clenched his fists, but remained silent.

"And Elton?" Fran asked. "What about him?"

"Ah, Elton was a true accident." Carma shrugged nonchalantly. "I was driving past your house that night and when Elton came barreling outside, I tried to swerve. Oopsie."

Fran shivered at Carma's callous attitude. "Someone attacked me at MacGreggor's Pub, then threw the grenade through my window, and set the fire at the café. Are you responsible for that as well?"

Carma laughed. "You really ought to think about putting dead-bolts on your doors. Locks are too easy to pick. And my plan to steal the butcher knife from your café worked at first—the police suspected you'd murdered Henry Whitehead."

"How can you be so cold and nonchalant?" Fran asked.

"Easy," Carma said. "I've never liked you and I hoped one day I'd get my revenge, which I am now."

"But—"

"Stop worrying, Fran." Carma laughed again. "You won't be around much longer, because I plan to put you out of your misery."

Fran sensed she was running out of time and strained at her bonds. Of course, they wouldn't budge now any more than they had before. "Carma, you need help. I'm not angry, and I promise I'll try to find someone to sort all of this out."

Carma waved her off. "I don't need your stupid help."

Biting her lower lip, Fran made no further comment, but her mind was screaming silently.

"Since you so conveniently came up here and found me, I've decided to end it once and for all," Carma said, grinning. "I'm going to finish you off in flames, the way it should have happened days ago." She grabbed the brown paper bag on the table, reached inside and produced a box of wooden matches. "The brush and grass around here are dry as bones. No one will think twice about a forest fire burning down this cabin. You, unfortunately, will be inside."

"Mom, don't do this." Danny walked toward Fran. "I'm going to let Fran go."

"Don't you dare," Carma growled at him. "Back away. Now."

Carma's plan seemed perfect, except that she hadn't counted on Danny becoming alarmed. At least he'd finally seen through his mother's madness. Nevertheless, Fran didn't think it was going to help.

Keep her talking, a small voice in Fran's mind insisted. "Carma, back at the casino, why were you crying?"

She rattled the box of matches warningly. "None of your business."

"If I'm going to die anyway, why does it matter?"

Carma paused thoughtfully, then must have decided to elaborate. "I don't make a large income doing nails, so I took a casino server job up here to supplement my funds. Then Henry taught me how to gamble on the machines, and I hit some good jackpots."

"Seems like you should be happy about that," Danny said.

Carma frowned. "Lately I've run into a streak of bad luck. My bank account is practically cleaned out, both checking and savings, and my credit cards are all maxed. I'm broke on my ass. Before long, the bank will repossess the old car my mother left me when she died, my house, and my life."

Carma tried to light a match, but it sparked out. Frustrated, she tossed it aside and tried another.

Tears threatened as Fran's heart hammered. This was it. She was going to die because of a high school love affair gone wrong.

Again, Carma struck a match, and this one flared into life. Horrified, Fran watched the match fall to the floor, instantly igniting the pine needles and debris. Flames leapt into life. Carma and Danny stepped back. Through the wall of orange fire, Fran watched them run from the cabin.

Smoke crept into Fran's lungs as she struggled to free herself. Her eyes began to sting and water, and her throat felt scratchy. The fire licked her face with heat. She knew she'd die from smoke inhalation first, but the thought did not comfort her.

"Fran! Fran, are you in there?" a voice shouted.

Though she felt ready to pass out, Fran lifted her head and managed to say, "I'm here!"

Through the crackling flames, a loud crash resounded as the back door burst open. In the swirling gray smoke, Fran saw a tall figure race in her direction. *Gabe.* How had he known where to find her?

Gabe lifted her up, chair and all, and carried her outside away from the cabin. As he put down the seat and sliced through Fran's bindings with a pocketknife, she watched the cabin explode into licking flames.

As the ropes fell away, circulation returned to Fran's fingers. Supporting her, Gabe dragged her up a weed-choked hill, far away from the smoky, crackling inferno. Fran leaned against him, thankful he'd arrived in time

A red ladder truck, siren wailing, pulled up to the cabin. Firefighters jumped out and aimed a fat hose at the crumbling structure, dousing the orange glow.

"They arrived pretty fast," Fran said.

"When the guy at the gas station in town told me he'd seen Carma in there buying matches, I was afraid she had planned something like this. That's why I called 911 before I started up here. I figured no matter what was going down, it wouldn't hurt to have firefighters on the scene."

Gabe pointed at a dirt road that snaked toward a stand of fir trees. A squad car had pulled over Carma's vehicle and two police officers urged her and Danny out of the Buick. They handcuffed the two, loaded them into their police cruiser and drove away.

"How did you figure out that Carma had murdered Henry?"

"The phone calls and text messages and emails they exchanged told the story pretty well," Gabe explained. "Carma had threatened to kill Henry if he couldn't go through with murdering you. Also, Otis and I had finally narrowed her down as the owner of the black Buick Regal. We were close to making an arrest, but we were just waiting for the judge to sign the warrant."

Another shrill siren pierced the chilled air.

"The ambulance is enroute," Gabe said, holding her against his side. "I thought you might need medical attention."

A horrible thought hit her. "Lucy—"

"Is fine," Gabe reassured her. "One of the hotel maids found her and called an ambulance. They took her to the hospital in Westonville."

Fran relaxed, yet knew she owed a big apology to her sister for dragging her up here. That would come later, after they returned home safe and sound.

When Gabe produced a clean tissue from his pocket, Fran used it to wipe her nose. A wet flake landed on her cheek, and she realized it had begun to snow. More fuzzy flakes swirled around the forested area, blanketing the rocky, uneven ground with a shroud of white.

They'd been in a drought for years with barely a drop of water. Now it was snowing like crazy. That was Wyoming. Unpredictable and wild.

"How did you know where I was?" Fran asked, shivering.

Gabe removed his heavy overcoat and wrapped her in it. The protective gesture helped Fran relax.

"I happened to stop by Big Daddy's to see if you and Lucy were there. I wanted to talk to you two about Carma and my suspicions. Carl said you two had made a trip up to the Ice Queen Resort, and I got worried because I knew from text messages between Carma and Henry that they spent a lot of time up here gambling. You know, I often get gut feelings about cases."

"It wasn't a gut feeling," Fran said, punching him playfully on the arm. "You figured my sister and I had come up here to snoop, which we had."

He shrugged and said, "Guilty as charged."

"Okay," Fran said. "How did you know Carma and Danny had grabbed me?"

"A server at the casino saw the two of them dragging you outside. He mentioned the suspicious incident to me, which had occurred shortly before I arrived."

"One more question, how did you know where to find this place?" Fran asked.

"Easy," Gabe said. "Late last night, after Otis told me about the fire at your house, I went to Carma's house and put a tracker on her car. I suspected she'd been behind the attempts on your life and the other troubles, so I wanted to see what she was up to, maybe catch her in the act."

Fran stared up at him. "Now I know why you told me to lay low. You had a good idea who the guilty party was."

"Exactly," he said. "I wanted you to stay safe while Otis and I handled it."

"It's hard to be patient when you fear someone wants you dead," Fran said.

"Good police work takes time," Gabe said, lifting Fran's chin and staring into her eyes. "You can't go busting people without clear cut proof. Otherwise, you compromise the case."

"Yeah, yeah, yeah," Fran said, relenting when she heard the concern in Gabe's voice.

"Anyway," he continued. "You and Lucy got lucky today."

"For a moment, I thought it was all over." Fran shivered again, even though Gabe's overcoat and warm embrace had made her quite toasty. "Carma blamed me for getting the life she thinks *she* deserved. She and Dan were lovers back in high school and she swears I stole him from her. Danny's their son."

"I've done my homework, Fran. I know all about it. It's over now. She's going to prison."

"What about Danny? He claims all he did is help his mother with a few pranks to scare me."

"The courts will take that into consideration. If he doesn't have any other strikes against him, they'll go easier."

"That takes a load off of my mind," Fran said. "Danny tried to make Carma back down, but she yelled at him."

"I can imagine," Gabe said.

"I swear, she's delusional."

"That can happen when people get fixated." Gabe tucked strands of hair behind her ears, then added, "By the way, I stopped at Big Daddy's for another reason."

"Why?"

"I, um," He trailed off, then said, "I wanted to ask you out."

"I see," she said.

His face turned red and he grinned. "I've wanted to ask you out for a while for real, not just for questioning. But I'm a dork when it comes to women."

"The big, strong detective has a fatal flaw?"

He squeezed her shoulders. "Will you have dinner with me? I promise, there'll be no talk of murder or mayhem."

Fran smiled. "That sounds wonderful."

Born in Portland, Oregon, Cindy has lived all over the United States and spent five years in Japan. She has visited Canada, the Philippines, Samoa, Hawaii, both the western and eastern Caribbean and New Zealand.

Currently, she lives in Cheyenne, Wyoming, where Cheyenne Frontier Days is held each year. CFD's well-known rodeo is often referred to as the "Daddy of 'em all."

Over the years, she has won or placed in various writing contests. She has also written for and edited numerous newsletters. Her nonfiction magazine articles have been featured in "True West" and "Wild West." She was a book critic for Storyteller Alley and is a freelance editor.

Although retired from Laramie County School District 1's Community Relations office, she still contributes articles for the district's annual magazine, "Elevate," which has a circulation of approximately 47,000 readers.

From baby alligators to glow worms, Cindy has seen a variety of life's wonders.

www.ingramcontent.com/pod-product-compliance
Lightning Source LLC
Chambersburg PA
CBHW011510100726
47899CB00010BD/3312